On the Back of the Swallow

To Kevin

On the Back of the Swallow

A Novel
by

Danny Morrison

Roberts Rinehart Publishers

Published in the US and Canada by Roberts Rinehart Publishers,
5455 Spine Road, Boulder, Colorado 80301

Distributed by Publishers Group West

First published in Ireland in 1994 by Mercier Press

Text copyright © Danny Morrison, 1994

Library of Congress Catalog Card No 96–68568

ISBN 1-57098-101-9

The quotation on p. 44 is from Siegfried Sassoon's poem 'The Last Meeting'. The quotation on p. 135 is from Mahler's 'Das Lied von der Erde' ('The Song of the Earth'), a German version by Hans Bethge of eight-century Chinese poems.

On the Back of the Swallow is a work of fiction. All the characters and situations in the book are entirely imaginary and bear no relation to any real person or actual happenings.

Typesetting:
Red Barn Publishing, Skeagh, Skibbereen, Co. Cork, Ireland

Printed in the United States of America

1

NICKY AND ROBIN were mesmerised by the brilliant glow-
ing flame of the thick-veined red candle pinched from the back
of Sonny's shop late that afternoon. The plumpish bud rocked
up and down the shaft of the wick as if responding to the soft
undulations of the boys' semi-audible breathing. Around the
old shed's walls lapped waves of darkness which drove the
eight-year-olds – castaways upon the mysterious sea of life –
into greater communion.

They were sitting on threadbare potato sacks spread flat
over small crates, opposite each other, and watched as the yel-
low-white lozenge magically honed its energy into an arrow-
head but still could not escape the wick.

'It's started crying,' said Nicky, as first one tear, then another
and another guttered down the candle into a tiny terrace of
sinter at its base fixed on the snug lid of an upturned wooden
barrel. 'That one's happy. That one's sad. Happy . . . sad . . .
happy . . . sad . . .'

Robin ran his fingers through the shimmers and chanted
solemnly, 'ShoobeyDoobeyDoobey-Doo.'

Nicky copied him but said, 'ShoobeyDoobeyDoobey-Day.'

'That sounds good, doesn't it?' said Robin. 'I wonder what
it means.'

'It would scare you if you didn't know.'

'I know it would,' said Robin.

It had been Robin who had asked Sonny if he could use the toilet. Once in the store at the back of the shop he opportunistically rummaged about, found the huge candle, wrapped it in a cushion of old newspapers and tossed it over the yard wall and into the entry where he and Nicky collected it.

The boys became silent again as the waxing bronze light played on every curve and edge of every object within the conspiracy of the old garden shed. On the window-sill jamjars, some empty, some sealed, some brandishing paint brushes recently steeped in spirits. On the window were visible the ghostly fingerprints of the former owner of the shed and nearby house, a retired seaman, now dead two years. On this wall a riddle clogged in desiccated clay; on that wall a large wobbly saw and a flaccid coiled rope. At the back: a weighty tool chest, an ancient, short-wave marine transceiver, a lopsided stack of chairs and old pictures of seascapes in gilded plaster frames, and the barely visible front fork of an upturned bicycle frame. And in the far corners of the ceiling, the spiders in their grey hammocks, watching every move.

By virtue of superintendence and habitation Robin Coulter considered the shed his and Nicky Smith's property. It therefore fell to Robin to keep some order and to stem the incredible volume of household junk which was often dumped within from crashing out. The shelter was at its most snug when rain or hail drummed hardest on the tight skin of felt and bitumen which made up the sloping roof. It was like being in your pram during a downpour, said Robin, and Nicky thought, yes, perfect. Even on the hottest summer's day the hut, perfumed by the resin seasonally oozing from the pine timbers, provided a cool sanctuary where the twins could put their feet up and talk the child sense of intimate coevals; a few words and simple innuendo servicing a whole world.

Presently, Robin said: 'I was walking when I was about two months old.'

'When I was a baby,' said Nicky, 'I was thrown into a stream full of stones but didn't drown 'cause I swam to the bank.'

'Who threw you in?'

'Don't remember. But next you know I was rushed back to my cot and it was still warm.'

'Are you sure it happened?'

'It might've.'

The flame before them changed from being graceful hands joined in prayer to a squat genie.

'If you sit too long, you know,' mused Robin, rubbing his chin, 'you squeeze all the fat in your bum up your back and down your legs.' He stood up and tested himself. 'Tsst. It's bloomin' happened. We shouldn't have sat for so long talking.'

'I never heard of that before,' said Nicky, knitting his eyebrows.

'Want to see?'

'Oom . . . aye. But I think mine's okay.'

Robin pulled down his trousers and raised the hem of his boxer shorts, exposing a scrawny buttock with a rash of hard goosepimples.

'Looks all right to me,' said Nicky, blinking rapidly, his heart racing.

'Are you sure? Take another look,' said Robin, craning his neck over his shoulder.

'Oom, yeh, it's okay.'

'Let's check yours then,' said Robin, his voice slightly tremulous, as he zipped up, tucking in his shirt. Nicky had just pulled his trousers and underpants down to his ankles and bent over when the shed door shuddered in its swollen frame before opening, the bones of the bent hinges creaking in their metal joints.

'There you two are!' said Mrs Coulter, good-naturedly. She searched for the cord of the electric bulb which, never hanging where it is anticipated, eluded her fingers for a second or two. A second or two in which Nicky struggled frantically and uselessly to find his waistband. A second or two in which he experienced an eternity of shame. He moaned like a trapped animal as the light clicked, and as Heather, Robin's younger sister, proclaimed from behind her mother's skirts, 'Nicky's got no trousers on, Mammy! Look!' He was utterly confused and just shook. Mrs Coulter made some assessment, blocked her daughter's view and tucked Nicky in without a word. With the same equanimity she addressed her son.

'Robin, what were you told before about lighting things in here! Well? Come on, hand over the matches.' She broke the stalagmite off the barrel. 'It's late and time to go in, boys,' she said. 'Sure you can see each other tomorrow, okay?'

In bed that night Nicky agonised over his humiliation and what sort of trouble he and Robin were in. But there was no knock on the front door. In the morning he heard voices below his window and looked out. Standing at the end of his path was his grey-haired mother, her hands in the pockets of her apron, nodding repeatedly and listening attentively to Mrs Coulter at whose side Heather was doing what seemed like little triumphant dances.

Nicky dived between the sheets as his mother's tread on the stairs amplified with each step until his door opened like the jaws of an almighty beast come to devour him.

'Don't be calling for Robin, OK? Nicky? Did you hear me? Nicky!'

'Yes, Mammy.'

'He's got a cold and he's in bed.' She opened his wardrobe and poked around. 'Mrs Coulter's away into town. Billy's minding Robin and she said you can call over and see him when she gets back, if you want.'

Is that it? he wondered. Perhaps Mrs Coulter had never come down the garden path after all. Nor opened the door, nor switched on the light. Nor had he been near to tears. Perhaps Robin and he hadn't even played that game. Thank you, God! Thank you! Never again! I promise. He rolled over while his mother interrupted her humming.

'You all right?' She felt his head. 'Well, you're not running a temperature. Come and get up. I need your bedclothes for the wash.' She tried to pull back the sheet but he had it firmly in his grip. He shut his eyes, buried himself deep in the mattress and kicked wildly with his wiry, long legs at the beast trying to drag him from his tent. He only realised that he had dislodged his mother from the bed when he heard the thud of her fall on the floor. He anxiously looked down and saw his mother was still alive but muttering to herself. She looked up at him and smiled, acknowledging the funny side.

'Sorry,' he said. 'I was only playing.'

'I know, you rascal, but I'm an old woman!'

He leaped out of bed and ran to the bathroom.

Walking over to Robin's in the afternoon Nicky noticed a bird fly past to his right. It induced a feeling of good fortune which was heightened by the recollection of his mother's childish smile which made him smile too. He saw Robin staring out his bedroom window which overlooked the street. He seemed down. His chin was on his hands which rested on the trestle of a hunched leg. He immediately brightened when he saw his visitor and waved enthusiastically. Mrs Coulter was coming up the path behind Nicky, carrying her shopping.

'Hiya Nicky,' said Heather, sounding lispy through the gaps in her milk teeth.

'Nicky, take this please,' Mrs Coulter asked. Robin opened the hall door and crowded them.

'What have you got for me! What have you got for me!'

'Wait till I get through the door . . . Robin! Get away from that bag . . . What did I say! Heather, go and get changed before you go out to play.'

Nicky loved the atmosphere in Coulter's. Rarely did he witness a show of anger or intolerance. Even the arguments between Billy and Robin, usually arising out of something Robin had poached, did not last. In his house dinner was eaten in relative silence; here it was a babble and a clashing of cutlery. If ever Nicky's mother and father died in a horrific car crash he could come and live here, Robin promised.

Mrs Coulter gave each of the boys a mint chocolate biscuit. They tore off the gold foil wrappings, rolled them into balls and threw them at each other. Nicky headed Robin's and stopped a goal.

'Show food!' shouted Robin at the top of his voice and instantly Nicky obeyed. They faced each other with their mouths wide open, displaying a melting mash of chocolate catarrh and stringy saliva. 'Agghh! Horrible! Horrible!' screamed Robin.

Mrs Coulter got to work in the kitchen. Billy, whom Nicky found grumpy, asked something concerning dinner and left. The boys pawed over a crisp, new comic and Robin had Nicky falling off the sofa with laughter as he repeated jokes and mimicked the characters.

'There's Daddy, Mammy!' called Robin when he saw the roof of his father's car appear above the small privet hedge. Brian Coulter was a primary school teacher, off for the holidays and working part-time with his brother.

'What has Superman in pyjamas, then?' he joked.

'I've a cold and Mammy won't let me out.'

'Are you going to give it to Nicky?'

'He hasn't asked yet,' laughed Robin.

'And where's my Plum?' asked Brian of Heather.

'She's out playing.'

Nicky stayed until dinner time. Walking up the street towards his own house he saw his father turn the corner – a middle-sized, unsmiling man, whose eyes rarely looked up at the leaves on the trees, the mountains in the distance or the blue skies. As a toddler Nicky had never rushed to him for a swing in the street: he had never received the signal. He ran home before his father reached the door.

Often Nicky would return to Coulter's after dinner for games. On winter weekends he was allowed to stay over on a Friday or a Saturday night, an invitation that Mrs Smith reciprocated. But the boys preferred Robin's and that's where they were to be found: Robin patiently teaching his friend how to play chess; or, in bed, Robin reading to Nicky from abridged versions of their favourite books, *A Tale of Two Cities* or *The Scarlet Pimpernel*, whilst Nicky fell asleep, his head resting against Robin's shoulder.

One summer the boys became astronomers.

It was a pale, clear evening and they were observing the full moon through Robin's new telescope which his father had bought him for his birthday. The refractor was mounted on a tripod on top of the garden shed. The moon lay low in an off-white sky, visible between roof-tops, chimney-pots and the serrated canopies of trees. Robin, taking his turn looking at the craters, noticed a distant telephone line come into view in the eyepiece. As the moon slowly sank, the line appeared to bisect the image horizontally.

'Fuck me!'

'What! What is it?' screeched Nicky in a panic.

'The moon's breaking up! We'll be engulfed. It'll fall on top of us!'

'Let me see! Let me see!' Nicky was shaking but as he awkwardly bent his back and focused his eye he kept still and he saw that the moon was indeed sliced in half along its equator.

'Tell everybody! Tell everybody at once!' he shouted with a dance of his head.

Robin was wringing his hands as if it was the end of the world. He was moved by the sincerity of his friend who hadn't noticed his bogus terror.

Nicky took another look. 'Wait! Wait a minute. Something's happening!'

'What is it? What is it?'

'I think, I think we're okay,' he sighed. 'Look! I know what it is! I know what it is! It's a wire in the sky between that telegraph pole and that house! Look, it's only a wire! We're OK, we're OK!'

Robin bent down, saw the wire, adjusted the telescope and saw the moon intact, and said: 'Phew! That was close! I thought we were goners.'

Had Nicky known that Robin had been actively deceiving him all along he would have now felt very stupid. Instead, he smiled and was proud that he had discovered the explanation.

'Wait till you see this!' said Robin, one night. He took a refill of table salt from the kitchen cupboard as they slipped out the back door. On the flagstones around the side of the house his torch searching for garden slugs came upon first their silvery contrails and then, the dumb molluscs themselves, pacifically cruising across the path.

'Watch this!' said Robin, his glee almost palpable.

'Why, what are you gonna do?' asked Nicky, with an instinctive foreboding. Before he could stop him, Robin sprinkled a flurry of salt over the first slug and the effect was cruel and less than immediate. The granules liquidised the slug before their very eyes, reducing to a phlegm a creature which seconds before had design, beauty and purpose.

'What did you do that for!' shouted Nicky, pushing Robin back against the wall and snatching the container from him.

'What did you do that for!' It was the first time he had ever raised his voice against, or struck, his friend.

'What did you do it for?' he persisted.

Robin was shocked. His eyes filled and he blubbered: 'They're pests . . . Pests, Nicky. They ruin things.'

'No, no, no, no, no!' shouted Nicky. 'You shouldn't have done it. It's bad!'

This was one incident about which neither of them spoke again.

Another summer the Coulters took Nicky away with them for a week's holiday in an old country cottage. It was a magic time. The kids were allowed to run wild about the lanes though on Sunday they had to become civilised, get washed and dress respectably and accompany Mrs Coulter to church. At night time they could remain out late. The light of the stars rained down on Heather, Robin and Nicky as they silently lay on their backs on the itchy ginger stubble of a harvested field and squeezed hands, the current of pure childhood pulsing through them. One day, for a bit of adventure, the boys slipped away to the hills and away from boring Billy who, according to Robin, was in the middle of his period. They were crossing fields when Robin stopped, pointed to several swallows and described which were the parents, which the younkers. He said that swifts nested in the dirty cities but swallows kept to the clean, pure air of the countryside, closer to nature.

'They're preparing to migrate back to Africa. They fly thousands of miles without landing.'

'When do they feed? Do they not sleep at night?' asked Nicky in amazement.

'They sleep on the wing. They use the warm currents in the air but that only helps a bit. During the journey some of them get so exhausted that they feel they cannot go any further and just want to give up and drop to earth like a stone. It's just at that very moment, Nicky, that another swallow comes alongside and, using whatever language they speak, tells him to get on his back and take a rest, that he'll be able to do the same someday for somebody else.'

'That's fantastic!' said Nicky, breathless. 'That's absolutely brilliant!' He peered up into the sky and admiringly searched out a pair of swallows fluttering to a great height. Robin was touched by his innocence.

'You know so much. You are gifted,' said Nicky, whose own faith could turn water to wine.

2

THE BOYS PASSED from the same primary school to the same secondary school. Robin went into the top stream; Nicky fell back a class. Each year Robin inevitably gathered new teenage friends about him but the cleverest was a clodhopper in comparison to Nicky, who remained his soul mate. Nicky didn't care for the company of anyone else. He could live contentedly inside his own head or walk the streets or lie in bed doing absolutely nothing because he had that privileged satisfaction of knowing that he and Robin had been purposefully conceived in the same age and would run to the ends of the earth and the end of time by each other's side answering every question existence put to them.

It was the summer of their fifteenth year. They were riding in parallel in a bicycle lane. It was Sunday, just after lunch-time, mid-July. Robin kept up a stream of entertainment: did you hear this one, did you hear that one. He told Nicky the chilling story he had read in a newspaper that very morning, the story of a woman who had been pregnant for so long that her baby eventually was born with a beard.

'Poor thing,' sympathised Nicky.

'When the nurse slapped him on the backside,' continued Robin, 'the first thing he asked for was a shave.' Nicky looked at Robin, saw the glint in his eye and began laughing.

They cycled past a thatched pub which was shut. Nicky said, 'My mammy and daddy used to live somewhere out here when I was first born.'

'That's right, I remember you telling me that before,' said Robin without adverting to the shadowy details he had picked up from his father that the Smiths had been well off but that Harry Smith blew the lot on drink.

Robin noticed a stile behind which a path disappeared through a wood. He called upon Nicky to pull over. They rested their bikes against a creosoted fence around whose posts flared manes of rye grass and took stock. They had cycled ten miles from home. Part of the excitement was that no one knew they were away; another was that they had no idea of their final destination.

Initially, the main road was mostly flat; then it took a short cut to towns through a number of small knolls to avoid promontories or to service interests along the way, sometimes to the exclusion of an old or abandoned scenic route. Along such stretches the boys were often only a mile or less from the coast. Through the occasional thinning in woodland or forest the teeming sea had, for the past few minutes, been flashing with a compelling awesomeness.

'What say we go down this path and see where it takes us?'

'OK,' replied Nicky. 'But watch the dung.' Briquettes of horse manure studded the untarred lane.

'Did you ever see so much shit in all your life!' laughed Robin, as he pedalled hard or braked to avoid the most conspicuous mounds and their clouds of flies in frenzied swarm. Suddenly, as they turned a bend, the lane gave onto a whitewashed courtyard. A teenage girl in riding regalia was trying to mount a pony which was restrained by a stableboy. The pony snorted and bridled as if protesting that this was its day off. The girl and boy stared in astonishment as the bikers described a loop around them.

'Hiya!' shouted Robin.

'Bye-bye!' said Nicky, as they pedalled furiously out a gate at the other end and passed a broad gable whereupon they became stuck in the flinty gravel of a rectangular driveway which served the large house in front of which they now stood.

Curtains fluttered in an open casement and there was an ambience of authority and, despite the silence, an indefinable industry about the place which frightened Nicky. They dismounted, rushed the bikes onto the lawn and, to shrieks of horror from an old-boy pruning shrubs, leaped on their saddles and raced parallel with the driveway towards an entrance of tall, black, wrought-iron gates which lay open. Once outside they looked behind them and noticed the sign which in bold lettering read, 'Private – No Entry'. The road continued in a serpentine descent through alternate cool glades and hot, exposed patches of road, towards the seashore.

They let their bikes freewheel, occasionally curbing acceleration. Above them, hanging tassels of leaves rustled in a unison of fine whispers in the wake of each ribbon of wind. On those stretches where they passed through vaults of sunlight the mature bouquet of the season – a heavy botanical blend of verdure and efflorescence – rose in their nostrils and was relished in the palate of memory.

I wish this moment would last foreverandeverandever, thought Nicky, as he looked at his companion riding alongside, so richly alive that he was screaming out his joy to the birds in the trees.

Large, old-fashioned villas sat off the road in spacious grounds of otherworlds; then there were a few white and grey cottages. Tears trickled down Robin's eyes, drawn by the salty breeze berating his face. Nicky shouted that he had swallowed a fly but didn't stop and spat out for a half-minute until he shouted, 'It's away now!'

Their speed lessened as the gradient approached the horizontal. They crossed a railway line and cycled lazily along an open road where the sea, separated from them by a dry stone wall, bristled out to their left. They felt as if they had landed in another country having left their own illegally. They came to where the wall had been knocked into a field and its stones scattered and broken to form a hard, parking surface. The remainder of the field, in gradations of impoverished grass, came to an end in a causeway of bladder-wrack and big, rounded stones over which clashed the mighty rolling cymbals of the sea.

They dismounted, passed a couple of parked cars and followed a rough path which gave onto a small beach. The tide was in and they walked close to the breaking combers where the sand was firm and less inclined to stick to the tyres.

'Hold my bike a second,' said Robin. He went forward, bent down on his hunkers and received in the palm of his hand some incoming surf.

'I love the way it gently paws the beach,' he said dreamily, almost hypnotically. 'It's calling us back, into its depths.' Nicky knew exactly what he meant and felt the echoes of a primitive, ancestral rapport.

Below a Maginot Line of dunes, on a band of hot, white sand, sat a woman on a blanket, thirtyish, her full freckled face thrust towards the sun. Nearby, a boy and a girl and a toddler, all in bathing-wear, were making castles. Robin cut towards them. 'We'll ask her to mind the bikes,' he said. 'Excuse me, missus. Could we set our bikes here. We're going into the water.'

'Yes, certainly. Leave them just there.' And she pointed to a spot within her purview. Her hair was shoulder-length, her teeth were neat. But she had seen slimmer days: her gold ring conspicuously cinched her wedding finger. During the exchange the boys stole a glance up the harbour of her parted thighs to where a small fringe of black hairs showed on either side of the fleshy gusset of her bathing suit. It stopped Nicky from breathing and made his face flush even after he averted his eyes. They strode a few yards off to strip down.

'Aggh!' teased Robin. 'She's having the baby with the beard!'

'Watch you're not heard,' said Nicky, feeling embarrassed again.

'Black, too. My favourite colour,' said Robin as he stood taking in the small bay and beach and a headland nearby where stood a number of inclined trees pointing inland, their branches caught in a permanent shriek. 'Ah, this is the life!' he said. 'Now, a couple of girls in a tent would go down well! Could you imagine rubbing oil all over Madeline Taylor. Ouu-uummmm!' he shuddered. 'Have you noticed her, how her hips sway and tits swing when she walks? Absolute harmony! She's a great size for her age! Must be fifteen now. And her lips, especially the bottom one pouting. As thick as . . . as a lugworm! I'd love to be a mackerel sucking on its juiciness.'

All this waste of ink, thought Nicky-the-blotting-paper.

'I could get you off with her wee mate. Suit you too. She's as quiet as a mouse!'

Nicky screwed up his nose and never answered his wishful-thinking, empty-boasting, lovable friend who had yet to even find the courage to approach Madeline. He had written her a poem once, whose meaning Nicky had found incomprehensible, and given it to Nicky to push through her letter box but then withdrew it. He hadn't even signed it.

Robin read Nicky's attitude and laughed. 'OK! Race you to the water!'

They dashed across the dusty sand and continued in the same speed through the submerged shingle of tiny broken shells and screamed as the gelid water, its sheerness, ran its protean blade up to and over their belly-buttons. They eventually found respite in a band of warm current. Nicky, taller and heavier than Robin, waded out some distance before swimming. Other bathers were hundreds of yards away; and, apart from the woman with the pretty children, the beach, small, with no amenities, unsignposted and barely accessible, could have been described as empty.

Coming out of the water Nicky let air into his trunks to obscure the features of his genitals. Robin was already sitting in front of the woman, chomping on one of her sandwiches and talking rapidly. He had brought their clothes over.

It was difficult to determine her mood. She would laugh at Robin then become impassive. She expressed amazement that they had travelled all this way from the city without a puncture repair kit.

Robin secretly wished that she needed to dress and trusted him to drape the towel securely round her.

She gave Nicky a salmon sandwich and handed him a bottle of lemonade.

'What's your book?' asked Robin.

'Criminology. I'm trying to get a head start before the autumn term. Boring stuff. Social Sciences. I'm a mature student.'

'Can wives study?' asked Robin.

'With difficulty.'

'Where's your husband? Is he at work?'

Nicky wished Robin would show more tact.

'He says he's working,' she replied with a hint of sarcasm and looked out across the silvery leaves of sunlight curling on the sea's surface. 'I know where he's working!' she added with vehemence.

'Where's that?' said Robin. 'Golfing? Drinking?'

'Oh, no matter.'

Those three words. Oh, no matter. Nicky saw right through the pith of their meaning, down to their roots in the depths of an incredible sadness, a life gone awry. He stared unnoticed into her lovely brown eyes. At that moment he would have loved to have been a man and would have been proud to defend and comfort her. Nicky loved Robin from the beginning in an immediate, almost preordained way. But with this woman, a stranger, what impressed him was the chemistry of her potential. How could her husband miss it!

'What's he work at?' persisted Robin.

Her countenance changed to a momentary smile at Robin's naive relentlessness; and Nicky found himself for a few seconds behind the times.

'He's a police officer. A detective.'

'A real detective! Has he ever shot anyone?'

'No!' she laughed. 'He doesn't carry a gun, thank God.' She broke off and called out the name of her toddler. The toddler was charging the sea, then retreating in screams before the tide even reached her ankles.

'*Nikolai*, go and get Jane before she drowns,' said Robin. Nicky got up and went after the child. As soon as he took the little soft chubby hand of the baby he was transformed. He pretended to trip, fell on the sand and rolled head-over-heels several times, like Charlie Chaplin. Jane's laughter was almost hysterical. She said: 'Do again, do again!' He said no, took her hand once more, lulled her, and then suddenly tripped. The child went into convulsions of giggles. He returned her to her mother at whose side Robin was abstractedly carried away talking about the solar system.

'And what speed do you think we're travelling at?'

'Pardon? . . . Oh, I haven't a clue,' she said.

'Go on, guess!'

'I just don't know.'

'We're travelling around the sun at 108,000 kilometres per hour! Isn't that something?' he said smugly. 'And the sun, the earth, the moon, the other planets are all flying through space at 200 kilometres a second! . . . A second! And our galaxy is flying through space at 600 kilometres per second . . .'

'It's all beyond me,' she said.

'You only think that.'

'It's a great day, isn't it,' said Nicky, who up until now had hardly spoken.

'Yes,' she said, turning to him. 'It's nice here. And usually quiet. And the kids like it. But all my friends would prefer a fortnight in places like Tenerife or Greece. I think I could spend summer and winter here. Even when it was stormy it would still be peaceful, if you know what I mean.

'And what about you two? Enjoying the school holidays?'

Nicky nodded. Robin became bored. 'I'll be back in a minute,' he said, wandering off towards a group of young people making a din in the distance.

'What's your name?' the woman asked.

'Nicky. Nicky Smith.'

'And your friend's Robin, isn't that right? Would you like some chocolate?' She handed him a bar, which had already begun melting in its wrapper, and took one herself. She shared out other bars with the kids. 'I know I shouldn't indulge, but it's a kind of drug,' she laughed. 'By the way, my name's Elizabeth.'

He was glad she told him: he didn't have the nerve to ask. He was infatuated. Jane was once again charging the waves and her mother called out to her. Nicky ran and lifted her up by the armpits and she kicked wildly in the air. On his return Nicky walked on a sharp piece of shell which pierced the sole of his foot. He tried to ignore the pain but Elizabeth had seen it happen.

'Are you OK?'

'Yes, I'm OK. It's just a wee cut.'

'Sit down and let me see.'

He sat down on the sand and she lifted his foot into her warm lap between her soft hands and gently dusted away the sand like an archaeologist with a precious artefact. Nicky felt his feeling pour into her and she looked at him innocently and solicitously.

'That's a deep cut. Wait and I'll put a plaster on it.'

'It's OK, honestly.'

'No, it's not. Now stay put.' She went to the water's edge, rinsed a cup and filled it. Then she returned, sat down and took his foot in her lap again. She poured the water over the cut and the sensation made his toes curl. In reflex he attempted to pull his foot away. But she held on and they both laughed. She dried his foot and applied a small plaster from her bag. 'There now. But no more swimming for you, today,' she said.

'Thanks,' said Nicky.

Robin returned with a tin of beer in his hand. 'We'd need to be moving,' he said. 'Here, want some?'

Elizabeth declined.

'What about you, Nicky?'

Nicky also refused.

'I've a spare towel if you want to get dry before going,' said Elizabeth. No – no – their shorts were almost dry, Robin insisted, although it was untrue. They changed into their jeans and tee shirts and said goodbye.

'My arse is bloody freezing,' said Robin as he pushed his bike along the beach.

'That was nice of Elizabeth, giving us grub,' said Nicky.

' "That was nice of Elizabeth . . ." ' mimicked Robin laughing. He felt at least twenty with his tin of beer. 'She *was* nice, Nicky,' he added reassuringly.

Nicky looked back. Once again her face was thrust to the sun. But where were her thoughts? She turned her head and smiled at him. He gave a small wave and thought, Good luck.

They reached the group of fellows and girls Robin had spoken to. 'Where are we going?' Nicky asked after a few brooding moments.

'See those rocks? Well, the lads said there's a short-cut to the next town and then back onto the main road.'

'Those rocks look dodgy. Look at the height of them. Are you sure you want to try it?'

'I'm up to it unless you're not . . .'

Phrased that way, Nicky made no opposition to the plan.

There was a little path which meandered through the rocks close to the petrified trees. For the first ten minutes they were able to push the bikes along by the saddles. Robin drank and sang and finished the beer. On occasions the path became just a ledge and so narrow that they had to carry their bikes on their shoulders and manoeuvre slowly against a veritable cliff-face. At gaps in the ledge Nicky leaped across first, then was handed the bikes before he helped Robin over. Twice they almost lost the machines. It wasn't long before they realised that they were trapped. It was impossible to go back and it seemed impossible to go forward. Below them a huge tongue of sea would rush into the cove and make a giant lick up its walls as the wind sent a stinging spray of spittle over them. They became cold and dispirited as they slithered along the grizzly black rocks whose passages lay in shadow.

'We'll have to leave the bikes,' said Nicky in desperation.

'Never!' said Robin. 'I only got mine last Christmas. Yours is the wreck. Leave it.'

'One bike, two bikes, it's the same problem,' said Nicky. 'We'll not get out of here in one piece if we try to carry these. Maybe we could come back for them once we've found our way.'

Robin pointedly ignored the suggestion, urged Nicky forward, then slipped. He grabbed Nicky's shoulder for purchase and missed. Nicky attempted to catch him with his free hand. Robin's weight on the nail of one finger dug into the back of Nicky's right hand and they both went tumbling over the side, the bikes clanging behind them. They fell onto a jagged shelf of rock, their fall softened by a lamina of bird flue and guano. Nicky had taken the brunt and broken three fingers. Robin's nail had also peeled a streamer of skin from the back of his friend's hand. Robin was lying moaning, though all his limbs were intact. His face, like Nicky's, was cut and bruised. His watch was smashed and he sat up and stared at it like a shell-shocked soldier.

Nicky winced and stuck down the roll of skin in a swollen ridge of blood. He used his teeth to rip off part of his torn tee shirt. 'Robin, Robin! Tie this. Tie this for me.'

Robin came to and bandaged the wound.

'Come on,' said Nicky. 'We have to climb out of this.'

'I'm afraid, Nicky. We'll fall. We'll only fall again.'

'No, we'll not. We'll not!'

It took them fifteen minutes of painful climbing, with leg muscles trembling and hands shaking, to get back onto a ledge, and what seemed another age to work their way out of the labyrinth. Eventually, they emerged on the other side but there was no sign of a town, just a shoreline steaming with an overpowering stench of beached matter.

'We'll have to take to the fields,' said Nicky. The fields were partially flooded, like rice-paddies. At times their runners were almost mud-sucked off their feet in loud slurps when the bulrush hassocks onto which they had leaped quickly sank. But, at long last, the bog fizzled out and the ground beneath them no longer squelched.

They disturbed some grazing cattle, provoking a series of lowing which carved the still air of the pasture and sent a number of wood-pigeons flapping from their perch in a clump of hawthorn trees. Nicky climbed over a gate into an overgrown lane. He helped Robin down.

A warm draught of air drifted through the green and foliage-shaded alley. Insect life drowsily hummed in air heavy with a pot-pourri of wild scents.

Smiling, Robin plucked and split open the pale magenta bells of the prolific fuchsia, squeezing the nectar from the flowers and voluptuously catching each droplet on the tip of his tongue. He showed Nicky how it was done.

'We'll get onto the main road soon,' said Nicky, 'and hitch a lift.'

'Two bloody hobos. We'll be so lucky. Hey! You should see your face!' quipped Robin, regaining his spirits.

'*My* face? You should see yours!'

They came to a long road where telegraph poles like driven crucifixes profaned the countryside. There was some traffic and they took the direction in which the cars had travelled.

They were in sight of the trunk road back to the city when a car passed, slowed and then stopped. As they approached it they saw Jane in the back, strapped to a safety chair, and her well-behaved brother and sister sucking on bribes.

'It's thon woman!' exulted Robin.

Elizabeth leaned across the seat and opened the passenger door.

'What happened to you two? Were you attacked?'

An explanation followed. She told them to get in.

'. . . Yes, about a hundred feet down a cliff,' Robin repeated, with the euphoria of one now safe and in exquisite comfort and who cannot take in the contrast in his luck. 'But Nicky saved us. He got us out, OK. He thinks his fingers are broken. Don't you, Nicky?'

She looked over her shoulder to Nicky who felt a fool, inadequate, dependent.

'I think we should go straight to the hospital, boys. You need to be checked up.'

'No!' said Robin. 'We would be obliged, missus, if you could drop us near a bus stop. That would do.'

'Well then, I'm taking you home,' she insisted. 'And don't keep calling me "missus". I'm not that old, am I! Call me Elizabeth.'

Nicky, using his undamaged hand, played 'Round and Round the Garden' with the kids and had them agonised with excitement as he prolonged the stages of 'one step', 'two step', 'tickly, way under there!'

The car pulled into their street and they thanked Elizabeth. Nicky didn't move from the spot until her car had turned the corner. His backhand wound would turn into a scar. The bones of his broken fingers would knit. With the complicity of his mother his father was never to learn the details of the day's events.

Robin's parents were appalled at what had happened. 'Your new bike!' his father had complained, only to be quoted a string of notional defects Robin had invented and rehearsed whilst limping up the path.

'The bike's not important,' said his mother whilst she cleaned Robin's cuts and grazes. She lifted up his chin so that their faces met. Behind the soft medium of his blue eyes his person, whose life had hitherto been so manifest, was evolving into the compound individual who would leave her.

Robin, the child, leaned over and kissed her on the cheek.

3

BLACK CLOUDS MENACED the city, making the afternoon a prolonged leaden twilight and enforcing a premature night upon the early evening. Then, during the small hours when floorboards contracted under the sudden cold spell and the wind whipped every loose end, the clouds broke and sent their showers of spears earthwards. There they snapped on the slate roofs or were blunted by the paving stones or pierced and disappeared into the soft soil of garden lawns. But by early morning the clouds had disappeared and the unperturbed sun once again radiated its celestial light and heat.

'What's wrong with your lip?' asked Nicky.

'I've a cold sore. Sure it's been the four seasons around here since the end of July.'

It was eleven in the morning and they were inspecting the shed for leaks. The roof was intact.

'Fancy going somewhere?' said Nicky.

'Sure we're skint.' Robin sat rubbing his hands as if the sweat in his palms were dust. He had been listless, rude and impossible to cheer since shortly after their disastrous day at the seaside. Sometimes he sent Heather to the door to say he wasn't going out. There was an awkward silence. Then he said: 'I'm away in. I'll maybe see you later.' He brushed past Nicky, who was left speechless.

Nicky experienced a tremendous loneliness and a desperate longing for Robin to shake off the devil that had him in its grip. He closed the door after him, left the garden, and walked down the street, smoking and chewing his cigarette, a great habit he had formed. He kept one hand in his pocket; the other with the broken fingers swinging by his side had nowhere special to go.

He turned the corner and continued to the end of the road. In the sun the asphalt footpath was quickly drying in an embossed, speckled pattern which stretched out before him like infinite galaxies. He imagined he was God stepping on constellations in giant strides across the universe and it was as he was thinking this that his eye spotted what looked like a twenty-pound note on the ground. Half of it flapped like a sparrow with a broken wing; the damp half lay motionless. He lifted it. It was genuine! He hummed 'Pennies from Heaven', the melody of which he had picked up as a child around his mother's skirts when she sang to herself. He laughed when he caught himself mimicking in his mother's off-key lilt the words, 'If you want the things you love, You must have showers . . .'

This will cheer up Robin, he thought, and turned to go back. He hadn't travelled too far when he encountered the whole Russell family, that had a reputation for being in the eye of much trouble and for lowering the tone of the street and the respectable neighbourhood. Their empty milk bottles were never washed and at Easter their Christmas decorations were still hanging. The mother, a widow, was highly-strung, pinched snuff, took a drink and did some shouting at those she suspected of poking fun at her family. There she was, with her four sons and daughter, combing the footpath and drain, and shaking the distraught daughter so hard that her socks had fallen down and her tears were shooting out like sparks.

'Did you lose twenty quid?' Nicky asked Barl, the eldest son.

'Why, did you find it? Hand it over!' Barl was aged seventeen and with his rotting teeth and maniacal smile looked villainous. The others weren't too bad. Barl snatched the note from Nicky and grunted. 'Now, where-to-fuck did you get it? Steal it off my baby sister, did you?'

Nicky towered over him but Barl was far heavier. He should be on all-fours and on his way to the market, thought Nicky, going on like that.

'I found it, Barl. Just over there.'

'Fuck, but you're lucky. It's OK, ma. I got it,' snorted Barl, turning towards his mother and cleaning the note along the sheen of his jeans. He pushed Nicky into a small privet hedge and walked off.

For a few moments Nicky sat where he was. It was quite comfortable among the twigs although some leftover raindrops splashed into the horn of his left ear, rolled about ticklishly and made him laugh. Nicky knew that had he wanted he could have punched out a few of Barl Russell's liquorice-black fangs, even with his undamaged left hand, but he just couldn't see any point in retaliation. Robin had once quoted him one of Newton's laws: to every action there is an equal and opposite reaction. 'That's a beautiful phrase,' Nicky had said. 'It also sums up the violent way of this world, doesn't it? But if we are to be better we have to rise above that and have a higher standard.'

'Nicky!' Robin exclaimed. 'That's very poetic, very profound!' Nicky didn't know what profound meant but he knew he'd been paid a compliment.

He picked himself up and brushed from his corduroy jerkin and blue jeans a few dead leaves that had been cocooned in the hedge since its early summer trimming.

He still had nothing to do so he began walking again. He was not conscious of roads, streets, hills, corners, the bridge, traffic lights or the pedestrians streaming through the busy city centre. He looked at his watch. It was almost noon. He looked at it again: it was now half twelve. His feet throbbed and his brow was cool but immediately glistened when he stopped. He found a bench in the grounds of the City Hall, opposite his bus stop, and sat there with his shoes and socks off. Veins ran across the mounds of his feet like the exposed roots of a tree. He sat so still that some pigeons came right up to him, cleaned their beaks on his toes and cooed.

That's amazing. I can see the shape of my da's head in my big toe.

His imagination ran wild with the different ways he could possibly help raise Robin's morale but he concluded that he was talking nonsense and that time and patience were the only cure.

It was lunch hour and he watched shop and office workers and shoppers come and go. The smart young men wore the latest fashions. He laughed at some of them. Catch me dead in that gear! Some of the girls who passed by were very pretty. But he also noted that the pigeons puffing our their grey crayoned breasts had a nervous pathetic grace; the trees were a ramified trinity of crown, shadow and roots; and the heavens had a vast and infinite beauty which stirred the atoms in the unexplorable recesses of his being. All around him he saw his God. He marvelled at the birds, some of which could, within three seconds of leaving him, be perched on the dome of the City Hall should they so choose. Flight was a miracle. He tilted his head back and watched a mute jet steaming a contrail in the deepest blue of the skies. He laughed at the thought of Barl Russell's dog, which bayed at the sight of these tiny silver hyphens as they silently passed over the country. Even their dog's mad, said Robin.

He lit up a cigarette, blew the smoke out in a cloud, closed his eyes and drifted.

'Hello. Out feeding the pigeons?'

Nicky's sight was momentarily blurred by escaping, twin translucent creatures which swam in unison under the folds of his eyelids as if fleeing the girl's voice and image. He had trouble making her out, for although she stood directly in front of the sun, its light poured around her and resumed its course like water flowing around a boulder. He could smell her perfume, the pheromones of some kind of lavender joyriding the cascading motes.

Then he recognised Madeline, the daughter of Jack Taylor, their local postmaster, muse to the greatest poet since the last one died, Robin Coulter.

'Where's your baby brother?'

'Eh . . . Hello. No. In his house.'

She giggled. 'You *are* funny! Mind if I sit down? Is there something wrong with your feet?'

'Like what? You smell something?'

'Oh, I don't know, but have you no shoes or socks?'

'They're hiding behind me. In the bushes.'

'What are they doing there, if you don't mind me asking?'

'Earning me money. We're skint.'

'Sorry? I don't understand.'

'I'm begging for money and letting on I've no shoes or socks.'

'You're joking. You're having me on, aren't you?'

'Yes, I'm only joking.' He was nervous and constantly needed the steel of blue smoke within him. He offered her a cigarette but she refused.

'You had me worried there. I thought you had flipped. Why do you smoke? It's not good for you, you know.'

'It is for me.'

'You don't say much, do you?'

'I don't have much to say.' Nicky thought he was handling this encounter brilliantly. The score was easily a draw so far. Not once had he stuttered or talked real nonsense. Rarely could he speak calmly to girls, other than to Heather or perhaps a cousin. Elizabeth of a few weeks back had been a woman so that didn't count. It was entirely new to him and not as daunting as he had expected. The girl was attractive. He used to think her fatter. He could see why Robin liked her. A lot of girls were silly, though.

He braced himself. 'You must be very smart, working in the post office and all.'

'Oh, I only help out during the holidays or after school and on Saturday mornings. I like dealing with the public. I'm an extrovert.'

It was beginning to get a bit deep but Nicky continued.

'My mate Robin says you must be very intelligent. He's very intelligent himself. He's a poet.'

'He's very skinny, your mate, isn't he? You'd think he'd cancer or something.'

'How could you say such a thing! Don't you know it's unlucky? That's horrible, horrible . . .'

'I'm sorry. I'm sorry, I didn't mean any harm.'

Nicky leaned back quickly and retrieved his socks and

shoes. Then he discovered that he couldn't tie his runners properly.

'Shall I do them up for you?'

'No thank you,' he said firmly, and tied them in stupid knots using his fingers and staves.

'Are you going for the bus? I'm going as well.' She sounded a bit flustered but Nicky had to ignore her, for conversation with her went off in dangerous directions. 'I'm really sorry!' she shouted after him.

'It's OK, you didn't mean it.' But he still walked off.

She watched his rangy gait. It was a kind of march without the militarism: proud bearing without the swagger. He has a nice, firm backside, she decided.

With the few pence he had in his pocket Nicky bought himself a packet of salted peanuts for the walk home. Each time that it felt empty he shook the packet and another few nuts rustled at the bottom. There's millions in this bag, he thought.

He dandered out of the city centre. He would watch the swimming on the television, get his tea, then call on Robin to tell him about the extraordinary meeting he had with Madeline – though he would have to edit some of her remarks. Still, she didn't like cigarettes and Robin was a non-smoker and he could state, without telling a lie, that she had asked where he was, an expression of interest which Nicky could present as Robin having one foot in the door. He stopped in the street. What am I lying for? He had tried to go through life like a witness perpetually under oath. In his home there had been no religion. When he had been about five or six he had divined God without any external prompting. He would address God in his bedroom ceiling or in the sky as if it were the most natural thing to do. He associated God with good so that he thanked God whenever good came his way or when he narrowly avoided misfortune. He had yet to realise the incongruities of evil and suffering with his idealisation of the world.

He had also independently established his own inchoate morality, feeling unease if he were dishonest, greedy or bullying, or saw something immodest.

Nicky shook his head and acknowledged that had there been any great fervour in Madeline's interest in Robin he would have felt some jealousy and would certainly not have been as enthusiastic about presenting the truth as he was now about presenting a distortion. But hadn't I attempted to interest her in the first place? Oh! he hated these moral debates! He couldn't see that it was only really honest people who suspected the integrity of their own intentions. Since he himself didn't like to be deceived he decided against even mentioning Madeline. Lying could bring you bad luck.

'I wish we still had our bikes,' said Robin. 'We'd be home in no time.'

It was late September and Robin was cursing and indecisively selecting books from his school locker whilst Nicky looked on. They left through the science block, ran quickly across the football field to avoid being recognised by teachers, leaped a stream and climbed through a broken fence at the back of a factory. Nicky, being the taller, gave Robin a fireman's lift up the perimeter wall. He himself was still on the wall when he heard panic and terror in Robin's voice from the street below.

'Nicky! Nicky!' Robin shouted up to him before collapsing.

'What's wrong! What's wrong!'

Nicky jumped down. Robin's face had turned purple. His body was lifeless. Nicky loosened his tie and unbuttoned the top of his shirt where the collar seemed too large for his thin neck.

'Help! Somebody help me!' screamed Nicky.

People heard the alarm and rushed out of their homes. Some traffic stopped. Nicky felt himself losing primacy of place in the human crush around Robin and began shouting. 'For God's sake, give him air!'

Robin's eyes remained open but he didn't appear to be conscious.

'Are you his friend?' someone, a man, asked.

Nicky nodded.

'An ambulance is on its way. Where does he live, son, and I'll get word to his parents?'

Nicky answered automatically. He held and stroked Robin's

hand and kept whispering in his ear that everything was going to be fine.

'Robin, Robin? Do you hear me, do you hear me?' He saw an incongruous smile come and go. 'He smiled! He hears me! He smiled, everybody! He's going to be OK!'

He was allowed to travel beside Robin to the hospital.

'Where am I?' Robin asked.

'You're in an ambulance,' said Nicky. 'You fainted. Don't you remember? Your mammy's on her way.'

'Where am I?' said Robin. Nicky became frightened. But Robin smiled again, serenely. 'Yes! I see you! Don't fall! I'm coming, Nikolai...'

Then he became unconscious.

Nicky was sitting on a seat in the hospital corridor, his head cast down, two schoolbags at his feet. Billy was next to him, mindlessly putting his wrist watch through the repertoire of its special features. Mr and Mrs Coulter emerged from a conference with some doctors. Mrs Coulter was surprisingly calm and Nicky felt reassured.

'Robin's in theatre, Nicky. Being operated on. It'll be some time before we know the outcome. There's no point in you hanging on here. We'll get a taxi to take you home and we'll let you know what happens. OK? You'll be the first to know.'

'I can stay, you know. I want to stay,' said Nicky, feeling extremely disappointed and not wanting to desert his post.

'We appreciate it,' said Brian Coulter, 'but Robin would understand you having to go. We don't want to be in the way of the nurses and there's nothing anyone can do but pray. You've been great, Nicky. We'll get word to your mammy later.'

No word came that night. The Coulters' house was empty. Nicky couldn't face school and for what seemed like days walked the streets instead. That Robin would die was unimaginable. 'I would kill myself,' he said, as he stared obliquely into the river, his body restrained by the broad, pock-marked granite parapet of the bridge. Even here they had stood a hundred times, always making wishes. He smiled at Robin's mischievousness. He remembered his saying that when Mrs Russell looked over the bridge the river stopped in its flow, turned back and ran upstream! All the stranded fish told her to get to fuck out of it. Now a lone swan patrolled the turbid black water. Some cold mizzle, driven by a ball of wind, struck his cheek like a piece of wet gauze and brought him out of his reverie. He turned up the collar of his jacket and headed into the squall. Within a half-hour he was outside the hospital, pacing up and down the road like a sentry. He was desperate for news and yet did not want to intrude. He felt guilty for being healthy.

'Mrs Coulter was here and said you could visit Robin this afternoon.' His mother was standing in the kitchen with a tea-towel draped over her arm. On the worktop an electric kettle was beginning to boil.

'That's great news!'

Nicky had been distracted for almost two weeks. He had called and spoken to Billy several times but Billy was unforthcoming and would only mumble that Robin was in a bad way. Later he asked if Robin could recognise anyone. Billy said that he was conscious but groggy, though he was expected to be sitting up in a day or two.

The tin in which Mrs Smith kept the tea made a little gasp as it was sprung open and exuded a scale of pungent smells ranging from tea dust to leaf granules. She took cups and saucers from a cupboard, poured a little milk into the cups, opened and closed the fridge. Something about his mother's ponderousness made his stomach sink.

'Nicky.' Her tone was grave. 'Nicky. Robin is very, very seriously ill, do you understand?' Her eyes filled and then tears, like beads of a thick, clear oil, fell in heavy drops from the middle of her twitching lower eyelashes, curving along the two wrinkles which described her small jaw. It was very slow, dramatic and poignant.

Nicky burst into tears. Robin was going to die. *Robin*! the only true friend he had and whom he loved beyond all description. He couldn't believe that this was happening. Nicky howled like an animal, sat on his hands and rocked back and forth on the wooden chair, tears pouring out of him. His mother placed a hand on his shoulder but withdrew it when there was no response. She saw again the child she had lost one day in a busy store. She had finally found him by the noise of his wailing which penetrated the circle of shoppers and sales assistants gathered to comfort the little boy who was crying without having shed a single tear. Now she felt like one of those shoppers on the circumference of his life.

She went to the worktop and pulled some tissues from a box. Nicky shared them with her. He blew his nose and sobbed. The air was whorled with the fumes of brewed tea.

'He can't die! He can't! He can't! What'll I do without him. I'll be alone. I'll be nobody. I'll be the loneliest person in the world.'

'Oh, son, please don't say that. We love you.'

'No, mammy!' he shouted angrily. 'I mean, yes, you love me OK but I've always felt you put my da first, always took his part. He was your big child, needed your time. Do you ever really look at him? Walking around with vinegar in his mouth, hardly ever talks, has no friends. Do you think I never detected how you fussed over him?

'Do you remember when I was four or five, that time I was getting out of hospital and my da came to collect me? It was just before Christmas? I had been all excited about coming home and I kept talking about Santa Claus and what I hoped he would bring me and what he was bringing the other kids. My da stopped in the middle of the reception, bent down and told me there was no Santa. He was drunk and refused to budge until I repeated after him: "There's no Santa; toys come from shops in town. There is no Santa; toys come from shops in town . . ." '

'Did he hit you, did he hit you?' she asked urgently.

'No, he didn't hit me, I don't think. But he was forceful and intimidating. I was miserable that Christmas and the next. And the boxing club! Imagine sticking me in a ring at the age of ten to beat hell out of another kid. And you let him!

'Fortunately, by that stage I had a friend. Yes, I was an orphan – an orphan! – until Robin Coulter came along. It was only when Robin came to live here that my childhood started.'

'Oh Nicky, that is so hurtful . . .'

Hardly had the last syllable sounded when Nicky jumped

up from his chair and threw his arms around her, angry with himself for laying his pain on her.

'My daddy and you have been great and given me everything I've wanted. I'm sorry for what I said. I'm sorry, I couldn't control myself. I'm back to front at the minute. Forgive me.'

They stood in the middle of the kitchen, Mrs Smith's head buried in Nicky's chest, his long arms around her. His mother was lost in the paradox of a sudden current of close happiness in the midst of sorrow and imminent grief. Nicky dabbed his mother's eyes and she smiled.

Life: smiles and tears.

'I'm sorry,' he said again.

'It's OK. You're upset.'

'Does Robin know – about – about you-know-what?'

'Oh Nicky, no. He doesn't know. You have to be very careful. I should've kept it back from you but just couldn't. He thinks he's getting better. They may actually let him come home, depending.'

'What time have I to be at the hospital?'

'They asked for you to be there at two. Do you want me to travel in with you?'

'No. No, thanks. Does Robin know I'm coming?'

'Yes, yes, he's been asking to see you but the doctors had only been letting family in until now.'

Nicky arrived early and went into a shop across the road from the hospital which catered mostly for visitors. He didn't know what exactly to get that was appropriate and couldn't bring himself to ask the advice of the friendly assistant in case this led to routine but for him emotionally problematic queries about the patient's illness and condition. So he bought flowers, a box of Black Magic chocolates, a bottle of Lucozade and a book of crossword puzzles. He also brought their copy of *A Tale of Two Cities* which Robin used to read to him and which he had preserved in its old dog-eared condition.

Outside the ward sat Billy and Heather, she looking forlorn like a lost lamb. They had been there since mid-morning and were waiting to go home. Mrs Coulter's parents were at Robin's bedside and so there was some delay. Nicky felt precious time being stolen from him and anxiously bit his nails.

But after just a few minutes the opaque plastic doors were pushed open, the relatives came out nodding encouragingly and a haggard Mrs Coulter beckoned Nicky. She looked at the flowers and chocolates. A gentle smile broke her dry lips and she shook her head, pleased, the gesture embodying her affection for Nicky and his simplicity of devotion.

'Hey!' shouted Robin when he saw his mother lead Nicky into his room, a side-ward. 'You win *Crackerjack* or something!'

'Here's the man himself, Robin,' said his mother before addressing the visitor. 'He hasn't shut up about you, Nicky,' she said with a light air. 'Now remember to take it easy, you two. I'll leave you alone. I'll give those flowers to the sister.'

Robin's eyes had lit up, the way they had of old when Nicky called to the house. His shaven head was swathed in a bandage and covered in muslin.

'Wanna see the colour of brains at puberty?'

'You're crazy!' said Nicky.

'Horrible, horrible,' said Robin, slurring the words for emphasis.

As Robin spoke, Nicky couldn't help but be impressed, though it was a commonplace observation, by the characteristics and idiosyncrasies which his friend shared primarily with his mother, but also with his brother and sister and which would perhaps be inherited by some of their children in turn. It was a very unsatisfactory, poor form of immortality and Nicky discernibly shuddered.

'You getting a cold?' asked Robin.

'No. I don't think so. Hey, what's it like in here?'

'The nurses are always trying to get a peek when you're on the bedpan. And the sky pilots! When you see them hovering with their Bibles or rosary beads you know the carpenter with his measuring tape isn't far behind . . . Actually, everybody's very good, really. I'm in the hands of the Lord,' he said, but Nicky didn't know whether the remark was a reproach. 'Are you not going to ask me what's wrong with me?'

'Think I don't know,' jested Nicky. 'You old bluffer, letting school get on top of you! You should be in our class,' he said self-deprecatingly, 'playing with plasticine all day between

sleeps and smokes . . . "Teacher, teacher, the dog ate my homework! Teacher, teacher, my da ate me ma . . ." '

Robin laughed. 'See here! Too much brains aren't good for
you!'

'Anyway, how do you feel after the operation and all?'

'I feel a lot better. I'll be here for another two weeks maybe.
Then rest at home.' He leaned forward and half-whispered
though no one else was in the room: 'They could be telling me
lies, Nicky, couldn't they? I wouldn't want that. I'd want to
know.'

'I couldn't see it,' said Nicky with an air of reassurance, acting nobly in his treachery. He was surprised that he didn't give
the picture away because guile did not become him. He was
further surprised to find how easily one white lie smoothed the
way for the next.

'Guess who was asking for you?'

'Who? . . . Who!'

'Go on, guess.'

'For God's sake, it could be anybody.' Robin went through
a number of names to each of which Nicky in chess jargon
answered 'check'.

'Do you give up?'

'But I've guessed right!' protested Robin.

'Not this one. See that card on the locker. Where do you
think it came from?'

'You sent me it. Oh, I get it. You were asking for me,' he
said.

'No. The person who gave me the stamp was asking for you!
Boy, was she asking for you! "Is it twu, is it twu, Nicky.
Whabin's having his head seen to?"'

Nicky chuckled and smacked his thigh.

'Checkmate! But I have to say that that is the worst impression of Madeline Taylor I've ever heard. But are you serious?
Did she say anything?'

Make every lie convincing, God. Wash every word before
it leaves my mouth. 'I picked your card in Sonny's, right?'

'Go on, go on.'

'I went into the post office for a stamp. . .'

'Yes, yes, continue.'

'Robin, I almost had to swim to the counter! "What's wrong with you?" I asked Madeline, as if I didn't already know. "Oh, Nicky," she sobbed from behind the wee bars. "I've just heard the news. Robin Coulter's in hospital." I said, "So? So what?"'
'You said, "So what?"?'
'Yes. This was to draw her right out. Understand?'
'OK. And then what?'
' "So what?" she said, imitating me. "Some friend you are! I don't know what Robin sees in you." You can see how my attitude got her to reveal her hand. Then she was all sad again. "Robin's real nice but I've never had the chance to talk to him properly," she cried. "He doesn't smoke; he's so intelligent and nice looking. Has he ever said anything about me, Nicky?" she asked.'
'She said that?' interrupted Robin, raising his eyebrow, but Nicky ignored him.
'I told her that despite what your poem said it wasn't her big breasts or backside you were interested in but her personality. She seemed pleased it was her personality that – '
'You didn't say *that*, did you!'
'Naw. I only threw that bit in there now. But the bit about the personality's true. She said, "I would love to send him something. Would you bring him some flowers? You don't have to say I sent them." Then she opened the drawer and gave me a tenner. Boy, are you all set there!' said Nicky with a flourish.
'I've been trying to get off with her for ages, too! So the flowers are from her. I wonder would she like to visit me. Although, to tell you the truth I wouldn't want her to see me in this beehive,' he said, pointing to his head.
Nicky looked affectionately into his friend's blue eyes and sensed the Trojan Horse of death poised within. He wanted to take Robin in his arms but had to forego such a signal touch and allow him to continue in the relative peace and complacency of deception. For a few moments nothing was said. Much to Nicky's embarrassment Robin kept studying his scrutable face. Then, over the blueing scar on Nicky's hand he ran his finger in a physical union of their mutual tenderness.
'Still sore?' he asked.

'Not now,' replied Nicky, softly.

There was a short hiatus before the conversation suddenly erupted again and turned to cheerful reminiscences – those memories upon which only gold-dust settles and which sparkle the more at intervals of fresh re-inspection. They went over all their adventures and funny episodes. Then Robin said: 'Do you remember the song we wrote?'

'You mean, you wrote,' replied Nicky modestly, refusing an undeserved accolade.

'Yes, but you helped me. Come on and we'll sing it!'

'Here?'

'Yes, I feel like singing and you've to spoil me!'

'What about your head?'

'Fuck my head! I'll not move it, OK?'

'Oh, I'm not sure we should. I was going to read to you.'

'You'll only send yourself to sleep. You never heard any of the stories I read you. You were always snoring! Read to me the next time. Come on! You'd better join me!'

To the air of 'Bloody Mary' from the musical *South Pacific*, and with great brio but with his head in a burlesque of fixed coordinates, Robin began singing and Nicky eventually entered into the crazy spirit of the situation.

Ma-aa Russell lives in Twenty-four,
That's the house with the dirty door.
Ma-aa Russell lives in Twenty-four
Now ain't that too damned bad!

She's got no teeth and wears a pinafore,
Vari-cose veins, by the score.
She's got no teeth and wears a pinafore
Now ain't that too damned bad!

She's doing a line with Joe McClatchey's da. Ugh!
Who's doing a line with Annie Kelly's ma.
    Horrible!
    Horrible!
They're all involved in a man-adge-a-twa,
Now ain't that too damned bad!

'Robin! Robin!' cried Mrs Coulter admonishingly, as she rushed into the room. 'You're not supposed to be moving about! Do you want to . . .' She cut herself short. Robin was laughing so infectiously that Nicky couldn't help but giggle and then Mrs Coulter herself smiled. Then she said it was time for Robin to get some rest. Nicky rose and stretched out his right hand like a man for Robin to shake. All these years together, thought Nicky, and we've never shaken hands before. We have never fallen out. Robin pulled Nicky down towards him and with his other hand held the back of Nicky's head close so that he could whisper.

'I know the score, Nicky. You'll never make a liar. You're my mate; you are *very* special. And I love ya.' Robin kissed Nicky below the ear, sending a *frisson* down the latter's spine, the suffused waves of which spread through him with the pain of a thousand little arrows.

An irate sister and doctor had come into the room, the singing having been reported to them by a ward nurse. They quietly pressed on Mrs Coulter the seriousness of her son's condition – as if she didn't already know.

Viscous tears stood in Nicky's eyes, flooding his vision, and he stumbled out of the hospital. He found seclusion within a nearby park, leaned his head against the dusty, gnarled trunk of an oak tree and shook with emotion. He wept for Robin, for himself, for the feeling of helplessness in an unresolvable universe. He would have assumed Robin's place in the tumbril in an instant had it been an option under providence. He sat down on a damp bench.

Time became lost. Then the bell was rang, each single dong travelling forever and ever and ever. It was rung again. He was startled by the attendant's hand on his shoulder. The park was closed.

4

NICKY WOKE INSTANTLY when he felt the depression on the side of his bed. His room was bright – he slept with the main curtains open – and intuition told him that it was still very early. He looked up as his father was just about to rouse him. He saw close-up his old man's perpetually bloodshot eyes upon which seemed to drift the empty boats of his brown pupils; the lozenged wrinkles below his eyes; the black-and-grey moustache; the grey bristles on the face of this distant man, a stranger even to this bedroom.

'What's up?' Nicky murmured, noticing also his mother standing, almost hiding, in the doorway, her face blotched and smeared.

'Irene Coulter's brother's just been,' said his father gravely. Ugly little crescents of a milky substance, like the bitter juice from a dandelion stem, stood in the canthi of his eyes. 'He came to say that Robin died shortly after midnight. They hadn't been expecting it for a while yet . . . It's as well you saw him yesterday. . .'

'Do you want anything, a cup of tea or something?' his mother offered, advancing.

There was a space of silence as Nicky's entire world – years of symbiotic love, laughter, emotion, thrills, adventure, excitement – disappeared through a plughole in two or three seconds.

He turned over in the bed. Mrs Smith stepped forward again but Nicky was peremptory.

'Just leave me,' he ordered and they slipped out of the room, to speculate on the stairs as to how he was taking it.

He stared at the ceiling – white, blank, taunting.

So, life had changed to death. And I believed in miracles and that there was a purpose to everything. There is only the drudgery of life left. He has been taken and I've nothing to prop me up. Nothing!

He became frightened at the thought of death as the end, death without purpose. The foundations started to break beneath him and he felt the nausea of his hollow stomach mirror the sickness of an empty world.

Oh Robin, I need you. I'll never get by without you.

'I need you!' he shouted. 'I need you!'

'Haunt me, Robin!' he begged aloud, sitting up in bed. 'I know you're out there. I cannot believe that I am talking to just your memory. I don't believe it. I *won't* believe it! You got a bad body, that's all. Fate was cruel . . .'

'Haunt me! Rattle the window; throw the radio on the floor; tear the sheets off the bed; kick me in the stomach; but haunt me, haunt me, haunt me, my friend!'

Nicky was choking with tears, with frustration, with anger. His mother and father heard his shouts, looked at each other across the plate of toast and ran immediately for the stairs. Neighbours on either side heard the commotion and stirred, some rushing to their doors.

Nicky, completely naked, had gone on the floor on his knees, his fists raised high to heaven.

'God! I took you at your word!' he screamed. 'Life was sacred, a sparrow couldn't fall without you knowing! Where are you now when I need you, when I need reassurance! You're full of crap! Where's your justice! Hold your head in shame, you bastard!'

He was insulted by the sun continuing to shine, by the earth turning on its axis, by the sea not observing a moment's silence.

'I hate you, God! You permitted this! You fucker! Do you hear me! You murderer, torturer, you rapist. You toy with us!

You are the devil! I hate your world, your hunger, your diseases, your cruelty, your crimes, your lies, your death! I fucking hate you!'

He ran towards the sash window and with both arms outstretched and using his fists as rams he smashed through the net curtain and top pane. His head and upper body flopped through the upper window but the old wooden horizontal frame of the lower window wouldn't give. It checked his fall, bore his weight and saved him from being sliced open.

Mr and Mrs Smith reached the room together and together they struggled to pull Nicky in. Mr Smith cursed his wife's efforts as being pointless and she gave way. Nicky, thwarted, was shouting abuse at a milkman and newspaper boy staring up at him half-hanging out of the broken window like the puppet Punch hanging out of the seaside tent.

'See enough, do you? Wanna fucking see me do it again?' he cried, big tears running down his cheeks.

After a minute or so father and son fell on the floor in a heap, both exhausted. Amazingly, Nicky was virtually unscathed; there wasn't a cut on his hands or face, just some redness on his chest and stomach. He put his arms over his eyes as if the ceiling were full of grotesque images and wept. His mother cried and whimpered, catching her breath, and through the gaps in her thin teeth and receded gums came little bubbles and a dribbled string of saliva. His father sat on the floor with his back against the wall, fathoming in Nicky the fuel of a bewildering vigorous love. Nicky pulled a sheet over himself out of modesty. His desperate response to Robin's death had seemingly calmed him and after a few minutes he spoke.

'Mr and Mrs Smith, that's the last time your son is going to kill himself,' he said with a hint of mirth.

'Thank Christ for that,' said his father in the same vein, trying to relieve the atmosphere. 'I'll go and get some hardboard and nails.'

His wife dabbed her eyes with the ends of her apron.

'Nicky?'   .

He didn't respond.

'Nicky?'

When he did lift up his eyes to her she said nothing but

gestured condolences with a pitiful smile. Nicky acknowledged her, nodded and said, 'Thanks, mammy.'
    She felt it was safe to leave him. 'Are you OK?'
    'Yes, yes. It's all right.'
    'You'll get dressed and come down?'
    'Yes, I'll be down in a sec.'
    'You're sure you're not cut or haven't broken anything?'
    'Ma, I'm certain. OK?'
So, she left.
    He thought about Robin. From nowhere Robin's voice came
into his head, a story from religion. ' "Without me," God says,
"you would not exist." – "But without me," asserts Abraham,
"you would not be known!" Discuss. Understand that, Nicky
or shall I repeat it? It's a good one, isn't it? Do you want me
to repeat it?'
    'No, I get it. What Lincoln's saying is . . .'
    'Lincoln???'
    ' . . . Shoosh and let me finish! What Lincoln's saying is that
God's as much a product of man as man is of God. If we didn't
exist who'd know or think or talk about God? Think about it!'
    If you existed, Big Fella, thought Nicky, raising his eyes
heavenwards, you wouldn't be so dumb as to damage your
own cause.
    Nicky's beliefs had been simple: there could be no one true
religion; it was better to give than to receive; and God does us
no harm.
    'God does us no harm, huh! Fuck you, God. May you roast
in fuckin' heaven.'

The suddenness of Robin's death had taken the medical staff
by surprise. He had slept soundly for several hours after
Nicky's visit and awoke in bright, good form, joking with the
nurses and domestics. His father had arrived in the room
which in recent days had ceased to hold terror for him and
which was no longer strange, his son having managed to stamp
his character on it by having some of his belongings brought
in: a poster on the wall and his mascot, Brian the Snail, tied
to the bedpost. The patient had also been given an extra table
for his cards and magazines and on his locker, in a small frame,

was a photograph of the inseparable twins, circa 1975, which Nicky had sent. In it they were sitting on the step of Robin's front door. Both their faces were black with dirt, they wore shorts, their legs were brown from the sun, they had skinned knees and each had an arm over the other's shoulder.

Brian Coulter and his son exchanged small talk until the conversation came around to a subject which the Coulter children had only pieced together from occasional badinage – the story of their parents' courtship and marriage. So, with dad relaxed and temporarily basking in a false sense of assurance, and Robin avidly listening, father became engrossed in his own narration. And the tale, for all its plainness, was found by Robin to be fascinating and enthralling because the start of him was in the middle of it. He had history and substance.

Brian Coulter experienced a glow of conceited satisfaction and deep pride in reflecting upon the charm of his children.

His eldest son, Billy, was over-studious and generally inscrutable, and usually had to be compelled to go on holiday with the family. But still they had a good rapport. Brian could never have predicted that out of them all Billy would be the most badly affected by Robin taking ill and would have been so overtly emotional.

Heather had been his little pig-tailed princess with the gappy teeth whom he called Plum. She would break hearts. She had her mother's looks and she borrowed mannerisms and opinions from the rest of them as suited her beguiling purposes, making it impossible not to like her, because she possessed the traits and qualities one cherished in oneself.

And Robin. He was the rebel, with his sharp, double-edged sense of humour, whose risqué jokes fortunately went over Irene's head. Yet in many ways he was still a child and Brian mistakenly viewed Robin's friendship with Nicky, which was otherwise a mystery, as something juvenile.

Robin's mother had arrived about half eleven that night to relieve her husband. 'Don't tell her what I confessed,' his father joked when he was leaving.

'What was all that about?' she asked Robin and he proceeded to quiz her about love and marriage to see how strong her memory of it was. Robin was talkative and made her laugh a lot. Then he went quiet. She sat on her chair and looked at her dead baby with whom she was all alone. Every second of their nine months and fifteen years together took on the weight of a heavy, devastating loss, tearing at the heart in her breast. She lay her head along his protective arm as if it were she that needed babying and she sobbed for them both and accepted God's will without question.

At the wake Nicky sat in a kitchen chair close to the open coffin and was both proud of, and amazed at, the non-stop procession of mourners. There were relatives (some of whom had travelled hundreds of miles), neighbours, friends, school acquaintances and teachers. Mrs Russell – the Mrs Russell – bent down and touched Nicky on the hand, raising him to the status of a Coulter. People are so good, he thought. Sonny shuffled in and offered condolences. Every child should have a shopkeeper like Sonny, thought Nicky, about this big fat man who always threw an extra sweet in your bag and who believed you if you told him you lost your money coming down the street.

At one point the beautiful Madeline Taylor came shyly into the room with a plain-dressed, plain-faced girlfriend who acted as something of a foil to the former's prettiness. The two were always together – a bit like Robin and Nicky – though Nicky hadn't given it much notice until now. He stood up, moved a few steps towards Madeline and whispered, 'He was asking for you on Wednesday. He was very fond of you.'

Madeline acknowledged the remark, went to the coffin, and then at the sight of death – reminded of her mother – began sobbing copious tears. She turned and fled the room, abandoning her companion, Emma, who was embarrassed and froze on the spot. Nicky stood beside the anaemic girl and spoke for a few moments in a low voice. He didn't know what he was saying and, naturally, she understood but the occasional word, though she avidly nodded throughout, and anyone who looked across could be forgiven for mistaking them as a close, teenage couple. At the first opportune pause she asked him to leave her to the door, which he did, chivalrously, conducting the occasional internal monologue with Robin though he knew it to be stupid and pointless.

In the afternoon the mourners emerged from the cremation chapel and began to disperse, all the lifts having been arranged. Exhaust fumes from the black limousines, the scores of cars and three school minibuses, hung distinctly in the air for a few minutes and then the veiled form vanished and with it all evidence of a funeral.

Nicky stayed behind and strolled deep into an avenue of the adjoining hillside cemetery. The older part was conspicuous by its splendid tombs whose gates were welded by rust and over which stood guardian angels drained of any hint of the celestial with their cracked eggshell faces and bodies covered in an impetigo of clustered lichens. White obelisks and grey stone columns marked the important people of their day. The place signified loss, grief, heartache, tragedy – yet offered the irony of a sense of peace.

Many of the oldest headstones, gaunt, eroded, lightless, were sinking or being strangled by ivy or appeared as if they were in the process of being tumbled by vines of thornbush connected to an army of Lilliputians hidden among the low weeds and matted grasses. The black of their inscriptions had long been eaten out, making identification impossible, the way the worms reduce to an anonymous skull the distinct features, the once brilliant eyes and fleshy face, of an individual.

A butterfly flitted past, went into the shade and lost all power. Nicky picked it up and rolled it about on the palm of his hand but it too was dead. He set it down gently and walked on aimlessly. He stopped at the war graves and read the inscriptions to the fallen dead. Further along, he whispered to himself the words on a memorial tablet to an eighteen-year-old soldier, dead seventy years:

> Look in the faces of the flowers and find
> The innocence that shrives me; stoop to the stream
> That you may share the wisdom of my peace.

Clumps of bushes, overhanging trees, some shedding their leaves – the general dereliction – made an asymmetry of the radial layout, giving the place a disordered but mysterious character.

It was a clear afternoon apart from one small mustard-coloured cloud which was imperceptibly crossing the sky at the rate of a camel moving through a vast desert. The density of sweating humus in the autumn air and the faint sweet sickly smell of decaying floral tributes varied within each lane. He passed wooden crosses marking the graves of the poor and unknown, then row upon row of black and white marble which he imagined as so many tongues pointing to the sky.

When I was younger everybody was alive.

All the long-gone souls, mused Nicky. Billions have passed through the world, really to be remembered only by their family and friends who outlive them by just that – and he flicked his fingers to express years passing in a trice. Every road around him seemed to lead deeper and deeper into nations of graves and he shivered and looked anxiously for that single track which would take him out of here and into the future, all alone – for he rejected the implicit egotism that someone, somewhere, was listening.

5

ON THURSDAY MORNING the June sun was thrusting itself
through an immaculate opal sky. The fitful wind was sharp but
beginning to diffuse into several silky rustles and an elemen-
tal zest permeated and refreshed the air.

Nicky walked jauntily through the empty neighbourhood,
throwing pieces of bread about for the baby sparrows with the
yolky beaks and the mafficking young starlings. He was experiencing the cheer inspired by the fecundity of the season. He
felt the growth on his face; he would shave later, before heading for work. His parents were still asleep when he quietly left
the house. Through their half-open door he had observed his
mother lightly snoring on her back in her single bed. Across
from her his father in their old double-bed with the back of
his head barely poking out of the humped-up checkered duvet
looked like a tortoise deep in hibernation.

Nicky ran his fingers through hedges and across a xylophone
of smooth, green wooded railing which made a low, clacking
sound. He looked up at the dentist's big house, the gas chamber at the end of a dreaded pathway. Automatically, his tongue
apprehensively tested his fillings for perfidious holes. Then he
crossed the street, over the green and passed the local library,
Montside Post Office, the chemist's, the bakery, and stopped outside Sonny's shop, now renamed 'The All Nighter'. The shops

and green occupied a block and grass strip parallel with the sweep of the street as it rounded and halted respectfully at its junction with the main road. From this point the heart of the city, two miles below, and its array of buildings, the docks and glimpses of the lough, came into view as the mist lifted.

The young man entered the shop, which his old friend Sonny owned jointly with his brother. Sonny was an insomniac whose surgery was visited in the early hours by the waifs of domestic rows, desperadoes, the lost and lonely, who all departed somewhat salved if not completely disburdened by this old-fashioned, family-doctor type who listened sympathetically, observed, nodded understandingly, and often laid down no prescription – the cure having been in the shriving.

'You're a bit late for the early shift,' said Sonny from his stool behind the counter. Nicky usually called into Sonny's for cigarettes and chewing gum when he had to be in work at 5.30.

'Call this a uniform!' joked Nicky, pointing to his old jeans. 'Don't start to later. I'm on the vans. I'm out for some milk – and for a dander.'

Sonny's body was pear-shaped as a result of a sedentary life and a sweet tooth. 'Do me a favour,' he asked. 'Hold the fort a second to I nip out to the toilet.'

Nicky flicked through a magazine. Outside, a vehicle pulled up sharply, its rear end almost lifting off the ground. Water dripped from the tongue of the exhaust pipe and Nicky imagined the engine panting. Sonny's brother David – or Hyper as Robin had called him, because he was always agitated – got out and opened the hatchback. A young boy – his son – emerged from the other side. David lifted the first heavy pile of newspapers from the vehicle and struggled into the shop. He was younger and leaner, and hungrier for trade, than Sonny. Not many liked him. Sonny returned and Nicky went out and gave David a hand. Soon all the papers were shifted. In the shop David gave his son a grubby old knife with a bone handle to cut the plastic binding. 'That's it,' he said encouragingly when the boy did it correctly. The various dailies were then counted and sorted.

A small front-page item in one of the broadsheets caught Nicky's attention and he picked it up.

'Four Billion Years Missing,' ran the headline.

'We have virtually proved,' one scientist was quoted as saying, 'that the universe, which began in a Big Bang about 12 billion years ago, contains objects such as globular clusters that are 16 billion years old...'

Well, well, well. Them globs is everywhere and just when you're least expecting them, chuckled Nicky.

Sonny said he was making tea, would Nicky like some? He thanked him but declined, lifted a carton of milk from the glass-fronted cooler and placed a pound coin on the formica counter. Sonny waived payment with a shooing of his hand but David lifted the money, rang the till and gave him his change.

Outside the shop Nicky was smiling. People are so different. What makes one person sociable and another hostile? One man a thief, another honest? Some kind, some cruel? Four billion years! Where did they go? You're going to have a long life, he remembered the sexy widow saying, as her finger circled his palm as in 'Round and Round the Garden'. A barely perceptible touch that sent his blood pumping so hard he almost fainted. Then she opened her dressing gown and placed his hand on her crystal ball, blue-veined towards its nipple tip.

He cut through the entry at the back of Sonny's, just for a change of scenery. Shaggy branches from birches in the spacious rear garden of a home for elderly people spilled over green metal railings and there came the noise of dough being churned and the smell of baking bread from Holden's. Nicky walked along and looked idly up at the yard walls with their ivy climbers and coping stones covered in jagged pieces of security glass. Then, at one window, he saw a naked girl yawn and stretch and look up at the sky. He stopped for fear of movement being noticed and his eyes gulped her sexuality. Even from this distance he could see that against her white body her nipples were big and very dark, her breasts full but not protrusive. Using her forefinger she uplifted each breast in turn and cursorily examined herself before turning back into the room. He hurried to the end of the entry only to discover the bottom gate locked, but climbed over a small wall at the side of the library and into the street.

For the first time he felt desire for Madeline Taylor. In his last year at school he had sometimes seen her at a distance. If he met her on the street he would nod or say a brief hello. But he had never thought about her sexually. She now worked in her father's post office full-time and she was always jovial with Nicky when he collected parcel mail.

He whistled softly so not to disturb those in dreamland. Do you know something, he addressed the sky. It seems like four billion years since I've had a boiled egg!

'Good morning,' he greeted his mother when she entered the kitchen, bleary-eyed and pulling her apron over her head. Two light-brown slices of bread popped up from the toaster. He had set the table for breakfast, three eggs were almost boiled and he was just about to pour himself tea, the fresh brewing of which hung in the air like brine off a bubbling sea.

'No, it's not your wedding anniversary,' he smiled. 'We were low on milk – which I drank I was that thirsty – and I popped out for a bit of early morning sun as well. Then I thought, I'll make breakfast.'

She was pleased, sat down and he poured her tea. Above, the hum of an electric razor ceased and a few moments later Mr Smith appeared in the kitchen. He wore a V-necked navy-blue pullover but the white shirt beneath was buttoned at the collar and a tie hung from his neck.

'Nicky made us our breakfast.'

'Very good,' replied Mr Smith. As he moved on to his chair he carefully pulled it securely under him as if for years he had been the victim of some practical joker. He cut the top of his egg, releasing a faint, short-lived puff of steam. A bright yellow yolk glistened. 'Very good,' he repeated, lifting the salt cellar. 'Just the way I like it. Hope you are taking notes, Mrs Smith.'

Nicky felt proud. His father was usually taciturn.

'Did you know, Mr Smith,' she said, cutting her toast into soldiers, 'that a hundred inventors in five continents have been working on a washing-machine that will automatically unravel smelly socks but have so far failed? Until they succeed, unfortunately it seems that busy people like yourself are just going to have to learn to unroll them by hand instead of leaving them in a wee ball at the bottom of the basket.'

Nicky smiled and looked at his father.

'Nicky, do you taste soap off your spoon? I do,' he said.

'How else to wash your mouth out,' answered Mrs Smith, clapping her hands together in triumph.

Towards the end of breakfast Mr Smith once again took up the cudgels: 'To think that I gave up a rib just for it to nag me,' he said, appealing to the kitchen generally as he began knotting his tie.

Mrs Smith came back at him: 'Consistently tight-fisted. One rib. But of course that's a nonsense. Women came first – it's obvious.'

'Came first in gabbling. No contest there. Right, that's it! Debate over. Man has to go hunting or there'll be no dinner – all due respects, Nicky. Thanks for the breakfast. My socks are at the bottom of the laundry basket if you get a chance. I know I can trust you to rinse the spoons. But just leave the bed. It's hard to make with Mrs Smith lying in it. Byeeeee.'

'What a headcase,' said his mother, laughing. She cleared the table and Nicky strolled off with a mug of tea into the sitting room, the wide window of which looked out onto their back garden: one lawn, demarcated on the margins by broken soil and a neat hedging, and divided down the middle by a path of crazy paving. At the end of this path his father, indulging a belated interest in gardening, had had a greenhouse and shed built at considerable expense. For three years past he had successfully nurtured tomatoes and cucumbers. But in the open air nothing with the exception of the most hardy of plants would thrive for him: the herbicidal sweat of his green fingers murdered every youngster of a rose-shrub transplanted from the safe environs of its nursery. If he didn't drown them in water, he choked them with manure. What he failed to destroy, the greenflies finished off.

Nicky lifted and browsed through a nature magazine which his father, a store manager in a bookshop, had brought home. He relished with a warm, childish satisfaction the affectionate rapport between his mother and father at breakfast, though he still harboured some ill-feeling towards the old man.

He couldn't concentrate on his reading and he kept thinking about Madeline's naked body. She wouldn't have expected to be prey to a peeping Tom at that hour of the morning. He felt ashamed for breaching her privacy but he wondered what she had been doing. He knew very little about women, found them strange.

One night his colleagues had got him drunk in the post office club and later they all retired to a party in somebody's house. A drunken woman took a keen interest in him. Her misshapen teeth did her looks an injustice but she was very affectionate. Upstairs he lost his virginity to her. She went home and he fell asleep on the floor because another drunken couple needed the bed. He often pondered the incident for some sense of drama or grandeur, for its being a turning-point, but it was quite devoid of splendour. What was the most memorable about the experience which imprinted itself on him was the initial affection the woman had shown him.

His only sober sexual encounter had been within the past year. He had delivered a registered letter to a country cottage. An agitated red-headed woman in her twenties appeared over the flower-box of a tiny upstairs window and said she would be down in a minute. She came to the door, signed for the letter and spoke in an unending stream of sentences that had an insidious current. She was a widow, missed her husband, and too few people visited. He was wheedled into the living-room for tea. She said he had beautiful fingers, like an artist's. He was flattered. She said she would read his palm. He allowed her to take his hand and laughed. She took offence. He apologised. She said he was going to live to a great age. Her dressing gown was hanging half-open and she placed his hand inside. That Wednesday morning was spent on the sofa; another Wednesday on the carpet; and the third in a big brass bed where she casually confessed that she had been sending herself the letters and wasn't really a widow. Instead of being aroused by her guile he was shattered. He had started looking forward to seeing her and would shortly have begun telling her about his life and asking her if she could put meaning to it. Why had she lied? What had she wanted from him? He departed in a hurry. About three miles from her house he stopped his van, got out and paced the road, cursing himself, hurt and angry. He hadn't had sex since then. He went walking, he went swimming, on his nights off. Always waiting. Waiting and waiting on the elusive thread of an answer to his life.

When he had stepped out of adolescence he had found the world more hardbitten than he had ever imagined. He mistook cynicism as honest expression until he learned to read the difference between what people said and what they meant. He didn't surrender lightly his innocence but over the years surrender to the regiment he did in tiny, temporary and not so temporary compromises.

Windsor knot in tie, spray-starched light-blue shirt, navy trousers, sun flashing off the toecaps of his black polished shoes: Nicky felt good and looked good in uniform.

In work he was proud of the fact that among his colleagues he had the lowest count of mis-sorts. Furthermore, he was sharp-eyed and fast and dealt the letters into his sorting frame like a hustler with playing cards. Sometimes he had to be told to take it easy. It was the same the first time he went out on the vans. He was too efficient and if he consistently returned early from rural deliveries the supervisor would be seeking to extend the run. Similarly, he had to be encouraged – for 'union reasons' – to take it easy on his walks and to remember that he could make look lazy the man on next week's duty who might not be able to walk as briskly around the drives and avenues, the parades and crescents.

Walking down the street on his way to work, the kids, off school because it was a holiday, spotted him and ran after him, crowded him and clung to his legs. He gave them pieces of change amidst cheers, sharing out the money as best he could according to their age or size. Above the noise an adult's voice attempted to be heard.

'Yo!'

Nicky looked around.

'Yo! Young Smith!'

The ferrule of the sun obscured Nicky's vision but he soon made out an overalled figure leaning out of the upstairs window of Robin's old house, beckoning him.

'Come up to you see this,' laughed Dan Leckey, an ebullient, red-cheeked, stocky man. The Leckeys were the second family to have occupied the house in eight years, having moved in about three months previously and almost immediately begun befriending the street. As far as Nicky was concerned the first family were public vandals and for eight years he avoided even walking past their house, using the other side of the street instead. He was glad to see them go.

Dan shouted down to his wife: 'Jill! Open the front door and send Nicky up!'

Nicky wondered what was going on. He always allowed himself plenty of time for getting to work – in fact, was so conscientious that he was habitually half to three-quarters of an hour early. So he wasn't under any pressure apart from a feeling of eeriness from entering this house again. At a glance he saw that the carpeting and furniture and knick-knacks were changed thus half-diluting old memories. But as he climbed the stairs with the use of the banister rail on the left, and looking up saw the corrugations of the net curtain respiring in the draught of the open landing window, it became too familiar and for a second he was a giggling wide-eyed eight-year-old with a dirty face running up the stairs behind his farting friend. Then he tumbled from heaven to earth in an instant, was utterly, utterly alone again and felt anger at the past for having the power to elate, then to demoralise and crush.

'Where are you? Are you coming up? Just be careful coming in the door, I've dust sheets down.'

When Nicky entered the front bedroom there was a smell of damp paper and the pungent humidity given off by dank plaster. Dan stood ankle-deep in peelings, a scraper in his hand, a welcoming smile on his ruddy face, and nodded to the bare and scuffed sallowy wall a few feet above a small, blocked-up fireplace. Nicky looked at the sketch on the wall and read the writing in heavy pencil which the plaster had absorbed and preserved in a slightly faded fresco. They had been about fourteen then, had been messing about in this, Robin's room, just before it was repapered, probably staring out the window and passing comments on the world, but had had a tiff over something silly. To break the ice Robin often used to place his hand in front of his eyes as if Nicky's nose was dazzling and say, 'No, your nose isn't big; what makes you think that?' and Nicky would surrender and laugh at his impudence. On this occasion Robin had picked up a pencil, stood and drawn on the wall a huge nose with a large pendulous drip hanging from it. After a few seconds of suspense he wrote below the sketch: 'Not your nose. OK?' Nicky smiled and added, 'OK.' The correspondence continued:

'Friends?'

'Friends,' wrote Nicky.

Little arrows like the footprints of a mouse then ran to just above the skirting board where Robin had written: 'Yours isn't dripping!'

The mouse ran up the wall where its feet changed into the reply: 'Yours will be!' and more exchanges:

'Ah bruder. Meeza joke, OK?'

'Bruder? Some bruder!'

'Bruders!'

'Bruders!'

Below 'Bruders!' Robin had written his name in closely-packed horizontal capitals and Nicky had begun his name downwards at an acute angle starting with the N at the end of Robin but with more spaced lettering. From a short distance the two names looked like the figure seven or the symbol of a bird in flight. Often too they used to write this same logo on each other's arms, like tattoos.

Nicky searched in vain for a date.

'I laughed when I was reading it and then, just at that moment, I saw you coming down the street like the Pied Piper,' said Dan Leckey. 'You two must have been some pair. You didn't mind me calling you in, did you? It's just that it'll be papered over in a few hours.'

'No, Mr Leckey. It's no problem. He was a great friend to have. And what happened wasn't fair. But he's dead . . . I'll head on now . . . Thanks.'

He walked down the stairs and out the door. If the old vegetable patch was dug up, thought Nicky, they'd find a sealed coffee jar containing coded messages from us. But the past should remain buried.

Robin, ohhh, Robin. Your blood runs through my veins yet. But you are gone and can't help me. A million times I asked for a sign and was snubbed with a dead silence. You used to tell me that the most magical word in the world is And. It means there is more. It was superior to Yes or Amen. It means there is no end. It was like everlasting love. But you lied.

They could have trusted me with a sign. I knew I was a nobody but they could have trusted me. I knew it would have been a miracle but Robin and God could have trusted me to say nothing to no one. Huh! Life after death! What a figment! We have what we hold – nothing else. Nothing else.

Nicky got out of his van with a parcel and twinged his knee. Growing pains, he laughed, and gave it a little rub. A group of school friends were at the gate of the bungalow he was delivering to.

'For the last time, I haven't got any money!'

'OK, lads,' said Nicky, coming the adult, 'let's by there.'

'Over here,' said one of the youths, tugging the shoulder and attempting to frogmarch a recalcitrant, grim-faced, bespectacled teenager who was distinguished by his school uniform and who gripped his brown leather case like a security guard handcuffed to a wages consignment.

Returning down the path Nicky heard a cluster of menacing voices and felt that something ominous was about to happen. The leading bully among the youths had produced a small can of lighter fuel and sprayed it over the face and chest of the boy. He had been flicking his lighter for a flame when the boy kneed him in the balls, provoking howls of disbelief and an assault on himself. The youth's glasses went spinning across the ground. Nicky leaped in the middle, a voice of authority, a decisive change of circumstances. He began shouting, shook the main aggressor by the shoulders and forced him and his allies to withdraw.

'We'll get you again, you fuckin' wee cunt,' shouted one of the youths through patently false teeth. The victim picked up and examined his unbroken glasses, sniffled, and nursed a cut finger. Nicky felt the pocket of his navy trousers – Mrs Smith had been there – and from it he produced a clean handkerchief and tendered it to the boy.

'Thank you,' he said. 'Thank you.'

Nicky noticed a tremble in the boy's left leg and felt sorry for him. He himself had been the butt of bullying in his younger years because of his lankiness and introspection and the assumption that he was a coward.

'Are you OK?' he asked.

'I'm fine now, thank you. My home isn't far. I think they've gone, haven't they? That's the second time they've attacked me. Lucky for me you came along. I think your uniform frightened them.'

'Why were they after you?'

'That's simple! I live over there and attend a college. They live in the new estate up the road and in the afternoons to get my bus I have to pass those of them from the secondary kept in detention or late in coming out. They were looking for money but damned if I was giving them any. They think I'm a snob, you see, because my father, Gareth Williams, owns The Sitting Room shops. Do you know of them?'

'Yes, I've delivered to the main one down town. They're well-known. What will you tell him happened to you?'

'Oh, I'll not tell him anything! He'd want his friend the Super to curfew the entire neighbourhood! It was quite exciting, wasn't it! They almost set fire to me!' Then he said, 'Look. I've ruined your handkerchief. It's bloodstained.'

'Don't worry about that. It's okay. What are you going to do if they come after you again?'

'Run like the hammers of hell!'

The gardens smelt of lemon or lime and imparted some such hot summer day's piquant edge to the air. Nicky was enchanted and the teenager smiled coyly and charmed the moment even more.

'I'll have to be going now. Thank you, again. Oh, what will I do about this?'

'It's only a hanky. Throw it away when you've finished with it.'

Nicky watched him depart and then shouted: 'Hey! What's your name?'

'Gareth!' shouted the boy with a hearty laugh. 'Gareth Junior!' before disappearing into the next avenue.

Two weeks later Nicky was driving through a suburb having turned off the mountain road which overlooked the west of the city. He was talking to himself as usual. He didn't know why he was in such an expansive mood.

I feel like someone who has come out of his apprenticeship. I feel mature. I feel like a man, he laughed. Goose-bumps broke out along his arm and he felt excited by life. You must spread out. You mustn't be afraid where life takes you. There are answers along the way.

His attention was drawn to activity on his right. Workmen were cutting down a line of fir trees which had scenically set off this part of the road and were ripping up their roots. A billboard proclaimed the building of luxury homes on the site. Within hazardous vicinity schoolboys were watching a hypnotic chainsaw cutting through the rings of growth, through a record of the seasons, down to the sapling at the centre and out through later years. Nicky had slowed right down and his nose and lips were stuck so close to the windscreen that for a second he presented a twisted latex face. Is that someone waving to me over there? Then he recognised Gareth, smiled back, and pulled up along the side of the road outside a shop, forgetting to indicate. The motorist behind was forced to brake and angrily denounced Nicky with his horn. He was mortified, especially since Gareth witnessed his stupidity.

'You shouldn't have been so fucking close!' shouted Gareth at the motorist. 'It's your own fault! Dick!'

Nicky didn't like the idea that he had driven the boy to such a vociferous defence of himself. He slid back the door. 'Where are you going?'

'Home. Where are you going?'

'Your way! Want a lift?'

'Yes, that would be convenient. Are you allowed to carry passengers?'

'Not really, but it's OK.' In fact it was a dismissible offence.

Gareth threw his briefcase in first, climbed in and pushed his glasses back up the bridge of his nose.

'You're like a doctor with that thing!' said Nicky. 'Stethoscope, syringes, medicines. What are you studying?'

'History, English, French, blah, blah, blah. Exam time, starting in two days' time. It's cosy in here.' Without asking, he switched on the radio and found a pop station playing rave music, to which he sang. 'Daa, daa, daa, daa-daa-da. Daa, daa, daa, daa-daa-da,' and drummed on the dashboard.

'You like that?'

'Yes, it's brilliant. But I like classical music as well. Do you like classical music? We've a piano but it's mostly my mother who plays it. Chopin's "Funeral March" . . . "Bomm, bomm, bom, bommm . . . bomm bom . . . bomm bom bom bomm bommm . . ." I can play "Three Blind Mice" and, if pushed, "Für Elise".'

He turned and smiled and Nicky smiled back. He was a nice kid. 'Have you any calls to make along the way?'

'No,' said Nicky. Not strictly speaking, he thought, deciding to double back and make his drops later. 'Do you ever watch *The Sky at Night*? Patrick Moore? It has a great theme tune. I like it.'

'I've seen it on occasion but it's fairly late and I be in my bed. From *Pelléas et Mélisande*. Sibelius.'

He knows everything! How lucky to be so young and clever. 'Are you married?'

'No!' said Nicky. 'What made you think that?'

'Nothing. Just asking. There was a girl strangled over there.'

'Where!'

'Over there, behind that pub. She wasn't really strangled. She got away. It was in the *Telegraph*. I've a stick insect at home. I keep it in an aquarium. Of course, there's no water in it! It doesn't do much. Just sits there. Chews the odd leaf. Watching it is far more relaxing than watching goldfish go round a bowl. It helps me when I'm studying. Do you like pets?'

Nicky thought for a moment. 'Yes, I like pets.'

'Do you have any at home? Who do you live with?'

'I live with my mother and father –'

'Still? Wouldn't you prefer a house or a flat of your own? I would, if I were your age.'

'Oom, maybe. Come to think of it, I would like to be independent. I've a claim coming through very shortly for whiplash. An accident, about a year ago, badly hurt my –'

'That would be great! You could get a flat and I could help you furnish it!'

Nicky laughed at Gareth's energy and chatter.

'I've great taste,' he boasted. 'You could also get a cat. Or a stick insect! I wonder would they breed? I mean the insects! If they bred we could sell the little twigs to my college friends! But you were saying, about pets, sorry . . . Hold it! Slow down . . . There's that woman . . . over there!'

'Where, what woman?'

'Short blonde hair, tinted, sort of trollopy miniskirt, putting flowers into the Volvo Estate . . .'

'Is that the woman who was nearly strangled?'

'No. That's the woman I'm almost certain my father is fucking.'

'What! What did you say?'

'I think she's my father's mistress. She's a former girlfriend of my mother's as well. Not in the dyke sense! I listen in to their calls. I taped some of them but I've yet to catch my father and her *in flagrante delicto*. It's her OK. But sorry. Pets?'

Nicky was amazed at this young fellow. Pets. Oh yes, pets.

'I had a budgie once. Spent two years teaching it to talk. One day I came home from school and knew something was wrong by the look on my mother's face. I saw the cage empty and asked her where the bird was. She told me she'd get me a new one; it had died of a heart attack. She said she had buried it. I insisted on seeing the grave but she became flustered and then admitted there was no grave.'

'What had she done with it?' asked Gareth, staring wide-eyed into Nicky's face with an expression of concern that Nicky could have devoured.

'It had accidentally flown into the fire.'

'How awful! Was it an old open fire? Those open fires are so dangerous. There must be a high incidence of that in your houses. Were you upset?'

'Yes. I was. Nothing could have replaced him.'

'I'm sorry... Do you know that I don't know your name? How ill-mannered.'

'Nicky. Nicky Smith. And you're Gareth Williams Junior.'

'You remembered! Very good! I'm going to write about this in my diary. I keep it hidden in my study at home. My study is special. God, I wish I could show you it; it's a little sanctuary. When you pass through our front door the stairs are opposite you, parallel with the gable end. But at the very top of the stairs there's a camouflaged door, flush with the panelling. You press it open and enter. Hey presto! You're in my study. It is long and narrow and was built on to the gable by the previous owner as a kind of retreat or lounge but it's not as ugly an architectural appendage as it sounds. You don't notice it immediately from outside the house because the roof of the garage obscures your view. It's the quietest room in the place. I have a small library, which I'm slowly collecting, and an oak table to write on. We've a snooker table in our basement. Do you play snooker?'

'Not very well. I sometimes can't tell the brown ball from the reds.'

'Well, we could play pool instead. You'll be able to tell leopards and zebras apart! You're very tall. What's it like up there?' And he laughed again. 'Have you any brothers or sisters? ... No! Neither have I! My mother, after I was born, lost both ovaries after developing cysts that had to be surgically removed. Isn't that great! We're both only children. I bet we've lots of other things in common.'

The boy was electric with vivacity.

'We're almost there. That was quick, wasn't it? Just drop me at the corner, please, unless you have to go into the cul-de-sac. I see by your gauge that we did almost five kilometres.'

Nicky pulled up. He was sorry that the boy would have to be going. Gareth pressed open the silver catch on his brief case. It seemed as if he was going to pay for the ride. Nicky felt embarrassed. This was going to spoil things.

'Here you are,' he said. 'I knew we'd meet again. After my exams I'll be away for most of the summer but I sincerely hope we'll pick up in August. I hope you'll want to, Nicky. We're special.'

He jumped out, pulled the door behind him, pulled it open again and repeated, 'Special.' He closed it, slid it open again and said, 'Well?'

'Yes,' said Nicky. 'Yes. You're right!'

Gareth skipped up the street.

Nicky was astounded. He looked at the object in his hand. His handkerchief was brilliant white, ironed and neatly folded. He pressed it first to his cheeks, this cool cotton cloud of freshness: then to his nose. It smelt vaguely of cologne. A sense of extraordinary power surged within his chest. He felt that if he reached out his hands his fingertips could touch any point on the earth.

He gave an euphoric yell and accelerated away as if his van was a magic carpet.

6

THERE HAD BEEN WEEKS that Nicky didn't know about, time passed so quickly. Workmates struggled through until Fridays: but he was prepared to swap days, nights, complete shifts to facilitate them. Often, the only full stops in his life were those moments when he realised that he had just wished the ceiling goodnight and another day was done. But now that he had struck up an important new friendship, the recommencement of which had to be postponed until Gareth's return, time once again drifted in around him, measuring its passage in the grains of a desert queued up on the neck of an hour-glass.

I would love to have a yarn with him. Just sit down and have a long talk about life and things in general.

He would work July, the traditional holiday period, and take his holidays some time in August, though he never went anywhere. His parents sometimes went off for a week, leaving Nicky blissfully on his own.

Nicky went into Montside Post Office. He signed for parcels and registered mail which Jack Taylor passed to him, threw the bag over his shoulder and went out to empty the pillar box. Just as he crossed the door he failed to notice a pedestrian who bumped into him. It was Madeline with a bag of scones. Several times it seemed he had met her, just here on the pavement.

'I'm sorry,' she said. 'I should have been looking where I was going. I was miles away.'

'It's not your fault,' he said. 'People don't see me. I'm like a ladder,' he joked. She appeared upset. 'Is anything wrong?' he asked.

She bit her fat lower lip and hesitated.

'Oh, trouble in the factory. I had a row with the slave-master general,' she said, referring to her father. 'Doesn't like the hours I keep at home. And I'm over twenty-one, into the bargain!'

Beneath her white blouse her breasts heaved. Nicky quickly looked away.

'Eh, would you like to talk about it? Would you like go out for a drink tonight?'

Did I actually say that? I can't believe it!

'Well, where are we going to go?' she said.

'Eh, where would you like to be taken?'

'Somewhere quiet. I'll leave it up to you. But don't call here. I'll see you at the bus stop down the road. Next to the mission hall, OK? About eight o'clock.'

'The mission hall at eight.'

'See you then,' she said.

The remainder of Nicky's day found him whistling and wondering what was happening. He had a great feeling of adventure through which ran a deep vein of apprehension. He was amazed at the elation he felt when he let slip to Gerard, the workmate about fifteen years his senior with whom he got on best, that he had a date. It was as if his chest suddenly expanded and the world witnessed him in a new light. Gerard leaned on the walking stick that Nicky had surprised him with the previous Christmas as a token of their friendship, and clapped Nicky on the back.

'I'll be expecting a full report!'

At home, after shaving, he came downstairs and sat in the living-room. His mother was standing at the window.

'Look at him,' she said. 'He never gives up. Some day his roses will bloom,' she laughed.

Nicky looked out and saw his father kneeling on sacking at one of the borders, meticulously pulling from the soil yellow weeds which resembled little stars.

Mrs Smith recessed in her armchair. Her fair face was wrinkled in line with her years, her hair was blue-rinsed and permed. She hardly made any impression on the cushion of the seat. She was thinking about the big garden she used to tend behind the picturesque former gate lodge she and Harry lived in. It was a few miles from the pub, The Tavern, which Harry's uncle left him. Across the lane from the lodge was a sluggish little stream which at one spot ran rapidly over a submerged V-shaped bed of stones and pebbles, shingling the light into tiny hearts. In the summer evenings she squandered time waiting here for Harry's car when he returned home during his break. Or didn't return home. She had been pregnant with Nicky. Nicky!

'Are you going swimming tonight?' she asked him.

'I've a girl to see,' he replied. He said it with nonchalance and it thrilled him and he quickly put his head back into a book on astronomy. He felt an all-round edge.

'A girl! Big secret, is it?' His mother was excited, fascinated.

Nicky tapped the point of his nose three or four times and his mother took the hint.

My Nicky with a girl! Her mind raced into the future. She secretly desired a daughter in a daughter-in-law to share intimacies with, be a friend to, to spoil, to go shopping and seek bargains with, so optimistically and perfectly did she foresee their relationship falling into place. She hadn't had a confidante since her adolescence.

My Nicky with a girl! How had Harry Smith addressed her, Margaret Donaldson? There's my girl! he would exclaim, even though she was thirty-nine. She had been a clerk in a spirit merchant's and had noticed him often when he came in on business, shy at first, but later joking. A little clipped military moustache and dark brown eyes. He would start off his order with the whiskies: 'Five forty-ounces of Bush, One Black Bush, Five Powers, Three Scotch . . .' and she would say, 'You're not going to drink all that yourself!' and he would always reply, 'If you'll help me!' One day he produced from behind his back a red rose, presented it to her and nervously bowed. Thinking about it gave her a *frisson* still. That, and the other time, amidst the ruins of everything – the lodge being repossessed, the pub bankrupted, Harry repeatedly drunk – when he came to her in the flat they had just moved into. 'You know, Mrs Smith,' he said, speaking from the centre of his soul. 'You're the best thing that ever happened to me. If you have to go, if I drive you out, I'll understand . . .' She quickly placed her finger on his lips. She stayed on. There were a thousand disappointments spread over the next six years. But he eventually stopped drinking and with some money she inherited they had settled here. He had become more morose and cynical and there were many times when she felt cheated. But she became an authority on him. And there he was, out turning the soil, while below his dead tilth she discerned the threadroots of love and affection still – just like the other morning at breakfast. It had taken an age but Harry was coming round, she was sure of it. One day he would walk through the door and surprise her with a single rose, as if to say, Remember me? I'm back!

'Mammy, what are you smiling at? You've a big grin on your face.'

'Oom, nothing. Just thinking over a few things.'

Nicky went upstairs to get dressed. He put on a short-sleeved grey shirt and a pair of brown corduroy trousers. He peered out the window: it might rain. Downstairs, he put on his duffle coat: he felt it made him look shorter. His mother fussed over imagined dust on his shoulders and told him not to smoke until the way home. However, he needed a cigarette before he got to the garden gate.

I must be mad. Why am I putting myself through this? What am I going to say to her? I hope she doesn't want me to hold her hand. He usually walked with upright bearing but plunged his hands into the small pockets of his coat. Why don't they make these pockets bigger, he complained, as half his spare hands stood out. Then he remembered he had a cigarette hanging from his mouth like a gangster. I'm all upside down. His intestines frothed. The muscles of his legs shrank in their cavities. I don't know who I am and I'll be presenting a mishmash. He imagined Madeline taking his palm. Let's see, she says. Yes, Nicky, you're crazy. But that line there means you mean no harm and do your best. He passed the post office on the far side of the street but couldn't see through the upstairs windows because a shoal of light was caught in the mesh of the net curtains.

He stood under some trees a few yards off from the bus shelter near the mission hall and the church: the distance saved him waving ridiculous signs of, 'Don't stop, I'm only waiting on someone,' to the irascible drivers of the buses that breezed past. He had been twenty minutes early and Madeline was ten minutes late. He had that sinking feeling of already having been rejected for a half hour. Something hit him on the shoulder. He hoped it wasn't bird shit. He looked. It was only a lump of old rainwater calabashed in the tree for a few days until now. Another five minutes ratcheted past. She only lives around the corner!

He saw Madeline hurry along the pavement. He felt the thrill and the terror of involvement.

'Oh Nicky, I am so sorry for keeping you. Just as I came out the door the strap of my shoe broke and I had to go back and change it and that meant changing my dress and coat. You look pale; are you OK?' She touched his cheek with the back of her hand. That made him glow.

'Fine. I'm OK. I just thought maybe you couldn't make it, you weren't allowed out or that something had happened.'

Madeline unexpectedly put her arm through his and began walking.

'Let Jack try and stop me!'

'I thought we were getting a bus into town?' said Nicky.

'We shall. I just wanted to get away as quickly as possible from back there.'

They alighted in the city centre and strolled through High Street. Nightlife was bustling even though it was the middle of the week. Eventually they made their way to an old pub in Bank Street. Nicky got Madeline cider, himself a German beer. She did most of the talking – small talk at first.

I am sitting in a pub, smoking a cigarette, sipping a German beer, listening to a very nice girl talking. I wish Gerard would walk in and see me. He'd be real proud of me! Look at her eyes. She has laughing eyes. In fact, close up, she has the beginning of a tiny turn in one eye – but which one? It actually makes her

more attractive. Do you know, I could sit here all night! I feel
like nuts.

'Same again? Yes? Would you like some nuts or crisps?'

'No thanks, just the cider.'

When Nicky began to eat his nuts Madeline shared them as
she spoke about her problems with her father and they went
in no time. I think I'll get another packet. That one was half-
empty, thought Nicky, rolling up the bag.

'He was furious and said that the fella was married and I
shouldn't be seeing him. My father knew him, you see. But I
didn't know he was married, did I? Well, maybe I did, but he
wasn't happy. And he used to leave me in wee romantic cards
and things like that. And phone me at odd hours. Did you
know I was going out with a married man, Nicky?'

'Eh, no. I didn't. Where did you go?'

'Are you sure you didn't know?'

'Yes, I'm sure. How would I?'

'I thought you might have heard at work. Just curious . . .
Would you like to see some photographs?'

'Of him?'

'No, silly! I've changed the subject.'

Madeline's whole person came to life when she produced
some photographs from the inner frayed silk sleeve of an old
wallet. 'That's my mother. Isn't she perfect? That's her sister,
my Aunty Sheila. My mother's name was Madeline. It gets con-
fusing, doesn't it, but handing down names is nice.'

'Where was this one taken?' asked Nicky earnestly. It was
of herself, her mother and father sitting at the beach. Many
beaches look the same but this one was unmistakeable. Here,
on the sand, they looked happy: it was just before Mrs Taylor first suspected she was seriously ill. Nicky was convinced
that the beach was the same one where Robin and he had met
Elizabeth and her three children, but Madeline couldn't say
where the photograph had been taken. Often Nicky wondered
what ever became of Elizabeth, the first female on whom he
had a crush. Over several summers he had casually rambled
the coast, looking for the lane and road down which he and
Robin had cycled that day, looking for their beach, anxious
to tell her that he had died, Robin had died. But scour the roads

and lanes though he had, everything had seemingly disappeared so that doubt called conviction into question. He studied the photograph again before appreciating that he had interrupted Madeline's flow.

Madeline had worked out that her mother was pregnant when she got married. She chuckled: her father was always telling her she had been two months premature. As far as she knew, her father hadn't had sex since her mother's death but for one occasion at a party, from which he returned and went to his bedroom in a black mood. Having no sex is bound to build up in a man. It was probably part of his problem, his moods, she supposed.

How am I supposed to answer that? Is that a glint in her eye?

'Anyway, he gets into a foul temper, watches every move I make and accuses me of flaunting myself at men. I'm supposed to tell him everything about my life. It all came to a head this morning and I just snapped.'

'He's just worried about you. He loves you.' Nicky was impressed by his fluency. I sound like a man of the world.

'Yes, you're probably right, but it doesn't make things any easier. I've decided to stop seeing the other fella. Not because of my daddy, mind you. Just that it's run its course.'

She rummaged through the wallet and pulled out a final picture.

'Remember her?'

Madeline and another girl were standing with their heads touching. He guessed they were about thirteen.

'Nicky! It's not as if she's a stranger.'

'What do you mean?'

'My cousin. My cousin, Emma. She used to fancy you! Don't you remember her? Deficient in Vitamin C, skinny, blonde, no dress sense. She's very pretty now. You'd hardly recognise her. She was in France for a few years but came back last Christmas. And guess what! She's now moved in with her boyfriend and has a lovely flat. She's so lucky!'

Nicky studied the photograph. He sensed a memory, chased it but drove it away. It was as elusive as the recalcitrant word on the tip of one's tongue. He looked at Emma again and

again. Then he experienced a rush of, on this occasion, a plea-
surable sense of recollection. It had been a hot summer's day.
He had walked Mrs Coulter, Heather and Robin to the bus
stop to prolong being in the company of his friend. As those
three boarded, Nicky heard someone scream. A pup dragging
its lead had broken free and ran out in front of the bus, where
it panted and wagged its tail. The driver had seen what happened so Nicky stepped on to the road and brought it to safety.
The pale-faced girl who thanked him was Emma. Of course!
thought Nicky. Emma's companion that day, Madeline, had
that fresh, girl smell compromised by overripe rosy flesh,
barely contained in a bright crisp cotton dress stained at the
armpits. As the bus drove away Robin was standing looking
out the window with his mouth hanging open and Nicky just
shrugged his shoulders.

Cousins. I never knew they were cousins. How many others passed us on those streets, each a small part of the familiarity of the place, only to disappear unnoticed down the
roads, or, like Elizabeth with her kids and car, into the
anonymity of the city; away forever?

'What's her name? Emma what?'

'Emma Reid. Her mom and my mom were sisters. The other
photograph I showed you. You must remember Emma.'

'I do now,' said Nicky, emboldened with drink, feeling
humour coming through from nowhere. 'The best pair of legs
I've ever seen and pleading eyes . . .'

'Hey you! Wanna make me jealous!'

'Ha, got you there! Yes, I remember her. Shy girl – as quiet
as a mouse.'

'Just like you!' retorted Madeline.

Around half past ten they got the bus. Two stops past Madeline's they alighted to allow a walk back. At the corner where
they were to separate, each time he made to leave she held his
hand tight, raised her body on one foot and kissed him ten-
derly. She let him go, would run back to him and ostentatiously
hold him. In this way they spent about fifteen minutes.

Well how about that, said Nicky, as he walked home, fairly
pleased with himself. How about that.

7

NICKY HAD BEEN to the cinema just twice in recent years. He had gone with a few workmates to see films that were the latest rage but which he found disappointing. He didn't see what the attraction was. Consequently, he was excluded from yet another fertile subject for discussion around the table in the canteen.

On this occasion, however, he had a growing lump in his throat.

He tried desperately to think of something humorous. He tried to think of something symphonically mediocre but the heart-tugging strings of the film score deepened the pain in his chest. It was a devastating scene – a terminally ill young girl was surrounded by her distraught family and was bidding each one farewell. She was incredibly courageous but her little brother was in pieces.

Nicky glanced at Madeline: her attention was on the screen though her hand was gripping his arm. He blinked his misty eyes rapidly, hoping that evaporation would do the trick.

As the audience rose from its seats at the end of the film Madeline said: 'That was sad, wasn't it?'

'Yes, it was a bit,' said Nicky, helping her into her jacket, trying to eliminate the story from his mind. 'It's very smoky in here.'

Outside, the night was warm. Couples streamed in all directions, voicing audible opinions. Madeline linked Nicky as they walked and discussed the film. Though it had been a very sad film Nicky had really enjoyed the atmosphere of shared emotion in the packed cinema.

'Let's sit down,' she suggested.

'Do you want to go to a bar or café?'

'No, it was stuffy enough in the pictures. Let's sit on one of the benches over there. The air is nice and warm.'

They strolled across the road, turned along the small tarmac path and sat down on a bench, facing the wide screen of the City Hall's frontage, illuminated by the light of a dozen projectors. She cuddled up to him, then lifted her face to his.

'Do you think my lips are too big?'

Nicky laughed.

'Why are you laughing?'

'There's nothing wrong with your lips. And what put that strange notion into your head, anyway?'

'Oh, something somebody said.'

'Who was that?'

'The wee boys, years ago. I've had a complex ever since.'

Nicky kissed her. He felt sorry for her being so self-conscious because she was actually very pretty and he felt chuffed being seen with her. It was true that her lower lip was distinctive and had a bit of a curl to its fatness. He put his hands in front of his eyes.

'No, what makes you think your lips are big,' he said, blinded. She laughed and showered his face with kisses.

'You're so funny,' she said and languorously threw her feet up on the remaining space of the bench, tucking in her skirt and placing her head on his lap. Nicky thought of icebergs crashing into the arctic seas, cold, cold icebergs, and that did the trick – so long as she didn't move around. As they sat there he remembered the day she had come up and spoken to him years before just here and he was curious to see if she would mention it.

'I can see right up your nose,' she said.

'What are you trying to say – that you could park two buses up there!'

'Touch-eee! I can see right up your nose but I can't see through to your mind, O deep one. Penny for your thoughts?'

'I was thinking of icebergs.'

'Icebergs?'

'You don't get it?'

'I haven't a clue what you're talking about.' She rolled her body on its side so that she was looking out across the dark lawn. After half a minute she rolled back, a mischievous smile on her face. 'I get it now.'

Nicky harrumphed.

'Oh, it's cold thinking of icebergs,' she joked and shook her head shiverously, pressing it down into his groin. 'And bumpy!'

'Hey, stop it, there's people about,' he said, embarrassed.

'And what if there wasn't?'

This was their fourth time out together.

On their second date they stood kissing for a half-hour before she went in. For days beforehand he had been coaxing and speaking sympathetically to a pimple on the end of his nose, which seemingly acted as a barometer of his pre-date excitement. But she didn't seem to notice it.

'See those stars up there?' said Nicky. None was visible through the obscuring halo of the city lights.

'Where?' she said. 'I can't see a thing. It's too bright.'

'Can't you? I can see hundreds. Anyway, some of them are four light years away, others twelve. Next to the sun they are the closest ones to us. What you're seeing is a snapshot of the past. But what that star actually looks like right now, and what's happening to it, we'll not know for a few years until its light reaches us.'

'Well, I can't see a thing. But it's interesting all the same.'

'You're only saying that.'

'No. It is interesting,' she said, reassuringly. 'Light from you reaches inside me immediately,' she added in a lowered tone which slightly embarrassed her so she laughed it off. But the expression of affection touched Nicky.

After a bit they left and got the bus.

Nicky kissed Madeline with moderate pressure.

'Aw, aww, awwwwwhh–'

That's the second time she's made that noise. You'd think

her lips were cut. He moved his head back slowly until he could focus on her face. She had her eyes shut as if she were in a different world. She was standing on the middle concrete step of her own back door, one of several that gave on to the back of the shops. Further along the dimly lit alleyway a dog toppled the lid of a bin, sending it clanging. Madeline darted her rasping tongue into Nicky's mouth. It was long and pointed, cold for a tongue and extremely wet. Now and again she stood on one leg and her knee would press against his inner thigh, for balance he had supposed. But when he tentatively moved his knee deeper between her legs she went, 'Awwwwwhh –' again, very softly and sensually.

Well, fuck me. She's up to a million! I've raised her sexual passion! He felt slightly proud. He feigned indifference but her goings-on, rocking back and forth, whimpering like a dreaming puppy in its sleep, soft whisperings, soon had him feeling immensely virile. He kissed her hard and vibrated his head from side to side the way one would make the vigorous gesture 'No' behind someone's back.

No, no, no, no, no, went Nicky.

'Aw yesssss,' she growled from the back of her throat, like a ventriloquist.

Will you look at me! This is fun. He put his hand into her shirt. No sooner had he gently squeezed a voluminous breast than Madeline's hands, which had been ruffling his hair, shot beneath the shirt and unhooked the clasp at the front of the brassiere, letting her breasts drop free.

Timberrr!

The strangeness of the warm, naked flesh, its tensile texture, the incredible heaviness of her breasts, made him feel lustful but also momentarily sorry for bosomy women with these encumbrances. He would have loved to have whistled but that would have hurt her ears. As she exhaled sighs he played wantonly with her body. He measured her nipples against his thumb. He couldn't get over the size of them, nor the way their texture hardened like the floret of a cauliflower. He was a bit shocked when she began rubbing his crotch but the signals were now unmistakable, their actions unstoppable. Instinct, that involuntary, complex possession of the body, desire and masculine pride took over. He ran his hands up her legs and into the rounded patch of her sex. Such a powerful dark freedom, me doing this, stripping naked a personality. He tugged and pulled at her briefs until they became little more than a thin scroll of elastic around her knees. She pulled open his trousers and they slithered down his thighs. Nicky rubbed himself against her, a bit sore at first and then plunged into her warm sweet darkness. He thought of icebergs – icebergs! – and he held out for some time until nature shook through him.

Madeline nuzzled her head into his chest as he pulled the sides of his duffle coat around her, clasping her close like a daughter, incestuously truffling his nostrils deep into the oils of her hair and inhaling that delicate bloom with its ironic traces of infancy and innocence.

Then, out of nowhere, Nicky experienced little bursts of contempt and devilish, buoying triumphalism. Against his will he had the feeling that he had conquered her. But this was not what he had wanted. Something was missing, something grand.

After a minute or so he slipped out of her and felt ticklish.

'Just a sec,' said Madeline. As she adjusted her clothing he nipped the white threads of himself that connected them, tucked in his shirt and zipped up. He wanted to smoke but it could wait.

Somewhere nearby water dripped, as in torture.

A moth zigged and flitted by, its belaboured indecisive movements gritting Nicky.

A light went on, illuminating a significant part of the entry. Nicky gasped and pressed both of them closer to the door, like fugitives.

'It's only my dad,' laughed Madeline.

That's all I need now.

'That's the light on the stairs. Probably going to the bathroom. If you look up, beyond the landing, you can see the window of my bedroom. I've no curtains, as in Germany.' She pushed him away from the step so that above and across from the yard wall with its jagged pieces of broken glass he could see a dimly lit window – one he already knew. 'There, to the right. You can just make out the poster I got in Spain. I've had the same room all my life.'

A toilet was flushed and the light went out, and the stars teemed in the heavens, begging to be understood. Nicky looked up at the silent power. I'm seeing the past. The way perhaps that star, or that one over there, was at the time when me and Robin sometimes ran through this very alleyway when coming from the park, or, later, when Robin first noticed and fancied Madeline. Madeline, whose hair this is on my shoulder, whose body I've just been inside. He was about to ask her if she had ever been sitting at the back door with her dolls and pram when two boys passed but he held his foolish tongue.

'I'd really need to be going,' she said.

That suited Nicky, her initiating the departure. He felt drained and his mind was confused: sex and love-making weren't that distinguishable. He walked her through to the street.

'Is there something up with you?' Madeline asked. 'You've gone very quiet.'

'No.'

'But you have gone quiet.'

That embarrassed Nicky.

'I'm sorry,' he said.

'What for?'

'For being quiet. For being on another planet.'

'That's OK.' She sounded relieved. 'I thought it was something else.'

He knew it could only have been that she experienced a feeling of rejection. He moved to quash her doubts. 'So when do we go out again?'

She was delighted. 'What about dancing? You like dancing?'

'I've never been to a dance before. Not a proper one,' said Nicky.

'You haven't! You don't know what you're missing. What are you doing Saturday afternoon?'

'Eh, nothing really, I think.'

'Right. We'll go into town first, shopping. OK?'

'OK,' he said.

This time he took her up to the front door of the flat. She flung her arms around him and kissed him wide-mouthed. The earlier tingle in his lips returned and he got pleasure out of her farewell.

'Thanks for a great evening, Nicky. And I'll see you Saturday. Call for me, OK?'

'You'll see me before Saturday. I'll be here tomorrow on official business!'

'Oom! I love you in your uniform!' she whispered as she opened the door, turned and kissed him once more.

The next morning at work Gerard handed Nicky a postcard addressed to him which he quickly read.

Gerard teased him: 'Gemma? Geraldine? Greta?'

Nicky tried to get around him but he was boxed in.

'You're a bit of a dark horse,' said Gerard and Nicky's heart leaped at the implied compliment. I'm such a fraud, really. But his little conceit gave his mood an edge, like a little spice to the flavour of the dish.

Gerard was the only person really worth impressing. He had worked in the depot as long as anyone could remember. He had been a van driver before being involved in a fatal crash some years earlier, an accident caused by a drunk driver who perished in the smash. Gerard was disabled but after his recovery he worked as a daytime sorter. He had shown Nicky the ropes as an apprentice. Often even the supervisor deferred to his advice in times of crises or disputes. Gerard recognised Nicky's unassuming ways, his scrupulous attendance to duties. He saw how some of the others had had some fun at Nicky's expense and sometimes he himself drew off the flak. He didn't consider Nicky to be a woman's man and so he complimented him on the postcard. A pleasant surprise in life is always an occasion, however minor, and Nicky looked very pleased, excited even.

'So is it anyone we know?' he asked.

'No one,' said Nicky, secretively.

'Oh, I thought it might have been one of the regulars away on a holiday and missing you.'

'Regulars?'

'Yeh, you know. The widows whose husbands don't understand them. You might have come across them. Have you not come across Mystic Michelle? "Give me your hand and I'll tell you your fortune!" . . . huh?'

A shaft of light broke through Nicky's dim roof but the revelation was absorbed by the shadows and his eyes remained calm.

'No, I haven't been with her. But how do you think she'd feel if she knew that everybody was boasting about having . . . having . . . been with her? Do you think she boasts about having given what everybody seems to be boasting about having taken? You disappoint me, Gerard.'

'Wow! That's me told off,' said Gerard laughing. But he still liked whatever it was about Nicky. 'Just one more thing. How'd you know who I was talking about?!'

Nicky didn't reply but he went out to check his van for oil, water and diesel. He read the postcard again. It was from New York and read: 'Presently slumming it in Manhattan. Father all smiles but as false as fuck. Obviously missing Fanny Hill. He and big fat momma are leaving me here for a week with a dipso aunt. See you early August. What is the meaning of life? Love, G!'

To think that I haven't given him much thought recently, he said, chastising himself. He felt proud that Gareth still had him in mind and he remembered the silent roar inside his heart when they looked deep into each other's eyes. His young friend was crazy, funny, enigmatic, simultaneously deep and superficial. Nicky felt excited just by the knowledge that he would be seeing him in a few weeks. He put the postcard into his breast pocket.

When he entered Montside Post Office Madeline was more animated than usual, using his first name quite familiarly in front of her father, who was pleasant and nodded. She stamped and signed Nicky's collection docket, folded it and returned it to him with a knowing smile. A few hours later Nicky noticed a piece of white notepaper slipping out from below the docket. Whilst still driving he opened it and read the message: 'Can't wait until Saturday. Loves you! – Madeline XXX.' He almost crashed the van into a parked car and corrected the steering wheel just on time. He was stunned by the message and felt some annoyance because it could have easily fallen into the wrong hands and left him open to banter. But equally it was a powerful compliment and it had an occasional effervescent effect on him, increasing him in stature and giving significance to the neutral moments of an otherwise mundane day.

8

'WE'RE GOING TO DRESS YOU properly,' she declared on the bus, holding shut her thick eyelids to ward off any possible objection, a bit schoolmistressy, surprising him. He loved her decisiveness, her firm grip on fate. It was a nice feeling being taken in hand as the subject rather than an appendage. He had always associated shopping with being dragged behind his mother as a child or with going for groceries.

Madeline said that his clothes were fine but just a tiny bit old-fashioned. It was true he knew nothing about styles and had had a simplistic attitude to his dress. His eyes sparkled at the thought of her rigging him out. He wasn't concerned about the expense because he rarely dug into his wages, except to give his mother house-keeping. In fact, he had about £7,000, though £5,000 of this was still with his solicitor, Mr Baker.

What an adventure! he thought. The bus flew down the road on a carpet of warm dusty air as the italicised images of pedestrians and shop fronts whizzed past the window.

Shirt after shirt she rejected. He couldn't get over her fastidiousness. This was the fifth boutique they had visited and had all been so alike that they could have dulled and confused the observational sensitivity of even a newcomer: but not Nicky's. His mood was alert to detail, colour and atmosphere as never before. As Madeline flicked through yet another rack she suddenly expressed satisfaction: 'Ah, yes. Perfect!' She held the blue shirt against him. He was certain he had seen the exact same shirt at the beginning of the expedition. 'Try it on. Over there,' she said, indicating a booth. 'Yes, we'll take it,' she said to the salesgirl. At the till Madeline paid for the shirt despite Nicky's protests. 'This is on me,' she said firmly. 'It was my idea. Now don't spoil my day!' There was something almost childish about her sweeping behaviour. She chose washed jeans whose comfort he couldn't have imagined had he not tried them. She peeked through the curtain as he was changing and they laughed as Nicky realised he had rushed to cover himself.

And so the purchases continued: brown leather belt, stylish trainers and what she called matching socks. She even bought him boxing shorts and he caught fire when she whispered, 'Don't know why I'm getting you these. Sure, they'll be more often off!' Against his wishes she finally bought him an expensive jerkin and he felt absolutely undeserving. 'Don't worry, I'll get it all back!' she said, cheekily.

'From now on the cheques are all mine,' he insisted.

Yes, it was a brilliant day. But at about five o'clock Madeline said, 'Now it's time for my clothes,' and Nicky, sticky with sweat, felt just a bit weary. 'I'm only joking,' she said. He was much relieved. 'Think I'd do that to you! We'll go and get something to eat. Your choice.'

'I haven't a clue where to go,' he said.

So she took him down a narrow lane, sandwiched in shadow, whose remarkable existence he – a postman – had never been aware of, and into a small restaurant. Madeline did the ordering and they were served delicious slices of Italian meat-loaf glistening in a silky thick red mushroom sauce, served with gnocchi and fresh Parmesan cheese. They clinked glasses and Nicky felt indebted to Madeline for this new experience. It seemed a million years since he went about on his own, a billion years since he was a child.

'How do you feel?' she asked.

'Tipsy!'

'Aren't you tired?'

'Tipsy and tired then. But when I go home to get changed I promise not to fall asleep.'

'You can get changed in our flat,' she said. 'It'd be handier. Emma and Andy are coming back from town also and I told them to meet us there at nine.' Andy was her cousin Emma's cohabiting boyfriend.

'Are you serious? What about your daddy? He'd love that.'

'He's away for the day and won't be back until late tonight.'

'Are you sure?'

'Absolutely.'

'Waiter, more wine please!' called Nicky with a borrowed flourish. 'This is great, isn't it.' A low, overhead lamp cast a pale red spot on the space they occupied, though other tables were illuminated solely by candles. Nicky asked for one to be brought. The lamp was raised and switched off. Before Nicky's eyes Madeline's features were sublimated by the soft light and shadows into a living picture of tenderness. He almost told her that he loved her – something he had only ever said to two people – but it was a huge step and though he was drunk he hesitated. But his face went through a repertoire of a dozen different smiles, each held for a second or two, followed by a sigh of happiness.

'You're a real charmer,' she said.

'You think so?'

She thought his question rhetorical.

'Do you think so?' he repeated, slightly more loudly, leaning forward so that his waxy cheeks glowed in the flame.

'You're drunk!' she laughed.

'Am I?'

'Do you not know?'

'No. Not really.'

She smiled and shook her head. 'You're crazy!'

After climbing the stairs Madeline said, 'Welcome to my apartment!' She threw her bag down on the floor and kicked off her shoes. Then she pulled the drapes across the plankton of topaz light which permeated half the room beyond the window. Nicky set down his shopping and wiped his brow and made a mock collapse onto the sofa. Next thing he knew, Madeline came and sat on his knee, put her arms around his neck and began slowly kissing him. He manoeuvred her to his side for convenience and comfort as they began making love.

'You're positive he won't be back?'

'Yessss. Don't worry.'

They undressed each other slowly, drink having anaesthetised any feeling of embarrassment.

'Touch me there, gently . . . No, up a bit. Yes.'

Nicky surprised her and instead knelt down, moved her legs apart and kissed her where his hand had been, to see what it was like. Through the mask of her sex the smell was densely concentrated: the taste, slightly repellent, seemed to sear his tongue. Her finger came down between his lips and guided him to a spot which seemed to be exquisitely painful, causing her to roll her head, bite her lips and groan.

'Oh Nicky, that's lovely, lovely, lovely. Fuck, that's it, that's it, that's it . . .'

She was moving her hips in short thrusts and Nicky through his befuddlement was a bit shocked at her language. The root of his strained tongue ached. This wasn't such a good idea after all, he thought, as he swallowed.

At last he could feel her rising to orgasm and he matched the action of his tongue to her breathing so that he finished on gentle, almost expert tippings, and felt quietly accomplished. He looked up and saw her eyes fill. He almost cried himself, whatever it was. But she slithered onto the floor beside him.

'Quick. Put him in, put him in!'

Nicky entered her. It was smooth going but Madeline's eyes were closed tight and he was somewhat annoyed that her pleasure appeared independent of his participation. With the rocking her face became more fierce and as he felt himself reach the hardness that precedes ejaculation she drew her legs quickly together to tighten her muscles, forcing his legs to the outside, and dug her nails into his back, breaking his skin, so that pain and pleasure began coinciding, though it did not accentuate his pleasure. She tilted her head back and moaned, and her eyes suddenly opened to reveal no pupils, just their frightening whites.

Then the dust began settling on them where they lay.

'Gee, you were very daring. And I got quite carried away there,' said Madeline. 'Didn't I?'

'No, it was good,' lied Nicky, smoking a cigarette, smouldering in sweat and thought, did she call me Ricky in the middle of things?

'Let's see your back. Christ, Nicky, you're bleeding! Did I do that?'

'I can't feel a thing,' he said.

'Are you sure?'

'Yes, no problem.'

'Right, we're going to have to get ready. I'll run the bath and you can use the shower.'

In the bathroom she gave him a brand new toothbrush.

'What's that for?'

'Your teeth!'

She surprised Nicky in the shower, stepping in and putting her arms around his shoulders, her head into his chest and holding him. He always liked the part involving affection. Just a few minutes earlier, at the instant when they fused into the chain of passion and nothing should have separated them, he had felt as if he were on a different continent. After the ablutions she remained behind and said she wouldn't be long. Then, robed in a generous bath towel, and smelling like fresh peaches, she came and sat beside him on the sofa. He played the blow-dryer through the long wet trails of her hair, freeing the shining strands, as she made up her eyes.

When Emma and Andy arrived from town Madeline still wasn't ready. Nicky was anxious to see if he recognised the original Emma beneath the maquillage. Her face had certainly changed: it had filled out, making her prettier. Her hair was dyed blonde and clipped short, commanding attention or curiosity. So many of her fingers were adorned with rings of every shape and variety that the armoured effect made her dainty hands look and feel pugnacious, as Nicky realised when they were introduced. She spoke confidently and with grating emphases – not what Nicky had anticipated. If she had ever fancied Nicky there was certainly no trace that he could detect. Beneath the expert make-up he barely saw the waif she had been. Madeline had been wrong: Emma had become prettier but not more beautiful. Indeed, she had lost all the invisible characteristics that were her subtle attractions, including that most essential component of true mystique – humility. She took off her coat and showed a clingy singlet over a slim trunk. Her short skirt in contrast revealed voluptuous thighs – as if she'd been fed from the waist down.

Nicky rationed his glances for fear of being misinterpreted.

I wonder are we the same people we were ten years ago, or even a year ago? he thought. The saintly can become corrupted and former thieves honest. But even less dramatically we are always, always changing. I have struggled to remain myself and have failed. Nothing stands still; everything changes. Fuck, but I talk a lotta shite. But it's true – we're too close to ourselves to be aware of the contrasts between who we were and what we have become and whether the difference represents an almost new personality.

'Madeline says you're a postman, Nicky,' said Andy. 'Do you do much travelling?'

'I get about. There's a rota and shift work. I'm mostly on vans. At night-time you'd use the Ford cargo lorry for long distance . . . It's under the articulated limit.' Fuck, that sounds so boring . . . But, here, you get to meet a lot of widdahs hanging out of top windahs. And Nicky smiled at his little internal joke.

Andy talked enthusiastically, somewhat bumptiously, about his own work. He was twenty-five and had his own electrical business. He ran a permanent advertisement in the *Telegraph*. His phone never stopped. His men couldn't cope with the overtime he had to offer.

How come you're out tonight, thought Nicky, as he smiled and shook his head in wonderment. Andy was athletic, played squash and exuded a capacity for boundless energy, like the sun's heat and light. He gelled his black hair, the sheen suiting his swarthy, slightly pitted face. He clasped his right knee with his hands and rocked back and forth on the armchair, smiling at the cousins who were in a world of their own.

At the dance Nicky was extremely chary about getting onto the floor but after a few drinks and Madeline's persistence he relented and they joined Emma and Andy. Nicky lost his inhibitions and gyrated like everyone else. He couldn't get over how good the band was. Each of its songs sounded just like the original on the radio, often even better. Many of the lyrics were suggestive and provocative and these were the songs that dancers mouthed in their partner's direction. Some of the show-offs were funny, clapping their hands, jumping in the air and turning 180 degrees before landing.

Nicky loved the music, the flashing lights, the gregarious, happy atmosphere – a world of which he had had little previous conception. All these beautiful people, no two dressed alike, he thought. Where were they all before? His new trainers felt like slippers they were so snug. Hanging over his chair was the new jerkin Madeline had chosen for him. Tonight he had paid for the taxi and admission and pushed his money on the waiters when the drinks arrived; he felt more secure for it, though Andy's objections occasionally won out.

Madeline's neat, short, crepe-like pink dress was low-cut and when she returned from the dancefloor or the ladies and bent down to take her seat you could see her breasts made oval and glimpse her dark brown nipples. It lasted only a split second and Andy devoured the sight. Nicky experienced a feeling of pride and was surprised that he wasn't jealous or affronted.

Andy was speaking loudly in his ear, commenting on the bodies of the girls negotiating the packed tables and all the while he threw loving smiles at Emma who was well on the way to getting plastered. Then, before he knew it, they were all up dancing again for perhaps a stint of fifteen minutes.

'You can stay the night with us, Nicky,' announced Andy when they arrived back at the table. 'You'll never get a taxi now. It'll be simpler and it's only a walk away.'

'But my mammy's expecting me home,' said Nicky.

Andy laughed. 'Fuck, the way you said that I thought you meant it!'

'But Madeline's to be home as well. Her father's very strict.'

'Jack? He's not that bad. He'll not be expecting her home now. It's not the first time she'll have stayed over.'

'What's up?' asked Emma, leaning across the table.

'Nicky and Madeline's staying over, love. OK? Hope there's drink in the house.'

'Yeh, there's plenty of wine.' Emma's speech was slurred. 'Chinkers. I wouldn't mind a chinkers. What 'bout you Madge? Fancy a chinkers?'

'I'd love one. It seems yonks since I've had something to eat.'
She turned to Nicky and whispered: 'If you want to phone
home, go ahead. Don't worry about Andy.'

'It doesn't matter,' said Nicky.

They queued at a Chinese take-away and then walked the
short distance to the flat through the soft warm air. Nicky felt
that he could so easily have left them all behind and taken off
on his own towards the sea or the hills and walked until the
answer of dawn such was the revelatory thread which ran
through the night. But the spell was broken when Andy
announced their arrival and they turned into a brightly-lit
mews and a modern apartment block.

Madeline sat on the floor below Nicky's armchair as he
picked rice indifferently off her plate. He never knew three people to make such noisy conversation. While they gabbled about
holidays in Spain, Cyprus and Greece and drank liberal
potions of wine he turned his attention to the apartment and
how the couple, or perhaps Emma, had carefully made it into
a homely space of some character. It occurred to him that it
would be possible to have a great love for and attachment to
a nest of one's own creation.

The place breathed an unique aura. From the kitchen came
the caffeinated piquancy of ground coffee and the drift of
spices; from the privacy of the bedroom the dressing table littered with jars and ointments shed its perfumes, a commodi-
ous wardrobe the lightness of crisp clean linen and the
pot-pourri of laundered clothes; from the bathroom the toiletries exerted a subtle pull the length of the hall. The living-
room, spotless and expensively furnished, was a blend of
polished teak, new carpet and leather. An orange bonsai tree
rooted in a heavy glazed cauldron stood in an eternal spring-
like pose by the side of an open casement window and smelt
of kumquat.

Nicky, now sober, resented the way his obligation to phone
home had exposed him to Andy's riposte – not that it was
Andy's fault. He resented his own accountability to his mother
and father. He drank more wine but the alcohol had died in
him. He felt weary and unenthusiastic for dancing to the CD
player but got up anyway. The lights were low and the music

slow when they changed partners. Emma could hardly stand and she threw her arms around him in a lock. She tried to kiss him, her mouth wide open, but he avoided her thin, elastic-band lips. He looked at Madeline who was leaning against Andy. She gave Nicky a drunken wink which could have meant anything: isn't this great; she must still fancy you; just humour her; you and I are here together and we're what counts, love.

Enjoying himself he was not.

About half two Emma fell asleep between Andy and Madeline on the sofa. Andy removed her unfinished glass from her lap. Then he raised her head and using his fingers and thumb cruelly worked her mouth like a puppet.

'"Andy, I'm really hot. Would you cool me down, please,"' he said, mimicking her.

'Certainly, honey.'

Nicky was astounded to see him pull her singlet over her head and off, revealing her small brown breasts. He wondered what the hell was going on and looked at Madeline, expecting her to angrily object, but she just giggled, a giggle that seemed to Nicky a signature of a most unlikable characteristic – disloyalty. Nicky was about to say something when Emma came to, seemed to be aware of what had happened, but did nothing. 'Put me to bed, Andy,' she grumbled. Andy struggled but fell back before succeeding. Only then did Nicky realise that everyone was extremely drunk. Andy returned with a duvet which he dropped over the back of the sofa.

'Night, now,' he said, and went back to the bedroom.

'Gin-joy yourself?' slurred Madeline.

'Up until Andy's stunt. It must have been very humiliating for Emma. That really annoyed me.'

'Shure she goes topless everywhere.' Then she laughed: 'Gitchya going, did it?'

Nicky experienced a conflict of feelings for Madeline, like the bile of disgust for food that to the palate seemed good.

'Help us off with this, would you,' she said. He helped her undress and, wearing just skimpy briefs, she rolled back on to the sofa which was long and wide. She twisted her finger through Nicky's hair. 'I'm too drunk to come, but you go ahead.'

'It's OK,' he said. 'We'll just sleep.' He extinguished the lamps, lay down beside her and pulled the cover over them. Talking about coming and whatnot, making it so common.

She fell asleep quickly and began snoring. The dead weight of her hot body was difficult to shift. Her snoring eventually became unbearable. He tossed and turned and wondered would she ever stop. He got up, crossed the room, sat in a chair and lit a cigarette. How come she's louder the further away I go? He felt a chill in the air so he closed the half-open casement. Towards dawn he eventually dozed in a cramped position. He awoke at after seven and went to the kitchen to quench his thirst. She had quietened so he now lay down beside her. Then she started again. He nudged her hard with his elbow and she stopped long enough for him to fall over.

'Did you do some snoring last night!'

'Me!'

'Yes,' said Madeline with that sure edge to her voice which brooked no contradiction and which yesterday he had found attractive. 'You went out like a light and almost right away you started.'

'Fuck away off, Madeline,' whispered Nicky out of frustration, the filament of his anger suddenly blazing. 'I hardly slept a wink.'

'Nobody tells me to fuck off, you odd bastard!' she said, her face pure white with rage, snatching the duvet from him and rolling over, leaving him speechless.

'Morning campers!' announced Andy cheerfully as he peeped out from the bedroom. 'Are we decent?'

Madeline sat up, naked, with a devil-may-care attitude designed to show Nicky who was who, and said, 'Yep, come on in.' She asked Andy to throw her her dress from the chair even though it was on Nicky's side. He moved off the sofa and pulled on his jeans.

'And what size is our heads this morning?'

Nicky answered that he was fine. Madeline abruptly left to see Emma.

'Would anyone like breakfast or lunch?' Andy shouted after her, laughing.

'No thanks,' she replied.

As Andy tossed bacon in a pan and Nicky leaned against the door frame watching him, he once again began talking shop about work, work, work. Nicky vaguely remembered him saying that he regularly worked Sundays.

Nicky knocked on the bedroom door which was slightly ajar, and was summoned in by Emma. He negotiated his way around a half-packed holiday suitcase and put down two coffees.

'Oh, you're a dear,' said Emma, cupping the mug. Madeline continued to ignore him and talked incessantly about her last fella, how he was prepared to leave his wife and children. He turned and left.

Andy said that the bus service on Sunday was close to non-existent but that he could drop them over to Montside. Emma, attired in a dressing gown which hugged her, walked them to the door. On Tuesday she and Andy were for Greece so they wouldn't all meet again for two or three weeks, she said.

'You hope,' added Madeline gratuitously, her barb cast with specific intent.

People out of sorts with each other can never walk comfortably and Nicky and Madeline were acutely aware of this handicap when they alighted from Andy's Shogun jeep. Nicky wondered was this the end of their relationship, incredible as it seemed given the intimacy of the previous afternoon.

They reached Madeline's and she told him to wait in the street; she would get him his clothes. They had been hidden in her bedroom and for convenience he said he'd get them another time, but she was insistent. He felt the eyes of parishioners on him as they emerged from the service across the road, many congregating around Sonny's for a bit of a chat. Madeline came down the stairs and handed him a plastic bag. Neither of them mentioned another date. He stretched to kiss her but she avoided his lips. He turned and left, expecting her to call him back. But she didn't. He heard the door close silently, with indifference which was even worse. Then he humped off down the street carrying on his back the mortally-wounded Nicky, publicly humiliated, a condition which he knew was partly self-inflicted, a result of his venturing outside his true nature.

Momentarily he felt a certain admiration for the church-goers in their Sunday best, the chains of their faith a consolation, however marginal, in times of trouble, personal hardship or grief. But his envy was fleeting. What we hold is all we have, he repeated to himself. In the vast ocean one real plank of wood can save a dozen souls: the mirage of the shores of paradise drown all swimmers.

He went home, vexed that an explanation for his absence would be required. His mother was in the kitchen. She glanced at his new clothes and his refugee parcel.

'You're alive then.'

'Don't give me that,' he said. 'Sure I said I mightn't be back, didn't I.' He hoped his firmness would carry off the lie of her possible memory lapse. But this only piqued her.

'No. When did you say that?'

'I said it yesterday. Not remember?'

'Nicky. If you had said that then I would have remembered. Instead, I sat up half the night worrying about you. I never slept a wink. I told your father you were stopping with friends.'

'Well, I did end up staying with friends. We went to a dance and it was late and we were drinking. You know how it goes.'

She looked at him with displeasure – drink having been to her the cause of immense unhappiness.

'Did you stay with your girlfriend?'

He nodded.

'You've never told me her name. What do you call her?' she asked, warming a little.

Nicky suddenly felt the need to substantiate his recent past and establish for himself that it hadn't all been some kind of illusion.

'Madeline. Madeline Taylor.' He found himself becoming exuberant, tapping into the cheer of their pleasant times together – the pictures, the walks, the shopping, the meals, expecting to sweep his mother off her feet, naïvely hoping this his airing would have wings and somehow reach Madeline and move her to telephone. 'We danced to all hours!' he laughed.

'Madeline Taylor? Where from?'

'Father's Jack, owns Montside Post Office, beside the All Nighter – Sonny's.'

For her pension his mother used an older establishment on the other main road into town where she would also catch the

Number 8 bus. She still referred to Sonny's shop by its former name of West's after its long-deceased proprietor.

'Madeline Taylor? Is her mother dead?' She turned down the gas as the pot of potatoes had begun to boil.

'You know her then?' asked Nicky.

'No, just remember the poor woman dying. She was quite young. So when do we get to see Madeline?' she smiled.

'Oh, I don't know about that. One day at a time, you know.'

'Dins! I want my dins!' This was his father's recently-adopted puerile act when he was hungry and usually sitting at the table in anticipation with his knife and fork raised. It brought a smile to Mrs Smith's lips but Nicky found it funny no longer. She turned to her son.

'Would you listen to him, huh! . . . I'm glad you had a good time but in future let me know. As I said, I sat up all night.'

'Me too,' said Nicky. 'Andy, the guy I slept with – or didn't sleep with rather – snored the whole night. I should have come home.' This last point was enunciated humbly and sounded like a concession.

'Your hair's sticking up.'

'Have I time for a bath? Is the water warm?'

'Should be OK. You've about ten minutes. How's your stomach? Were you sick?'

'No, I didn't drink much,' he replied and went upstairs. He ran the bath. The water soon turned lukewarm. He climbed in anyway, topping up the bath every few minutes by struggling with the hot tap, using his big toe. There's people paint with their toes – beautiful pictures that would put you to shame. The phone rang and he sat bolt upright, listening intently, but it was a mumble and he wasn't called. I hope my ma hasn't said I'm in the bath, phone back. Or worse, begun interrogating her! Naw, she'd have shouted. He sank into the water. He thought about Madeline's temper and what she had done to him. What a bitch! What is she? A b-i-t-c-h. Ah, but yesterday, kid, she was Miss Wonderful, spending a fortune on you. It's you should be phoning her. No way! And what if she rejected me again? There's loads of sides to her I don't like. Her moaning and bad language. You'd even think her neck was dirty but that's just the colour of her skin. And so

much for her father being strict! What other lies has she told
me?

Nicky experienced a bout of paranoia. Had she someone
else? Was she still doing a line with her married man? Or
Andy! And was the bit about Emma fancying him merely a red
herring? Phone, phone! Please! Phone me to say hello! Letting
Andy pull Emma's top off wasn't nice. Yet I let him too. Nicky
remembered a funny incident on the dance floor when he
picked Madeline up by the waist and almost dropped her. He
remembered her sensual kisses. But he also remembered how
candid and unrestrained she was. She'd fucking frighten you.
Getting wet at the slightest touch and talking about coming
and fucking. He climbed out of the cold bath and began drying himself. When he opened the door the steaming diaspora
of succulent, macerated beef from his mother's potroast filled
his nostrils and his stomach grumbled. He changed and went
down.

'Was there somebody on the phone?'

'Wrong number,' said his father, as dinner arrived. Nicky
was tempted to ask if it had been a woman's voice and the
desire grew like a thirst for a flask within reach but which upon
opening might prove empty.

'A fella or a girl?' asked his mother, setting down the roast
in her slow, careful way.

'Some fella,' said his father. 'Doing a survey on what people are having for their Sunday dinner.'

'But I thought you said it was a wrong number?' said Nicky.

'Nicky. He's having you on. It was a wrong number. Don't
listen to him,' said Mrs Smith.

9

NO PHONE CALL CAME. Each morning for a week he passed Madeline's flat on his way to work wondering was she lying awake thinking about him, on the verge of telephoning him perhaps. Several times when rain gave him the excuse he loitered in Sonny's, a few doors down the block, just to be near, but without ever having the nerve to ask about her directly, just making small talk.

Despite his frequenting the shop and feeling a tacit kinship of no mean depth with the avuncular, middle-aged bachelor which stretched back to his childhood, Nicky was surprised and somewhat disillusioned to find that Sonny, whom he believed to be the repository of all unsolicited local gossip, indicated absolutely no knowledge about his relationship with Madeline. Nor any appreciation of the suffering that Nicky was experiencing.

Instead, it was Sonny in grim mood who did most of the talking.

His brother David had recently suffered a stroke which had left him severely paralysed down one side. It was unlikely that he would ever walk again. Oh yes, Hyper, thought Nicky vaguely. Sonny said that David's family – his wife, three daughters and son – were devastated. The eldest's wedding had been cancelled. He knew David wasn't the most popular but still he was his only family: he had partly raised him, though young himself, when their parents died within months of each other. The doctors feared a second stroke would kill him.

Nothing would ever be the same again, he mumbled. Nothing would ever be the same again.

Each morning these daily reports on David's condition went completely over Nicky's head. He couldn't concentrate. No one has a notion of what I'm going through! No one.

At nights he walked out the airport road or went swimming as in the old days, except now he was in the deepest melancholy with a recurring pain in his heart and lungs.

On the second week he was on collections out Montside way and meeting Madeline was unavoidable. I don't love her, yet look at the state of me, he said, the trepidation knocking his knees together as he left his van. This isn't good for a person. Underneath it all it's nothing but a struggle for the restoration of pride, you know.

Nicky stood aside for a pensioner who was leaving, then he marched in.

'Is the weather still holding?' said the cheerful female voice from behind the counter, as parcels and registered mail were handed out to him. It was as if they had been acquaintances all their lives.

Nicky was perplexed by the sight of the stout, blonde, fortyish woman who gave him his collection docket.

'Yes, yes, it's fine,' he said. 'Fine.' He looked at the next counter and Jack Taylor was chatting amicably to a grubby man who looked like a wino. Jack counted out the pounds and pence through the guichet, recognised Nicky and winked as if in complicity. Winking runs in the fucking family. Nicky winked back, catching, as he left, Jack recommencing some funny story of the he said/she said variety which resulted in his new assistant roaring with near-vulgar laughter. Had Madeline been ill Jack would not have been in such good form, he deduced. So where was she?

Back at the depot he ran into Gerard.

'Two things. Firstly, somebody phoned but don't ask me who because it was Charlie who took the call. Maybe a girl, I don't know. Secondly, a wee word in your ear . . .'

'Who did you say called? Did you catch the name?' Nicky became excited.

'I'm not sure . . .'

'But you said it was a girl. It wasn't somebody called Madeline was it?' As soon as Nicky said her name he knew he had made a mistake. He had that sinking feeling of self-disappointment which often follows the cajolement of the confession of a close secret.

'Madeline, eh? Is that so?' said his workmate sententiously. 'Listen partner, we'll come back to that in a second. Come into the toilets to I have a word in your ear.'

Inside, Gerard told him that an enquiry was being carried out into a parcel containing, it seemed, pornographic videos which had gone missing in transit. It wasn't unheard of for a man to take such a film home, view or copy it; then when back on duty to delight in delivering the damaged package to an embarrassed customer, preferably the customer's wife. On this occasion the videos hadn't been delivered, nor was there a record of their having been sent to undelivered post. Furthermore, it was an unabashed, extremely irate customer who was kicking up a storm and the supervisor was going spare.

Nicky had covered the particular run but so had two other drivers around the relevant times. He thanked Gerard for the tip but the theft, if it were a case of theft, had nothing to do with him.

'Nicky, can I ask you something?'

'What do you mean? Do you not believe me?'

'Oh, the videos? No, not that. Something more important. Something that you said. If you don't mind me asking – who's this Madeline?'

'Why, why do you ask?'

'I'll explain in a second. What's her name?'

Nicky delayed for a few moments then said: 'Madeline Taylor. Works in Montside Post Office. Lives above it. Why do you ask?'

'And are you going steady with her?'

'Ye-yes,' said Nicky.

'Have you been out with her long?'

'About five, six weeks. Why? Why all the questions?' He was irritated.

'You watch yourself there. OK?'

'What do you mean, "watch yourself"? I haven't a clue what you are going on about.'

'I'm saying no more. Just be careful.'

'Fuck's sake, you can't just say that!' Nicky's poor mind didn't know were it was.

'OK then. If you must know. She's a chaser. A fucking ride. Get the message?'

On the surface of Nicky's skin every follicle horripilated with the burning frost of Gerard's ugly remarks. Then his temperature visibly rose in his cheeks as a prelude to violence. Gerard knew what to expect but he was still caught off-guard. Nicky kicked away his walking-stick from under him, punched him in the jaw and proceeded to hit him, blindly possessed by outrage.

'You bastard, you bastard!' screamed Nicky as he defended Madeline's honour. But Gerard, with all the wiles of a street-fighter and despite his thirty-nine years, wrestled Nicky to the ground and was soon on top. He repossessed his stick and pressed it across Nicky's throat until he couldn't breathe. Nicky quickly recognised the weight which contained him and the restraint and patience exercised by the older man. It had a calming effect but emotionally he was in turmoil and he felt ashamed for hitting a cripple. Gerard rose slowly in case of treachery. His mouth was cut but he ushered out of the room several colleagues who had rushed to the source of the commotion.

'If you ever put a finger on me again I'll take your arms off. Do you hear, Nicky? I'll wipe you out.'

When they learnt that Nicky had thrown the first punch, several of his erstwhile mates had wanted to fix him well and good but Gerard declared the matter closed. Instead, Nicky was shunned and made feel tiny.

He had one more day before the start of his holidays. He couldn't understand why Gerard should have said something as cruel as he did. He had always considered him his friend yet he had deeply wounded him.

He was travelling citywards when a Shogun jeep just like

Andy's turned onto the road in front of him. At first he wasn't sure but curiosity got the better of him. He followed the vehicle through the city centre and right out across the town. I wonder are Emma and Andy back early? Fuck me, I'm stupid. It's probably just one of Andy's workers using the jeep. Eventually, it indicated parking and, finally, with ironic satisfaction, Nicky saw Andy alight. He bumped the van's horn and waved. Andy approached the passenger's side.

'Whowee! You certainly get about!' he shouted.

Nicky smiled. What an actor I am. 'Everywhere! I go everywhere!'

'I wonder how the girls are getting on! You got your postcard yet?' asked Andy, before realising that Nicky's look of bewilderment meant total ignorance.

'Nicky. I thought you knew! I couldn't make it and Madeline stood in for me . . .'

I know nothing. Nothing. I know nothing about women, about love, about trust. I know nothing about life. And I've just been stabbed, right through the heart. That's what it feels like – a spear right through my heart. It all must be true. That bastard. He felt sick and just wanted to escape the immediate humiliation.

'We . . . we had a row, as you know . . .' He was unable to string his words together.

'But she told Emma and me – well, certainly me – that she called you and that you had encouraged her to go.' Andy added jauntily, 'Sure, you'll make up when they return and we'll have another good night together. You know what Madeline's like – she's crazy. She wants everything that's going. And speaking of going, I now have to go and pay the worker bees. I'll see you about. OK?'

'Yes . . . bye, Andy.'

Nicky floated at the deep end of the pool, his ears being plugged and unplugged with the wow-wow of lapping water. His heart was extremely sore. He felt very lonely. But the person who could possibly alleviate his loneliness was the very person causing him pain.

There are people ten times worse off than me. There are wives in happy marriages for years upon years who feel emotionally and physically secure. Suddenly their husbands desert them. How do they cope? How can they cope with the wretchedness, the constant anguish, the disillusionment, the utter hopelessness, the humiliation, the boot being put into their self-confidence?

He was lucky that his audience was really only a few people.

But what if you had to explain yourself – without knowing what the explanation was – over and over again to the children, to friends and relatives, to every neighbour who secretly pitied you, misunderstood you, gratuitously advised you, or gloated over your misfortune?

The thought of her going topless on the beach came into his mind for the thousandth time. And for the thousandth time he suffered intense jealousy and hatred. Self-pity disgusted him – but without self-pity the barely ticking heart would cease altogether. He thought of her making love to another man, another man teasing and caressing out of her her lyrical song of soft moans which he now belatedly treasured. Yet he wanted to rip out his brain and destroy this treasured memory and its hold over him.

Nicky! Nicky! Get a grip! he cried. This is all pride. You could never have loved this woman. Look what she has done to you! You knew her only for a few weeks which were really no more than a few days, perhaps even just a few hours. Yes, but she filled my life. Calm yourself! Think rationally. Easier said than done. And he suspected that the most rational thing anyone could do would be to die.

Between his legs a head of fair hair, a face appeared, with a grin stretched over perfectly even and brilliantly white teeth.

'Hiya!' said Gareth, eeling his body in the water to keep afloat. 'Not see me waving to you from behind the glass? You must have been a million miles away.' On the bridge of his nose, where his glasses had rested, his skin was red and below his eyes were two vague crescents. He looked strangely beautiful. He filled the whole world.

'I didn't see you. I didn't see you at all. Who are you with?'

'You!'

Just then a squabble had broken out among clamouring children at the shallow end and the lifeguard had blown her whistle.

'Hugh who?' asked Nicky.

'I'm with you! We're together!'

Gareth floated on his back and blew out a fountain of water which seemed never-ending. Nicky smiled.

'Now you try it. Just fill your mouth, purse your lips tight and blow like a whale!'

Nicky's first attempt was inept, his second try even more comical, with water streaming down the sides of his mouth.

'I can't seem to do it.'

'Don't be silly! Of course you can. Watch!' This time Gareth's geyser reached an amazing height of three or four feet. He rolled over in the water, surfaced, pushed his finger into his ear like a spigot and more water shot from his mouth over Nicky's face.

'Ha, ha, ha! You didn't expect that!'

Nicky ducked him; put him under with all his weight. But when he released his head after about twenty seconds Gareth's body was limp and remained submerged. Nicky panicked and his heart palpitated. He could touch the bottom of the pool with his toes and was able to support the boy's body and push it to the edge. He climbed out, then reached down to haul Gareth out by the arms. He blasted Nicky's face with another mouthful of water, and, using his legs against the side of the pool, simultaneously pulled on Nicky, causing him to somersault into the water.

'That wasn't bloody-well funny!' complained Nicky when he surfaced, but the young fellow was coughing and spluttering with laughter and really taking in water this time. He pointed to his mouth and chest and signalled for Nicky to help him out. 'Phew! I paid for that,' he said when he was recovering, though tears of extremity stood in his eyes and he continued to cough. They sat on the green cross-hatched tiles, side by side, with their feet paddling the water. A minute passed – moments of contentment – and it didn't seem to matter that no words were exchanged.

Then Gareth noticed something.

'What's that?'

'What's what?'

'Those scratches on your back.' Gareth ran the papillae of three fingers over one set of the fading marks on his left shoulder blade and Nicky moved the grain of his skin into the path of his friend's soothing touch, like a cat its erect tail through the rub of its mistress's hand.

'Oops, that's ticklish . . . I was in a fight about two weeks ago and got a scraping.'

'Are you serious! Tell me more.'

'No, I'm only joking. Thorns of a rose bush did that in our back garden. Ruined a good T-shirt into the bargain . . . I have to say, Gareth, you're a good swimmer. Do you ever swim in the sea?'

'Not much. My parents were always over-protective that way, and it's only now that I'm fifteen going on sixteen that they show some deference to my age. Thus you see me out on my own! Their attitude's up the left because, actually, the older I get the more dangerous I feel! But they were always afraid a crab would bite me and give me blood-poisoning or an albatross fly away with me! I love poking about the rocks and I've a great collection of shells – some from Crete, some from Brittany. . .' He thought for a few seconds and then said: 'Did you know that there's a species of shrimp native to our waters whose sex is determined by its environment?'

'What do you mean?'

'If they are born when the days are long they can choose to become either male or female, and if born when the days are short they eventually become females.'

'How odd.'

'The males are bigger than the females and they carry the females around on their backs for a few days until they mate.'

'On their backs?'

'Yes, on their backs. And do you know where a shrimp's heart is? A shrimp's heart is in its head,' said Gareth, self-importantly. He continued: 'Do you know what I love about our coasts? The seaside as you slowly approach. The invisible mist of salt in the air, the smell of brine. The sea is the mother of us all, you know. Then there's the tide . . . I love the way its combers gently club the beach, early life stretching out its paw towards the land . . .'

Gareth spoke as if he were there, sitting on his hunkers, witnessing the sparkling roll of the ages, time a vintage champagne streaming through his open fingers. Nicky shuddered.

'You getting a chill or has somebody walked over your grave?'

'No, no. I'm all right,' said Nicky. 'It's cold out of the water. Let's swim some more.'

In the changing room Gareth said: 'Don't you think I've shot up?'

'In such a short space of time? I doubt it.'

'I have! I'm practically as tall as you! Over here, quick. Beside the mirror. Before anyone comes in. Turn around.'

They stood back-to-back, their heads turned, looking in the mirror, and as their wet skins kissed Nicky experienced a gorgeous *frisson*.

'You still haven't reached my shoulder,' he stuttered as he turned around and began dressing, avoiding Gareth's wondering eyes.

In the cafeteria Nicky bought the refreshments and when he came looking for Gareth he found him in a far, dark corner. He was wearing his glasses again and looked the schoolboy. Gareth had asked for three chocolate biscuits and unashamedly dunked each in his tea, tipped his head back and swallowed them intact like oysters.

'Manners maketh the man, my father says!' Slurp. Another biscuit gone. 'But what does he know!' he laughed rebelliously. 'Do you get on with your people, your mother? . . . I mean, really well?'

'I can't say I've given it a lot of thought. There's always a gap between the generations, isn't there? And in my case my mother was forty-two when she had me.'

'Good God! She was old enough to be your granny. Women are so vain. My mother's always trying to knock five years off her age. Although none of us can really talk. Everything modern eventually becomes quaint. Time is ruthless . . . Are you not eating that bit?'

Nicky didn't know why – possibly tradition was the explanation – but he, like his parents, always left something on the
plate, be it a crust, or a pea, or a tiny bit of potato.

'There are no little people around here needing to be fed!'
said Gareth, picking up the half-biscuit from his friend's plate.
Nicky loved the discursiveness of the boy's fast and fascinating speech.

'Yes, I rifled through some old suitcases and came across her
birth certificate. Do you know what a basque is? My father
practically drinks with the Prime Minister, sees the floozie
florist on the side, does a reading at church on Sunday and col-
lects pornographic novels – sorry, erotica. Hey! Did you think
I was going to say that he wears a basque as well? That would
be a scream! No, I found the basque thing hidden in a locked
drawer of my mother's dressing table. If she's going to wear it
to keep daddy at home she'd need to be boiled down first to
half her weight! Any sign of a flat yet?'

'I'm house-hunting at the minute.'

'Great!' said Gareth. 'And if you need furniture we'll get it
discount or out the back door from one of our shops!' He
stopped and, as if the matter had played on his mind, said in
a quieter voice: 'I hope you don't think I'm snobbish and conceited, Nicky. If I were I would have gone on endlessly about
New York and Manhattan, but I didn't, did I? You don't
always know what you're saying or what effect it's having. But
what about you! I'm always talking about me. What did you
do this summer?'

'Well, my claim came through. Mr Baker, my solicitor, got
me £5,000!'

'Is that all? He mustn't be any good. If you'd used our firm
they could have taken the mean bastards to the cleaners! But
still, you can do a lot with £5,000. Beginning with a house-
warming party! Or a dinner! Beef stroganoff! Ever tasted it?
Oh Nicky, you'll love it and we'll have good wine . . . Côtes
de Beaune or Chambertin or perhaps you'd prefer a Bordeaux
or Beaujolais or a Côtes du Rhône. And we'll get blocked and
I'll get some dope out of college . . .'

'College!'

'Yes. You can get anything at our college. Ecstasy, crack,

wacky-baccy, poitín . . . But stroganoff – you'd love that! It's cooked in cognac and Dijon mustard. Slivers of fillet steak so tender that they only have to see the pan and they're cooked! All on a bed of fluffy rice! And wine on the table, on the chairs, on the speakers, on the floor! And I'll be able to get away from the boxing club for a night, thank God.'

'You box? I don't believe it. What a coincidence! I used to go to a boxing club.'

'No, I'm talking about the boxing club in our house, silly! Those two at each other's throats. One night my father held my mother's head in the aquarium because she gave him fish for dinner out of one of those chip shops. . .'

'That's terrible. What an environment.'

'Hey, I was only joking! But I wished he had. She's always bitching about the toilet seat. One evening she was going on and on and on about him leaving the shampoo at the top of the bath instead of at the bottom. Actually, it was me who left it there but that was irrelevant. Then, as soon as she left off, he started on about her table manners and her gross appetite. He said something snattery and the next you know my mother stabs him in the forehead with her fork . . . It was fucking brilliant.'

'Did it stick?' said Nicky, his mouth agape.

'No, it fell out. No doubt Rosebud kissed it better. By the way, have you got a girlfriend or anything?'

'No,' said Nicky.

'I didn't think you had but I wasn't one hundred. Well, what else did you do this summer, besides get a claim?'

'I delivered sixty thousand parcels, two hundred thousand letters and birthday cards and examination results, blah, blah, blah. I brought good news to some homes and news of death, tragedy and serious illness to other. . .'

'Come on, you did more than that!'

'Speaking of mail, the examination results came out this week. How did you do?'

'I walked everything. It's this year coming which is the important one. Now let's get back to you. Who are your friends? I want to know every single thing about you! What you think about this and that, what you do on your time off.

Well, we know that you swim! By the way, better not tell your mother who phoned. Just say somebody from work. It's simpler. Most people, I'm sure you've noticed, are afraid and suspicious of deep friendship. They're really afraid of themselves.'

Nicky nodded wholeheartedly for there was sense in Gareth's astuteness.

'What have I done this summer?' he thought aloud. 'Not much. In fact, my holidays have only started but I haven't planned anything. I don't have many friends except at work, and I rarely go away anywhere in the summer. . .'

'You don't! I'm not back to college till the first week in September. Let's do something together! Have you got a car?'

'No, why?'

'Hire one and we'll fuck off to the coast and round the countryside for day trips here and there! What do you say?!'

'Eh, yes. Yeh! But what'll you tell your mother and father?'

'You leave that to me. Unfortunately, it's time-to-go time. At this very moment I'm sitting in the home of my friend John and we're showing each other our awful holiday videos.'

Nicky didn't want him to leave but couldn't have expressed that feeling without throwing them into a cauldron of questions.

'I'll walk you to your bus stop.'

'Bus! I'm phoning for a big yellow cab!'

'You don't have to do that. There's a taxi firm not too far from here.'

'OK, then.'

Gareth handed in the towel and togs, having hired them upon arrival at the Leisure Centre to which he had traced Nicky.

They walked over the bridge but idled then stopped halfway and looked over the parapet like mystified children into the soundless swollen gulf of the harbour.

'Do you believe in God?' asked Gareth.

'No,' said Nicky. 'But I used to.'

'Oom. Me too.'

'Smell the river?' said Nicky. 'It's stinking tonight, isn't it.'

'You should see my mother!' said Gareth. 'She and I would be talking, when she'd suddenly interrupt me. "Just a second," she'd say, as if she forgot to turn off the bath. She'd leap out of her chair, run to the door . . . which would always be shut because I was taught to close doors behind me . . . take the stairs three at a time, and then she would appear about two minutes later as if nothing had happened and would continue the conversation!'

'What does she do that for?'

'To fart, of course! One day a minister was in our house and she rose and said, "Excuse me." But he kept on addressing her, holding his china cup and saucer ever so delicately in his hands and before she could get to the door the farts came trumpeting out of her! I swear to God, Nicky, the poor woman was on the verge of tears with the mortification. My father turned to me and said, "Gareth!" and I apologised. It was the closest we had ever been in terms of solidarity. And the minister, the scrounging, begging-bowl bastard, forgot his tact for a few moments and stared at my mother just too cleverly, then remembered why he was there, and looked at me with his little fucking forgiving Christian smile.' Gareth shook his head reminiscing. 'My father wrote him a cheque for £5 – it was four hundred and fifty short – and was my hero for about an hour.'

They arrived at the taxi firm and said their goodbyes. The arrangements were that Nicky was to telephone Gareth at home the following day calling himself, William Simms, the name of a college pal, just to check that Gareth would be able to get away and meet him at the rendezvous, the steps of the Central Library. Meanwhile, Gareth would have thought of something plausible to justify his absence.

Nicky had a choice of walks home and decided to take himself via Montside. There, at the post office, with its upstairs flat, the home of one ruthless woman, he stuck out his chest and marched proudly past. He didn't care where she was or whom she was lying with: she could no longer hurt him. He now found it difficult to recall, other than academically, the pain and humiliation he had been feeling just hours earlier.

He turned his head into the breeze and smiled. He thought he could hear the waves toss the dice of shingle up the sand of his beach, delivering him his long-awaited fortune.

10

'ZHEEEEE . . . WINOWWWWW . . . ZHEEEEE . . .' went the vacuum cleaner on the stairs, filling the hall with the piquancy of ersatz pine which he found unpleasant.

Nicky was biting his nails in anticipation of phoning Gareth. His mother switched off the machine. He listened to the cable being automatically yanked into its drum and the sound of his mother open and close the door of the closet. He went into the hall but then realised that his mother would overhear him on the phone claiming to be William Simms. He loitered to see if she had chores which would take her elsewhere.

'You want to use the phone? Go ahead, I'm finished with the cleaning.'

'Ah, no, it's OK,' he said and returned to his seat. But each time he approached the hall, thinking she was at the back of the kitchen, he could hear her humming. If he could hear her she would surely hear him. It was frustrating.

I'll just have to head on out. What'll I wear? Shite! What'll I wear? He knew that Gareth wouldn't mind what he had on but some dress sense had been aroused in him. He went upstairs and put on his dancing shoes and jeans but didn't like the top he had worn before. He was in despair. Then he decided to look in his father's wardrobe. He found a blue T-shirt which fitted him. Not bad! I'll not need a coat in this weather.

He came down the stairs carrying his sports bag.

'Mammy, I'm heading out for the day, OK?'

'Oh,' she said. 'Where are you going?'

'I'm going to hire a car and go to the beach.'

'Is Madeline going to the beach as well?' she asked with a little smile which produced a dimple in the crease of one cheek.

It was simpler to lie. 'Yes,' he said. 'Don't be worrying about dinner for me. OK? I'll head on now.'

'Nicky, that T-shirt suits Mr Smith but it isn't you,' she smiled. 'Come on upstairs and I'll get something for you.'

In the bedroom she flicked through the coat-hangers and produced a white short-sleeved buttoned shirt which she had bought him and he hadn't worn.

'Is it not too sort of formal?' he asked.

'No, it suits the jeans and it's smart-looking.'

He changed quickly and almost ran off. My kingdom for a phone. Five minutes later he was in a call box, placed his coin in the slot and dialled the number.

'Hello,' a woman said before the line went on automatic hold. Nicky swallowed hard. He pushed in his money but the bent coin of a previous user was blocking the inner chute. Oh no! Why me! Why now! At the other end the connection drained away. He came out. There was another phone box at Montside. It was on his way to the bus stop. My bag! I forgot my swimming gear! He ran back to the phone box and retrieved it. At the dentist's he crossed the road and went into the phone box between the library and the post office, outside of which stood a good half dozen people talking, among them Jack Taylor. Plenty of people about this morning!

Nicky got through this time and it was Gareth who answered.

'What kept you?'

'I'll tell you later. So. What's happening?'

'What's happening? Thunderbirds are go! What'll you be in?'

'In? I haven't got the car yet . . . I didn't want to get it in case you couldn't make it . . .'

'Oh, is it next summer we're going?' Gareth sounded irate.

'Don't worry. It's only a formality. I'll see you in what time?'

'Well, where are you now?'

'I'm, eh, in the city centre.'

'Oh, that's OK. I thought you hadn't left yet!'

'Where's your mom? Is she near?'

'No. I've sent her to the hairdressers! I asked her if she'd like to go to the museum to see the new dinosaurs but she shuddered. Ha! Ha! She's given us £40 for the museum and for the cinema afterwards!'

'How'd you manage that?'

'Oh, you can sell any compliment to vanity. I told her she was looking well and that the weight was falling off her. To be truthful, my mother is beautiful . . . but enough of that. Here! Are we going for a run or are we not!'

'Yes, yes.'

'OK, then. Synchronise watches. See you in one hour, *mon bon ami*.'

'11.30. See you.'

Nicky came out of the box. He looked over at Jack. Jack saw him and nodded. Jack, your daughter's eyes turn white and scare the shite out of you when she's coming. Then, from behind her father, Madeline peeked out a face so tanned that a blush would have been imperceptible. So you're back. She looked well. She smiled at Nicky and although all his hurt came back he nodded, but in a way that said, it's your loss. Then he thought, I'll have to fly. He was surprised at the large numbers of people about. He hadn't got time to ask Sonny or David what was going on and damned if he was going to make conversation with the Taylors. Suddenly, the clusters of people were drawn to the main road like surface bubbles that accelerate to the side of a glass. Nicky also stepped forward because whatever was responsible was holding up traffic and his bus. David's funeral procession had halted for a minute's silence across from the vicinity of the All Nighter. Sonny's head was bowed. He was big and fat and uncomfortably besuited, and he sweated profusely as if this was his road to Calvary. He sobbed and put his arm consolingly around the shoulder of his nephew, the son who sometimes accompanied David. David's widow and daughters were also in tears. Fuck, I'm so out of touch! I should be at this funeral. He supposed he felt sorry for David even though he had once boxed Robin

and him on the ears and falsely accused them of stealing bars
of chocolate. Robin had proposed burning down the shop,
wondered how petrol bombs could be made, and unnerved
Nicky while the idle threat lasted: Nicky could be kept going
so easily. But the only thing they ever took, or rather, that
Robin took, was the big red candle. Both the boys had been
honest and Robin had the additional influence of a churchgo-
ing mother who saw that her children went to Sunday school.

Nicky hoped that Sonny wouldn't notice his absence. Men
joined the cortège, behind which there was a long column of
funeral cars. Fuck me, said Nicky, how's my bus going to get
through? His anxiety was justified. His journey into town was
significantly delayed and when the bus overtook the cortège
he hid his head.

At the car hire there was a queue. But at 11.30 he pulled up
outside the Central Library in a metallic blue Ford Granada.
Gareth was sitting on the steps, absorbed in a book. Such a
concentration of life and potential, mused Nicky. He sounded
the horn. Gareth jumped, picked up a little travel bag and
showed a smile like that of an infant tickled under the chin.

He took his seat, pulled the door closed and unzipped his
jerkin, which he threw into the back. He was wearing a short-
sleeved white shirt just like Nicky's. 'Snap!' said Gareth. 'How
cosmic!' Nicky experienced sheer ecstasy just being in close
proximity to his friend.

'OK, Captain!' said Gareth. 'Let's fuckeen *go*!'

They shot through the town, all lights changing to green as
they approached They turned on to the motorway and immediately went into the fast lane. Gareth inserted a cassette and
gave it full volume and Nicky was in stitches at his young
friend's antics.

'No. No!

'No, no, no.'

'No. No!' they screamed in unison to the rave music as
Gareth shook his head from side to side and drummed the
dashboard.

He slow-waved every car they overtook except that of the
motorway police; he smiled at the officers deferentially while
giving them a one-finger salute below deck.

A few miles out Gareth said: 'So, where are we for?'

'I thought we'd drive north along the coast road, explore the glens for a bit, then maybe back down to the seaside and go for a swim if the tide's in.'

'No. We'll do that another day. Let's go into the country-side instead. Is that OK? It's just one of those days when you know the fields and woods are going to be steeped in colour and character and abuzz with nature. Do you mind?'

'Not at all. Your every wish is my command.'

'You are very kind.'

'It's a pleasure,' said Nicky. 'So, no real problems getting away? No posse on our trail?'

'No. My father's wrapped up in business or the Chamber of Commerce or the Rotary Club. Parliament's closed for the summer so he's at a loose end. He fancies himself as a bud-ding politician, you know. Probably explains his need for extra-marital ham! My mother is lost, I suppose, poor thing, but she can be so self-absorbed. She has her Capo di monte collection to keep her happy or time spent chasing up new cat-alogues of Mozart or Schubert. At the moment, she's into watercolours . . . Ah, you've a little pimple on your chin,' said Gareth, changing the subject. 'Can I squeeze it?'

'Yes,' grinned Nicky, bending his head over towards the pas-senger side whilst keeping his eyes on the road.

'Ping!' announced Gareth, as it burst. 'Phew, there was half a pint in that one!' He dabbed Nicky's chin with a tissue from the bag in which he carried the tapes. He took out a packet of mints, unwrapped the crinkly cellophane from one and said: 'Open!'

Nicky opened his mouth and Gareth popped the sweet in. He stretched and settled his arm behind Nicky's headrest and Nicky sighed contentedly. Gareth switched to gentler music on the radio.

They left the motorway and entered country roads, the boy giving arbitrary directions as the whim possessed him. They passed through a couple of towns and a picturesque village, after which the gradient sharply rose and radio reception began to deteriorate. After a while Gareth suggested that they pull over. They got out and walked to the side of the road and leaning on a dry-stone wall looked down into the deep green valley below where contented cattle munched merrily on thick juicy grass. Further down there was a small shallow lake frizzled along its far shore by the ripples of a steady breeze. Nicky stood with his hands in his pocket, his hair being ruffled by the fresh, strong mountain wind which blustered from the peak above.

'Brrrrr!' said Gareth. 'It's nippier up here than I thought.' He slid his arm through Nicky's and leaned his head against his shoulder, as a young son would do. Nicky was taken by surprise but glowed with pride. Suddenly, he was possessed by the most natural but sublime emotional feeling. My God! I love this boy! I love him! It's incredible but it's true. He means everything to me! Nicky couldn't suppress his feelings any longer. He loosened his arm, turned and held Gareth in a tight embrace to which the boy responded. Tears welled in Nicky's eyes because, while it was all so beautiful, it was also all so impossible. But it gave his life meaning and purpose.

'Oh Nicky! You feel the same way; you feel the same way!' cried Gareth, gripping Nicky's hand. 'Nicky! I'd die for you, I tell you. I'd die for you!'

'Gareth, Gareth! What are we going to do?' murmured Nicky, desperately.

'Do?' said Gareth, lifting his head off Nicky's shoulder and looking him in the eye. 'Do? Don't do anything. Don't say anything. Don't even think! Just keep calm. We'll be OK. You and I. We'll be OK.'

Nicky studied Gareth's face and although he was the one with tears on his cheeks he could see panic in the boy's eyes.

'You're going to end our friendship, aren't you? You're afraid. You're not going to see me again, are you? You're thinking of what people will say.'

'Gareth, this would ruin you and I'd be slaughtered...'

'There you go again, saying and thinking things. We'll use our heads, trust me. We're naturally secretive. No one will know.'

'Gareth, I'm eight years older than you. Eight years! You're fifteen. I'm supposed to know better. I'm probably even corrupting you just talking about this,' he laughed sardonically.

'Nicky, that's nonsense and you know it. Please, let's not spoil things. Let's not talk any more about it. And anyway, I'm almost sixteen. I feel far older than my years. I think I've been on earth before. Let's just enjoy each other's company. We're doing nothing wrong . . . Look! There's a hawk!'

'Where?'

'Just over there. Two or three fields, above the trees.'

'I can't see a thing. Your eyesight must be brilliant.'

'It's these binoculars I wear! There! It's hovering. Something's going to die!'

Nicky put his cheek to Gareth's blond-haired arm which was pointing the direction. 'Yes, yes! I see it now.'

The hawk plummeted to the ground, opening its wings just inches above its putative prey, though it rose empty-taloned.

Gareth rubbed his goose-pimpled arms for circulation and suggested they get back into the car. Resuming the subject he had urged they avoid, he said: 'Nicky, we'll talk about what this means to us another time, OK? You're worrying too much. Look, I have never felt this way about anyone before. Understand?'

'No wonder! You're only fifteen!'

'Almost sixteen, Nicky. We're so relaxed and natural together. I've hated my life until now. With you every second is magic. Nicky, each time I saw a post office van my heart used to skip a beat in the hope that you were driving. You've no idea . . .'

Oh, but Nicky had. He wanted desperately to be around Gareth. He realised that. Physical expression of their relationship beyond shows of affection were far from his mind. He was certainly happy – happier than he had been in a long time. But it was an island of happiness surrounded on all sides by a cruel, unforgiving world. Oh, fuck the world. Gareth is right. Why let it spoil the day.

Through the bouldered, heathered mountain passes they drove, down a drunken road which twisted alongside the downward course of a plump stream whose glinting, leadened and bottle-glass waters coruscated through rocks of granite and red sandstone. Again, Gareth called on Nicky to pull over. He jumped from the car and ran with his camera to the river where he removed his sandals and socks and paddled in the cool water whilst Nicky sat on a hot rock, unbuttoned his shirt and watched. Gareth took photographs of Nicky. He then set the camera on automatic for a self-portrait and struggled with the zip of his jeans. Before the shutter opened Gareth was pissing towards the camera. 'Look, Nicky!' he shouted. 'No hands!' He zipped up and splashed through the river.

'Nicky! Take your trainers and socks off and join me! Come on!'

Nicky shrugged his shoulders and did as he was bidden. The water was delightful.

Gareth ordered Nicky to stand still at a certain spot. Once again he aligned the camera, switched on the timer and jumped in beside his friend and posed. Just before the shutter opened he grabbed Nicky's left nipple between his finger and thumb and tugged on it, laughing. Nicky winced and was almost angry. 'OK,' said Gareth. 'We'll take that one again.' Afterwards, he said, 'We'll have to take more later. Meanwhile, how about something to eat?'

'Yes, but where?'

'We'll find a wee pub somewhere. It's always called the Farmer's Rest because, I presume, they're so fucking exhausted! If we see someone we'll stop and ask.'

About five minutes later they came across two tractors blocking the road. A trailer of hay prevented Gareth from seeing up the road. Nicky reported that the drivers were talking to each other.

'That's a bit ignorant,' said Gareth as the delay continued.

'It's their road,' said Nicky.

As one of the tractors pulling a trailer of black turf was passing, Nicky rolled down his window and beckoned the man in the cab. He turned out to be a mere youngster.

'Is there a pub about here we could get a bite to eat in?'

'About two miles down you'll come to an old stone bridge to the right of this road. Go over the bridge and about half a mile on you'll see The Ranch. Can't miss it.'

'Thanks,' shouted Nicky.

They found the place, which had character of a sort but was virtually empty, and lunched on steak-and-kidney pie and cheese sandwiches.

'It's fairly rotten, isn't it?' said Gareth, hanging his head over his plate and spitting out the gristle.

'Shoosh. They might hear.'

'What about a stiff drink to wash down the suet?'

'We'll drink shandies, that's all,' replied Nicky firmly.

'OK, Daddy,' said Gareth aloud, rocking on his backside. Nicky elbowed him.

A rheumatic collie trailed itself over the tiled floor to their table. Gareth looked at it. 'A case for euthanasia or what?' he said.

The collie's owner, a ruddy-faced old man wearing a dirty cap, both hands resting on a blackthorn, guffawed. 'I think he's lukkin for a bit of your sammeech.'

'Yes, well, he can lukk elsewhere,' said Gareth out the side of his mouth. Nicky rubbed the superannuated sheepdog about the head and then under the chin. It was panting and gleety strings of saliva hinged its jaws. 'Nicky! It probably has worms! Go wash your hands . . . Fuck off, dog.'

Nicky paid no attention to Gareth but enjoyed his expressions of concern and before that his little quips.

Afterwards they wandered around the back of the pub-cum-farmhouse. An old barn was stacked with redolent golden hay and continually shed chaff into the draughty courtyard below. Its sweet warmth lured Nicky inside and Gareth followed. In the eaves Nicky noticed the half coconuts of swallows' nests, empty and in a state of desuetude.

'Have we lost something?' asked Gareth.

'Lost – and found,' said Nicky enigmatically, turning and smiling. 'Shall we head on now?'

'Yes, let's go and get some real food! To think that I paid four fifty so that we could have the honour of eating that pigswill . . . Race you to the car!'

But Nicky walked.

The roadsides bulged initially with whin in full saffron bloom, then with buttercups. Above the shimmering thermals from the hot tarmac danced tulles of midge flies, hundreds of which were zapped against the windscreen.

'I'm a bit of a moan, amn't I?' said Gareth out of the blue.

'No,' said Nicky, warmly, stretching out the vowel. 'Never.'

Gareth, pleased, moved about in his seat: 'This is lovely, being out here, not knowing what's next,' he said. 'Out the window with you!' he shouted, throwing away the map which tore along a fold and blew some with the wind before cartwheeling down the road like a piece of tumbleweed. Then he took more pictures, some of the scenery, some of Nicky.

Suddenly, Gareth wormed his head into Nicky's lap with such a *risqué* connotation that Nicky gasped.

'Steady, driver! I'm taking a photo of you in profile from the South Pole!'

Nicky waited until two or three pictures were taken before shouting: 'Up, Gareth! Up, now!' in a voice tinged with anger, an anger directed as much at himself for revelling in the concupiscent sensation he experienced.

'I love it when you shout!' laughed Gareth. 'You don't mean it!'

That evening, after making arrangements for further meetings, Nicky dropped Gareth off in the city centre. As he drove home he was on a high thinking about the store of affection, magic and fun, not to mention sexuality, that was Gareth; and he laughed and shook his head in disbelief at the boy's cleverness and originality. But when he turned off the main road and noticed the All Nighter still closed and was reminded by the post office of a woman called Madeline with whom he had slept, when he came through the door to a welcome from his mother enthusiastically inquiring about his day, the contrast in his two lives depressingly emerged and he felt brought down a little.

Later, lying in bed, he told himself a dozen times that he was doing nothing wrong, that his friendship as such was not unusual. What was a few years age difference? They were like cousins. Or a young uncle and a teenage nephew. But as soon as he thought of the impulse that drove him to embrace Gareth he experienced qualms. Qualms soon drowned by an uncaring pride. He wallowed in the reciprocation he had received, their rapport. And when he recalled the words of diamonds and gems that formed on Gareth's beautiful lips, the words that were mined in the depths of a most precious heart, Nicky melted, sank his body into the body of the mattress and buried his head in the neck of his pillow.

11

ON THEIR FOURTH DAY together they decided to drive north. As part of a group made up mostly of foreigners they were given a guided tour of the world's oldest distillery and later visited on the slopes of a mountain the megalithic tomb of a warrior bard, the authenticity of which Gareth rubbished.

'Why do you not believe this to be a grave?'

'Nicky, use your head! It's all hearsay! It's like the Bible. The New Testament was written decades if not hundreds of years after the events it describes. How could the original survive so many tellings! Listen, you've heard of Abraham Lincoln?'

'Of course,' said Nicky. 'He was in the Bible too,' he joked, with a sudden memory of the past.

'Well, Lincoln made a famous address at Gettysburg. Right? Two reporters – expert stenographers – stood below the platform as he spoke and recorded what he said. And, do you know what? Their reports differ substantially in details! They were there but they witnessed and reported the same speech differently! So you can't be sure of anything. Even what you think you see or hear or witness!'

'Always said that myself,' said Nicky, trying to sound grandiloquent. 'We have what we hold. Nothing else.'

'Yes, well . . .'

In the afternoon they parked the car at a long cabin-like

restaurant on the edge of a forest which covered several hill-sides like a huge pelt. Nicky suggested that they explore the forest before eating and so they went for a walk up a dark steep pathway separated from a limestone gully and thickets of ferns in every shade of green by a protective wooden handrail. Con-fetti-shaped light barely penetrated the foliage high above whilst below were trapped the alpine balm of fresh decay and the disparate percussion of effervescing, gurgling, splashing water rushing through the deep wrinkles of the gorge.

After about ten minutes they reached a small cataract, the first of many. The higher they climbed the more fascinating and noisy the falls became until they reached a place where the spec-tacle was completely mesmerising, where the headwaters came tumbling over the edge of a cliff in constant, total surprise as if the carpet or bed of the river had been pulled from under it.

On the return journey Nicky said he would love to swim in the tiny green lagoons which, just yards from the base of each fall, turned the pounded water placid. Gareth, calling his bluff, told him to be his guest.

They didn't meet for the next two days, though Gareth had wanted to. Nicky said they needed to be careful. During those two days it had rained constantly.

On their next outing they drove to a popular seaside resort about fifty miles north-east of the city. They spent a fortune on the gaming machines, rifle ranges and dodgems in the var-ious amusement arcades. Gareth took Nicky onto a putting green and showed him some golfing techniques and Nicky allowed his unlicensed friend to drive their car around a dis-used airfield.

The sun came out in the afternoon, the weather having turned summery once again.

'Would you like to go boating?'

'Yes,' replied Gareth. 'But you take the oars.'

Nicky paid the fee and they climbed into the nervous boat. He put the oars into their pins and rowed out into the middle of the artificial lake. Gareth trailed his hand in the brown water and laa-laaad the 'Barcarole' from *The Tales of Hoff-man*, then with a sleekit smile he produced a hip flask, twisted off the top and offered Nicky a drink.

'What's that?'

'Should be navy rum given the occasion but it's brandy.'

'Brandy? Where did you get it?'

'It's my father's. It's really pretentious looking, isn't it? But it's the best of cognac. Underneath this leather pouch is sterling silver. The flask belonged to an officer in the First World War. It's pretty valuable.' He took a swig and his head involuntarily shook. 'Pooh! That's strong! Here. Are you certain you don't want some?'

'No, I don't, and you shouldn't be drinking at your age. What if they smell your breath when you get home?'

'They'll not. For God's sake, hasn't getting away proved much easier than we thought? I never realised just how much people could be absorbed in their own worlds. Anyway, we'll be having something to eat – I'm buying today – and I'll suck on mints before I go into the house.'

Whatever explanations Gareth gave his mother she probed him less than he had expected and he was required to use only the bare outlines of his detailed alibis. As the confederates relaxed with the success of their trysts, their arrangements tended towards convenience and Nicky would pick Gareth up and drop him off at shorter distances from his home.

Nicky rowed around a bush-covered island upon which some truant couples had beached their boats seeking intimacy. Gareth had the flask up to his mouth again.

'Careful, you!'

'Itsch fawkin great, Neekey,' said Gareth, deliberately slurring his speech to rile him, then laughing. 'Let me sing you a few songs.'

Nicky relented. 'OK, what arias are you going to give me?'

Immediately, Gareth launched into a country and western song:

Crazy. I'm crazy for feeling so loneleeeee . . .

'What!' shouted Nicky in surprise, interrupting him. 'Where'd you learn that? My mate Gerard in work sings that all the time.'

'My mother. She has Patsy de Cline tapes which she keeps

well out of sight. She listens to them when daddy doesn't come home and when she thinks I'm fast asleep in bed. She sits all alone in the dark with a cocktail, singing, and getting louder, the drunker she becomes.'

'But I thought she was into classical music and played the piano?'

'So she is but this is her other little secret passion, from some other life maybe – or perhaps it's the story of this her life. Do you think there's been another man? I suppose there has to have been. Over the years I've learnt all these songs . . .

Sweet dreams of you . . .

and

I fall to pieces . . .

When Gareth finished his medley Nicky stopped rowing and gave him a standing ovation. The boat rocked perilously and he had to resume his seat. The sound of clapping also came from a fella and girl on the island who had sat up with the singing. Gareth blushed, then said: 'Right Nicky. It's your turn!'

'I dunno any songs, I swear!'

'Come on, just one. Here. Take a swig.'

Rather than break the spell Nicky put the flask to his mouth but began laughing and spluttering at the thought of the particular words gathering in his throat and used the back of his hand to contain the fiery liquor and the rush of bubbly saliva inside his cheeks.

'OK. OK. Here goes,' he said. 'Here. Right now. Ready. Right.

'OK . . . Ahem . . .

Every time it rains, it rains
Pennies from heaven . . .

Gareth joining in, and the fact that he knew the lyrics set Nicky aglow with a love of life and humankind:

... There'll be pennies from heaven
For you and meeeee!'

'Ha! Ha! Ha!' they laughed.
'Fuckeen brilliant!' said Gareth.
Nicky was almost in tears he felt so happy. 'We're crazy,
don't you know,' he said.

... And I'm crazy for loving you

quoted Gareth. 'Oh, it's so good being around you. I wish we
could stay overnight instead of having to rush back home each
evening.'
'No,' said Nicky decidedly. 'That's not a good idea.'
But Gareth once again just trailed his hand in the water and
murmured, 'Ooom.'
'I don't know what that "Ooom" is for,' said Nicky.
'You don't? I want to be around you more. I want us to
spend a night together. Do you understand? Do you?'
'Gareth, don't do this to us. Please.'
'I don't know what I am to you. I feel like a bloody nephew!
When are we going to do something?'
'No more talk like that. No more, do you hear?'
'Ooom,' answered Gareth.

'Do you know two Madelines?' asked his mother when he
returned from another day's outing with his 'girlfriend'.
'Yes,' replied Nicky. At least two, he thought, ironically.
'Why ask?'
'Oh, that explains it,' she said relieved. 'The other one
phoned early this afternoon. Couldn't get her to say much!
Asked would you call her.'
Mind you own business, Ma.
'Right,' he said. 'I'll do that later.'
What could she want? How can I rebuff her best? He threw
his holdall under the stairs. He felt confused. Why is she com-
ing back on the scene now? What does she want? Maybe she's
lost something and just wants to ask if I've found it – a ring

or a watch or something. No. That's not it. She wants to be friends. She's sorry for what she's done. If I think too much about it the pain will come back. And there's now Gareth. Oh God, where am I going with him? He's sweet, funny, warm, understanding, beautiful. But he's too daring. He's single-minded in his convictions. He knows what he wants. All this inside his head and heart and he's only a kid!

The telephone rang and Nicky reached it first.

'It's you?'

'Yes.'

'Listen,' whispered Gareth. He sounded peevish. 'Something's come up. I can't make it tomorrow.'

'Why not?' said Nicky. 'What's the problem?'

'My father's being really inquisitive. I thought he knew something. He asked me how come I was spending so much time in museums, libraries and cinemas and eating out, and who was I associating with.'

A cold liquid shiver ran down Nicky's spine.

'We'll wait until Sunday,' said Nicky, whilst looking over his shoulder.

'Sunday! Why not Friday?'

'Do as I say or I'll not see you at all,' said Nicky. But immediately he added. 'I'm sorry, I'm sorry. I feel panicky. Listen, let's wait until Sunday, the library, eleven o'clock, OK?'

'OK. Sunday, Nicky. Are you OK?'

'Yes, I'm OK now.'

'I'll plague them and break things around the house until they're glad to see the back of me!'

'Right,' said Nicky. 'Bye for now.'

As soon as he put down the phone his mother appeared from the kitchen. Why to fuck is she always hanging from the ceiling like a fucking microphone.

'Nicky? . . . Nicky, when are you going to bring Madeline here? You know you can, don't you? Sometimes, I wonder,' said his mother with a hollow laugh aimed at disguising embarrassment, 'if you are ashamed of us.'

'What are you talking about?' he said, losing his temper. 'What to hell are you going on and on about? You never stop noseying, you're always hovering. Well, I'll tell you something.

Maybe you're right. Maybe you've hit the nail on the head. Who'd want to bring anybody here to see a grown adult – no! an old woman! – fuss around that big baby out in his playpen talking to the weeds and killing all the flowers he touches...'

His mother shrank. Her hands were joined at her midriff. Was this really her son? Though her feet were nailed to the floor, her shoulders shook. Tears streamed down her face and ran together underneath her chin like the knotted ribbons of a bonnet.

'Why didn't I get out of here earlier! I could have been in Germany or Paris, well away from, from this –' He stormed out, jumped into the car and drove off. The soul of him took a back seat and was terrified as it travelled inside an insane personality, this mongrel son of heaven and earth. Its timid voice was faint but it kept saying, Where am I going? Where's he taking me?

In town he parked in High Street, went into the upstairs lounge of the Hayloft and ordered a vodka and a coke and a bacardi, drank both, preferred the vodka and ordered another. He looked around and was glad to see that there were no faces he knew. He had another few drinks and his depression lifted slightly. He asked the barmaid for the copy of the evening paper sitting over by the optics. She gave it to him and he offered her a cigarette but she declined.

He went unsteadily over to an empty table with his drink, lit a cigarette and read the classifieds for rental accommodation. No time like the present, he thought, and tore out the advertisement:

> Apartments, Flats: Furnished rooms, good decor, Economy 7 heating, University area, £200 p/m. – Tel 46137, 7.30 – 8.30.

He asked where the phone was kept and was directed to an alcove.

'It's nice in here,' he said to the barmaid as he swung around and saw where she was pointing. 'Very nice, indeed. Could you give me some change, please?'

He was on the phone for several minutes, asked the other

person to wait a moment, then intimated to the barmaid that he needed a pen. He confirmed to the person at the end of the line that the arrangement was fine. No problem. The barmaid found Nicky quite funny: there was rarely an air of threat or menace about him despite his recent blow-outs.

He stuffed the advertisement in his back pocket and clicked his fingers smugly a number of times as he moseyed back to his seat. By now, the bar had filled up, mostly with young couples, and Nicky felt lonely and out of place. He missed Gareth and was heavily tempted to phone him just to hear the sound of his sweet voice. Better not. His da might have the fucking thing tapped. Fuck, drink makes so things clear, he laughed. Then laughed again at the juxtaposition which he reckoned his brain had done deliberately just to see if his mind could spot it. Smarter to be have than that me to catch!

He decided to move on. He drank in two more bars but each time found that he was among happy couples. The night is young. I am eternity! I am infinity! he laughed. He swept the world aside with the back of his hand he was so omnipotent and he strode down the street without once touching the ground. He thought about taking off Gareth's shoes and socks, then slowly removing his trousers, then his shorts as the boy lay languorously sprawled out on a bed. But the image was washed away in a wave of self-loathing and he shuddered at the reverie and felt embarrassed enough to check for witnesses. He found that he had been standing outside a window display of women's lingerie.

He bought a hamburger with onions and chips and ate them as he walked back to the car. He couldn't find the keys. Eventually, he saw them still in the ignition, tried the door handle and it was unlocked. He smiled, wanting to see good. Ach, I love the people of this city. They're dead on!

He drove eastwards and as he sped past Montside shouted, 'Hiya Madeline!' out the window, followed by the sound of her snoring: 'Hawwwwwwwwwwwshoooooooooo-Hawwwwwwwwwwwshoooooooooooo!'

About two miles down the road he saw a pub which took his fancy and so he pulled in to a side-street. This time he locked the car. In the quiet lounge he drank more vodka. I'd love to go for a swim. He stood two of his fingers on the edge of his glass. They jumped into the vodka, ice and lemon. My fingers have landed on their feet! He licked the vodka off them and poured coke into the glass. Tomorrow a new home, he said, sadly. He ordered more drinks. Must go for a leak. He stood at the urinal, his bladder the boss, and admired the stubs of his fingernails on his right hand. I haven't bitten them in days. He compared them to the nails on his left hand. Hold it! What's holding my dick while I'm pishing? Aw fuck! I forgot to take him out! A big stain covered his jeans. Nicky's drunk! Nicky's drunk, he said. He took off his jeans and held them up to the hand-dryer. For fuck's sake, how are you expected to dry your clothes in twenty seconds.

'Bit of an accident,' he repeated to everyone who came in.

Bit of a smell. The air'll take it away. Outside the air hit him. He couldn't find the car. The fuckers have stolen it. Where to now? It's almost half eleven. I'll go home. He staggered down the road and was tempted to visit Andy and Emma. They lived quite close.

Ask her if she remembered the wee dog under the bus. I'd ask her if she remembered Coulter the poet, stiff in his fucking coffin and me left to carry everything.

But he passed their street and forgot his questions. Why did Madeline fuck off like that? Why didn't she help me? The more I think of it.

He went up the entry behind the post office and waited and waited. A dozen times he decided to leave and a dozen times he came back after a few paces, persuading himself to stay for just one more minute – and see if she does anything for me. At last the light went on. She went back and forth across the bedroom, coming into view at the window for a split second at a time. She must be putting clothes away. His mouth was dry and his heart pounded. He stood on a mound of broken bricks and a bag of hard cement. He saw clips of her as she undressed. Finally, she came to the window and looked out, perhaps towards the stars and how they looked three weeks before, but he retreated into the darkness so that she was visible to just a corner of one eye.

She examined her naked breasts in turn, as before, assuming

privacy, stepped back into the room and a second later the light went out. I'd love to pull the fucking head off her. He licked and smelt the tip of his fingers, as if they'd been violently plunged into the still strange, forbidden territory of her sex and he experienced the raw power which had been atavistically hinted to him before, this mythical access to the knowledge of good and evil. Once again his soul burst through the night and took possession of his mind and he experienced a sense of extreme self-loathing. He threw his head about to see if he could shake out his evil thoughts. Fuck and fuck again. What am I doing? What am I doing! What am I thinking! He bumped into several bins and sent them clanging. Better get me out of here. He staggered into the street. Sonny's in. Must ask him how David's keeping. David's dead! Now and forever. Phew! Almost forgot!

Sonny took one look and could see his condition.

'Sonny, I'm sorry for your troubles. I didn't know until the last minute.'

'It's OK, Nicky. That's the way it goes.'

'Well, I'm glad you're taking it so well. I know how you feel . . . Ach, just ignore me. I've had a few troubles myself, Sonny.'

'Would you drink a cup of coffee if I made you one?'

'Naw, but I'd take a wee vodka if you had one . . . Sonny? . . . Sonny?'

'What is it?'

'Sonny, do you remember the big candle?'

'What big candle's that?'

'Oh, about this size. A big, big one. Like the bulb of a light-house!'

Sonny smiled. 'No, Nicky. I don't know what you're talking about.'

'You smiled there, Sonny. I think you do know, you fly man! But anyway. Sonny, what do you think of your woman next door? Well, a few doors down?'

'The girl you're going with?'

'Howdya know that?'

'Come on, Nicky,' said Sonny. 'Don't I work here? Don't miss much.'

'Right, right. Sonny, what do you know about her? Really know?'

'Madeline's a neighbour, Nicky. A good neighbour. And she's a good girl . . . What has you like this? There's something wrong, isn't there?'

'Major. It's major's what's wrong with me. I was in here four, no five, no six, no seven, ah fuck, whenever how many weeks ago. The morning I boiled the eggs. There was billions of years missing, 'member? Fuck, you should hear the one about the queer shrimps. No offence, Sonny. Eight weeks ago's only yesterday but I've been round and round the world since. You wouldn't believe it. You wouldn't believe where I've been, Sonny,' he said, leaning across the counter so that the fumes of alcohol were unmistakable.

'It'll be clearer tomorrow, Nicky. You're in no state to go into it tonight. But talk to me again. I know what the real issue is, Nicky. I've known for a long time.'

'You dooooo? Ho! Doctor Sonny knows, does he! Well, tell me when you see me. Huh! Gotta go. I gotta see Jane.'

'Jane? Who's Jane?'

'It's a song, Sonny. A song. Didn't know that, didya?' Nicky bumped into the doorjamb whilst exiting. 'Sonny, how to fuck do you manage to get in and out through this slit? No offence, mate . . .'

He stood for a few moments with his forehead against the frame and trembled. The child trembled and cried.

'Sonny. Sonny? I've never gotten over Coulter. . .'

He stumbled down the street and cried to the heavens. Then he got angry with the bastard above – the puppet-master – even though he didn't exist. Then he got angry with the world again.

Who's in my way now? Ha! Da Smith! Let him open his mouth and I'll take out his teeth with my toes!

He put his key in the door but it was snibbed. Is that the way yous want it. He repeatedly kicked the door. His father appeared at the landing window.

'Take yourself off, you ungrateful tramp, or I'll come down there myself. Don't have me do something, Nicky, that I shall regret!'

' "Don't have me do something, Nicky, that I'll regret." You need a stiff drink, that's your problem, sourpuss. Didya ever hear of taking your kid fishing? Or to a football match?'

'Nicky!' cried his mother, pulling on her husband. 'Nicky, son, please stop this. What's happening, son? I just don't understand.'

' "What's happening, son? I just don't understand." Open your eyes!'

'Oh Nicky,' she sobbed. 'If we let you in will you be quiet and not start any trouble?'

Nothing like this had happened since the time Nicky had tried to kill himself. She was mortified and didn't know how she could ever live the scandal down.

'Ha! There's the woman made me colourblind! . . . Take your time,' he shouted. 'I'm coming through the window!'

Nicky had began punching the glass window when his father hurtled down the stairs and flung open the door. The old man yanked him back by the shoulder and leathered into him. Nicky felt the great relief of blows, saw stars and heard screams and a siren. He remembered thinking, Fuck da, you've a quare punch there, before he found rest in unconsciousness.

When he woke up it was with the eeriest feeling. He was in Robin Coulter's bed.

12

THE DOOR OPENED and a familiar ruddy face peeped in.
'You're awake, then.'
Nicky was befuddled and desperately needed facts.
   'The missus washed your clothes. They're dry and ready. Oh
yes, those car keys and that bit of paper was in your pockets,'
said Dan Leckey, pointing to the advertisement Nicky had
torn from the *Telegraph* and which lay beside the keys next to
a bedside lamp on a small table to his right. 'Your wallet's in
your jerkin, if you want to check it.'
   'What happened?'
   'I take it you don't remember? You were locked out and tried
to break the living-room window. We heard the shouting and
by the time I got over you were fighting with your father and
somebody had phoned the police to say that a murder was taking place! Ha! They had been after a prowler behind the post
office – that's why they were on the spot so quickly. You were
almost arrested but I said you'd be OK with us. You were far
gone, Nicky. Your mother was terrified that you'd start again
so me and your da got you over here. So, how's the head?'
   'I get an electric shock each time I turn it. Even when talking.'
   'Here,' said Dan. He dropped a couple of soluble tablets into
a glass of water he had brought. 'This'll help. Always cures me.'

Nicky swished the ghosts of the tablets at the bottom of the glass and drank the medicine in one gulp.

'Brrrrh! Thanks, Mr Leckey.'

'Would you like some breakfast?'

'I couldn't face a thing. I've yesterday's dinner floating about somewhere inside me.'

'I suppose you'll be heading across the road to kiss and make up?'

'Yeh, I'll have to see them,' he said, reaching out, picking up and scrutinising the clipping. He looked at his watch. 'Half ten already! Where's Mrs Leckey to I thank her.'

'Jill's out. Don't worry, I'll tell her. I'll go and let you get dressed.'

Nicky sat up. Of course, this wasn't Robin's bed he was in but it was Robin's old bedroom. He remembered the stories his friend used to read to him in bed and the close shaves that their hero, Sir Percy Blakeney – the Scarlet Pimpernel – had with the French agent, Chauvelin. In one famous incident Chauvelin lures the foppish Sir Percy into a trap and has him surrounded. Sir Percy, as cool as ever, doesn't panic, but offers his wily opponent a pinch of the best snuff in Europe and the smug French man accepts. But the ingenious Sir Percy had meanwhile substituted pepper and Chauvelin takes a greedy pinch which brings on a crippling fit of sneezing during which Sir Percy makes yet another brilliant escape into the night.

Nicky had believed it a true story. I was once very innocent.

At the bottom of his consciousness lay the unpalatable, unfinished cud of elusive memory which he knew he must chew over however bitter its ingredients. He threw his feet out of bed and as he pulled a sock over his foot he suddenly made the connection between himself and the voyeur loitering behind the post office and the police being called out; and the police being redirected to a street brawl at which he was at the centre again.

I was also in Sonny's! What to hell did I say to him? Then the memory of his fantasy of spreading Gareth across a double-bed hit him and hit him with the force of outraged society's horror and disapproval so that he squirmed and turned cold and felt that his life was a real mess. I'm a bastard. Absolutely drunk I could have done anything. Anything. But they say that in drink there is truth. I could have robbed Sonny. I could have killed Madeline. Fuck! I could have raped Gareth! My God, what's happening to me! Up his throat came a mix of vomit and bile which he caught in the gag of a hand. But he forced the porridge of onion and oatenmeal back into his mouth and swallowed before he would dirty any linen in the immaculately kept room or otherwise abuse the Leckeys' hospitality.

'You owe us an apology,' said his father. 'As much for your insulting behaviour and abusive language when sober as for your carry-on last night. You owe us an explanation. You've broken your mother's heart. We're the talk of the street and I've missed a day's work over the head of you.'

Nicky stood in the living-room doorway.

His mother sat in her armchair. She was shaking and didn't speak. Her face was bloodless. Her husband affectionately held her hand and Nicky smiled sardonically at his solicitude.

'I was going to apologise,' he stuttered. 'But I'll be honest. I'm not so sure now. You made me a stranger, made me strange. Never liked me as a child. I've never liked the arrangements in this house and so I think I'll leave. It's true my life's messed up. It's really, really messed up. I need to be on my own. But if there is something the matter with me yous two must bear some of the blame, especially you, da.'

'You feel so sorry for yourself,' said his father. 'Don't you?'

'Yes, I do. But I am also disgusted with myself. Da. Tell me this. What's my middle name?'

His father guffawed. 'Huh! What do you mean?'

'What's my middle name? A simple enough question.'

His mother began to intervene: 'Nicky, you know fine rightly. . .'

'Shut up, mammy. Answer the question, da. Answer it!'

'Don't dare talk to your mother or me like that! Just get out! Go on, get going!'

'Huh, you don't know the answer! Just as I thought. I'll pack all I need in a suitcase. Mammy, I'll send you some money every week.'

'We don't want your money,' said his father. 'You'll come back with your tail between your legs when you appreciate the comforts that were provided in this home for you, when you learn that the world is not such a nice place and you can't get by without the love and support of family.' The father, as he spoke, was rubbing his wife's hand. Darby and Joan in their slippers, sipping Ovaltine.

'I learnt plenty from you about how cold a place the world is,' Nicky rebuked him. 'Maybe I'll go live in a warmer climate . . . I'll pack and go.'

He looked around the bedroom which had been his since he was about six. He would never be back again. Never. He felt sad because despite what he had said he still had many fond memories. But this was the price he had to pay. Anyway, it was just one more loss to go with a history of losses: a father with whom he could never connect; Robin, his best friend dying; the chipping away of his innocence through a thousand stages; Madeline who deceived him; his mother whom he loved but whose loyalties were divided. And, next, the loss of Gareth from whom Nicky had to flee because living the truth was impossible, unpermissible.

His mother ran to the door after him. 'Nicky,' she beseeched.

'Nicky? Where will you go, son? Where will you go?'

'Far away . . . England or Germany,' he said.

On Sunday morning he sat on an old-fashioned armchair in his new flat and stared in silence at the travelling clock he had placed on the table. It had a faint tick and the second hand advanced in fidgets. His breathing became pained, his lips trembled and his chin twitched as eleven o'clock approached. Outside, a soft drizzle fell. The acid of checked tears hurt his eyes and stung the membranes in his nose as emotion came up his throat several times. At eleven o'clock he felt the slow execution begin as Gareth lifted his eyes from his book to see if that was Nicky's Ford Granada coming through the lights – the vehicle which Nicky had retrieved and returned to the car hire on Friday. Gareth would smile and say hello to the occasional passers-by. He would check his watch against some of theirs in case his was fast. He would want to go to the toilet but would be afraid to leave the spot in case in the meantime

Nicky arrived, found the steps of the library empty and assumed he couldn't make it. So he would sit on in agony, agitated for a half hour, perhaps an hour. We hope forever, don't we, thought Nicky. We hope and we hope and we think that the next car to turn the corner will be the one we've been awaiting. Perhaps he has been delayed by a breakdown, Gareth thinks, and is now on his way on foot. Oh no! He's had a serious accident! No, he's far too careful is my Nicky. Finally, finally, there is a little anxious pinch across the stomach like a belt tightening. The thought occurs of having been stood up. But, no, put that out of your mind. Never. Not Nicky. My Nicky would tell you straight. Ten, fifteen more minutes. Gareth now begins to feel queasy. Is this what's happened? Cold feet? Second thoughts? Perhaps he lied. Was lying all along about how he felt? No. No. Nicky is real; Nicky is genuine; Nicky is good. Something has happened. I'll phone and find out.

They'll ask who is it, thought Nicky, and Gareth will hang up. He has a pretext for being away from home all day, whatever story he's told Williams Senior, so he will have to fill this long and lonely day on his own. Nicky felt like running down the landing and dashing into the city streets, seeking him out, screaming his name and defying the bastards of this world. But he knew that cruel sense had to prevail. He looked at the clock: it was ten past one. He sat back, his arms on the rests as if he was strapped into an electric chair or a spacecraft. He looked up and it was almost three. He must know by now. Yes, he suspects, or knows, and feels hurt and abandoned and bitter and hates me. At the thought of Gareth hating him the dykes broke and Nicky's tears poured over the lids of his eyes and streamed down his cheeks and he choked with emotion. He cried for almost three hours, by which time his eyes were red, swollen and bloodshot and he had bags and crow's feet resembling his father's. He switched on the radio for distraction but immediately turned it off again it was so excruciating. He sat on in the fading light.

13

THE SANDS WERE GREY and lumpy; the tide was hesitant or non-existent as in the Dead Sea. A few miles out, clearly visible through a squall, a large tanker carved an oily highway up through the lough. To his right were the dunes where Elizabeth minded their bikes when Robin and he went swimming, when Nicky played Charlie Chaplin with a child called Jane. He could still recall Elizabeth's sad face and he now understood something of her adult unhappiness.

She said she could have lived here even in the winter. I doubt it.

He walked his bike along the ghostly shore on this cold October afternoon. He pushed it up the path between the rocks, carried it on his shoulder when negotiating the ledge and laughed scornfully when he saw the place where Robin and he had fallen. It had been a distance of only about ten feet and they had never been in any real danger of being swept out to sea. As he emerged from the cove he saw that the town to which the drinkers had given them directions had advanced considerably, but not through development though. The drinkers had merely told the truth but the lens of youth had seen everything fantastically.

I shouldn't have come back.

He had now seen enough and sought out a road for the journey back to the city.

Their beach had been the last place he had intended to go. On the Monday, after he had stood up Gareth, he telephoned his supervisor and said he was handing in his notice. It was so unexpected that his boss was suspicious and asked him if he were in trouble. But Nicky placated him.

Between his insurance claim and his savings he had about £7,000 – more than enough to support him between times, until his head could again control his heart.

After he settled in his flat he phoned his mother twice when he knew she would be alone. He said he was sorry, he couldn't explain himself. By the solemn tone of her voice he knew he had deeply wounded her. She told him that after he left the house a man had rung a number of times looking for him but would leave no message and had ceased phoning altogether after a week or two when she just told the truth and said that Nicky had left home and was possibly out of the country. She asked Nicky how he was. He told her he was going to be OK. He had left work and was going to make a new start, was going to make something of his life. She began crying and he hung up. Through her tears the last thing he heard was her trying to wish him a happy birthday. When he replaced the handset he tensed his fist so that his knuckles stood out white. The truth was that Gareth was an unmitigable loss and that without him he was slowly crumbling. He phoned his mother a week later to see if there had been any more messages. There was just one: Gerard from work wanted Nicky to contact him.

He bought a racing bike and sought preoccupation in an exhausting physical routine, cycling out to the countryside in the early morning and returning late in the evening. His heart and lungs sang to each other in a eulogy of their prowess as he accelerated through dark and threatening byways or pressed the bike without demurral up and over lengthy steep hills. But his real heart was broken, its ichor in tumult. He would return to his flat drained, cast off his damp clothes and climb into the shower where he would sit on the tray with his hunkers drawn up under his chin, until the water turned lukewarm, cold, then freezing. He lived on bread, cereal, fruit and strong tea and continued to smoke like a chimney.

One day, on his return journey, he had crossed the road to help a woman change the tyre of her car which had been towing an empty horsebox. When they had it fixed and she drove off, he went to retrieve his bike from the fence, and there, on the other side, behind a hedge of five or six years' growth, was the lane down which Robin had persuaded him to ride. And that was how he had found the beach. Afterwards, as he cycled back home he asked himself how much more about his past was invented?

After an abstinence of several weeks he would occasionally have a few drinks at night which, combined with fatigue, ensured a fair measure of sleep. He liked the relief of tipsiness, though before he opened the vodka he always stacked chairs against the front door to prevent himself going out and doing something foolish, or at least to flash a red light in his stupored brain should he attempt to remove them. But he never did. He drank to forget Gareth but it never worked. He thought about him obsessionally. He dreamed about him regularly.

The back of his flat overlooked a garden into which lamplight seeped from the adjoining streets.

In the gloaming Nicky sat and sipped his drink as a German song played on the radio in the background. When it was finished the presenter translated it:

Thou, my friend, happiness was not given to me in this
    world!
Whither I go? I go and wander to the mountains,
I seek peace, peace for my lonely heart . . .

Yes, said Nicky. Yes. But there is peace nowhere to be found. Not on the mountain tops, not along the shores of the seas. I would love to see him but I daren't. Jesus! I would love to see Gareth!

Through traffic lights, down streets, past shops and offices, Nicky tore furiously through a thousand veils of freezing drizzle which hung like webs connecting sky to earth. He reached Gareth's college by half-past eight. He loitered around the site where the building of the new luxury homes had commenced. He was viewed with suspicion by two labourers until he explained that he was waiting on someone. The students passed through three gates into the college grounds and down a lane of tall spruce to the complex. Some stepped from buses opposite the main entrance, others were dropped off by car. Nicky had already reconnoitred The Sitting Room's main shop and knew that Mr Williams drove a jet black BMW. He knew his face from having delivered catalogues and parcels to the store but also from having seen published in the papers his photograph at various civic functions.

He saw the car arrive and he caught a glimpse of Gareth as he stepped out, made a parting remark and disappeared into the throng. Something about the boy had changed.

Nicky yearned for him. Seeing Gareth filled him with a burst of joy but it was a joy punctured by circumstances which left his heart in tatters.

He returned to the college at different times – now avoiding the mornings – and would consider a fifteen-second glimpse after an hour's furtive waiting as having been well worth it. His second sighting, however, confirmed what he had suspected the first time: Gareth was pale, had lost weight and rarely smiled.

Nicky then began cycling at a distance behind the afternoon school bus, overtaking it before it reached Gareth's stop, and positioning himself in the vicinity so that he could watch him for over a minute, though he half-convinced himself that he was really there to protect him from any thugs.

However, there were days when his subject completely evaded observation.

One Friday afternoon in November Nicky was standing outside a shop, down from the college gates, trying to resolve the riddle, being less conspicuous than usual, when a taxi drove from the college, onto the main road and towards him. Suddenly, Gareth's emaciated face was staring at him from behind a rear window, blurred by tears of rain which streamed across the glass. Shock registered on both their faces simultaneously, taking initially the form of disbelief. Nicky wasn't sure if he had heard the taxi suddenly stop and then reverse: he had impulsively leaped on his bike and cycled up a former cattle lane which ran behind an old house and up the side of the mountain. It was really stupid of him: a muddy stream repeatedly criss-crossed the rutted lane and rather than go back he had to dismount and push his bike to the very top until he came to the quarry road. Even here he felt apprehensive in case the taxi was awaiting him. How could he reprove Gareth when it was he who was doing the shadowing; how could he throw his arms around him with the happiness of reconciliation without causing public scandal to the boy and recommencing the relationship which he was desperately attempting to repudiate, but whose rupture was for him proving to be a slow suicide.

When he did emerge on the windy mountain road he was disappointed that it was deserted, that there stood just him and his bike on the mile stretch.

When someone rapped at Nicky's door that night his heart leaped in anticipation. But when he opened it, before him stood his diminutive mother who immediately misinterpreted the smile which fell from his face. He saw that he had discomposed her and moved to restore her confidence.

'Mammy, come in, come in! It's good to see you.' And he meant it. He had had little social intercourse in the two months since leaving home.

'So, this is where you live. Not that far away really,' she said, removing her headscarf. She saw her letter lying opened on a small table, upon which also lay several magazines and a stack of paperbacks, some of which, like his big astronomy book, she recognised. On the mantelpiece was displayed the birthday card she had sent him.

'So, this is where you live,' she repeated.

'Yes. Here, minding my own business, out of harm and evil's way. Let me get you a cup of tea – I was just making myself a pot.'

She followed him to the small kitchen. She saw the strainer: he used loose tea, like her. Though curious she didn't feel she had the right or the latitude to inspect the wall cupboards and units.

'Are you eating properly? You're terribly failed.'

'I'm fine. Honestly. I cycle every day. I'm as fit as anything. Workwise, I haven't started anywhere but don't be worrying

about that. I'm thinking of going back to school or college if
I can get a grant.'

There was a knock on the door: a woman, the tenant from
the other downstairs flat across the hall, left Nicky her key for
a friend.

Nicky asked his mother how his father was.

'He's OK. He wouldn't come with me. To tell you the truth,
I didn't want him to come because of what I've got to say
which he doesn't know about. But he did say yesterday that
the house was quiet without you, wasn't the same, was still
hard to get used to. You know, we've all been together these
past twenty-four years – '

'No we haven't, Mammy!'

'He's just proud. He misses you, like I do.'

'Mammy, what's really wrong with him?'

'Wrong with him?'

'Yes, does he think I'm not his or something?'

'I think you should apologise for that comment, don't you?
Why do you start this every time? This is my husband you're
talking about. My whole life.'

Maybe there are questions we should never ask of ourselves, depths to which we should never dig, thought Nicky.
But she was off:

'You've never accepted him, have you? Nicky, he was once
a wonderful man. For him just to have walked into the office
where I worked used to make my knees turn to jelly, he had
such presence. You never see that today in a man. He said the
nicest things to me. He made me feel so, so good. We would
sit down to a simple dinner, just the two of us, Nicky, and it
was wonderful. It might sound stupid to you. It might even
seem childish. But it was loving and it seemed it was forever.
I still have that treasure inside me. I've told you before about
the pub his uncle left him and how things got too much and
him taking to the drink. And then you saying those terrible
things to him about drinking! That was awful. He has been
afraid to go into a pub for over seventeen years. If this story
was about some other family you would listen to it, you would
accept it and probably sympathise. As a youngster you were
so kind and understanding. What happened to you? But to get

back to your daddy . . . We had rough times, he and I, but I do not regret my life with him. I'm an old woman – you were right about that. And now, now I just want peace in my old age, us all to be friends. But that's not exactly what I'm here for. There's something else – '

'Mammy, just a minute. Was there a stream beside the gate lodge where we lived?'

'Yes, there was. Why?'

'Was I ever thrown into it?'

'Don't be ridiculous. What are you talking about?'

'OK, did I ever fall into it?'

'No, Nicky, no! You were only a baby.'

'How can you be sure? Were you with me all the time?'

'Most of the time. What are you saying? If you are thinking your father ever tried to do anything on you, Nicky, put it out of your head. He has always loved you. And if he had done anything on you I'd have left him. I'd never tolerate that. Regardless of how drunk your daddy ever was he still maintained certain standards. There were some things he never stooped to. He never raised a finger. He never looked at another woman – and it wasn't as if he couldn't have, though I'd have killed him,' she laughed. 'There was plenty better looking than me! Why do you think bad things? You definitely weren't always like this.'

'Yesss, mammy. That's true. I think I've been obsessed with a sinister explanation for my daddy's distance rather than just the drink – or rather than just accepting that people, a father, can't respond to you in the same way as your mate's da. It started off small when I was small and just grew all the time and got bigger than me without me noticing. I'm probably making no sense. It's a stupid thing and I think I'm over it now.'

'Nicky. I had a visitor this evening,' she said, sipping her tea.

'Who was that?' said Nicky, lifting and lighting a cigarette and moving the ashtray along the table. Nicky felt as if his life was coming together. His mother visiting him made him sense his independence yet his kinship. There she was, drinking his tea. Sitting on his sofa, in his flat. He had branched out – he was the next generation, her progeny, and he appreciated her acceptance of his divergence.

'A young lad.'

'Who would that be?'

'He's called Gareth Williams –' the name euphonically rolled from his mother's tongue '– Says you know him. Did you know that his sister Patsy's pregnant?' She studied Nicky for his reaction, for a spark of paternity. 'He says you're the father – '

'He said what!'

'It's not that funny, Nicky, you getting his sister pregnant. Don't be denying it. It explains everything, doesn't it? Is that why Madeline broke up with you, because you were two-timing her?'

'How do you know we broke up?'

'I went round to see her after you left home to find out what the hell was going on. There was only one Madeline, Nicky, wasn't there? I thought she'd maybe had something to do with the way you were getting on. Her father was very nice, invited me up the stairs to their flat and left us on our own.'

'You were in her flat?'

'Yes.'

'Where did you sit?'

'Where did I sit? On the sofa, of course. Why?'

'Oh, nothing. Nothing. You have been busy.'

'She said that you broke up in early August, though she phoned once looking to have a talk. I remembered that. It was me spoke to her. But Nicky, you told me in the last week of August that you and her were going day-tripping. Was it this girl, Patsy, you were really seeing? Is this why you ran off the way you did when she got in trouble, breaking my heart, giving up a good job. You know we would have helped you, supported you.'

'Mammy, it's not true!'

'Oh Nicky, I don't know what's truth and what's lies anymore. Can't you see what you've done to us? For a long time I was convinced that you didn't even like girls. I was very worried about you, you know.'

Nicky was blasted in the face by the shot of irony but recovered himself because of the distraction of the door being rapped by yet another caller.

He opened the door.

Gareth crossed the threshold and looked as if he would faint when his eyes fell upon Nicky. But just before speaking he was surprised to see Nicky's mother.

'Oh, hello, Mrs Smith. You still here? I thought I saw you leaving.'

'How did you find here?' asked Mrs Smith. 'Nicky,' she continued, 'He wanted to know your address but I wouldn't give it to him. I didn't give it to him! He must have followed me.'

Gareth ignored her and said: 'Nicky, why haven't you called our house. My parents want to see you immediately. You've left our Patsy in some pickle. She's wondrin' what in the world did she do. To think that I introduced you and this is the way you repay me.'

Nicky had difficulty restraining his giggle at Gareth's superb performance. Everything was going to work itself out! Everything was going to be perfect! He was drunk with happiness for the first time in months, seeing Gareth close-up again, but his mother couldn't understand his levity.

'Mammy, do you mind leaving us? It's really a misunderstanding, I swear. I promise that tomorrow I'll come over and see you and that I'll make up with daddy, OK? Tomorrow I'll phone Gerard and see what's happening at work. Tomorrow we'll discuss Christmas and sort everything out. Tomorrow, OK?'

'Will you really?' she said. 'Do you promise?'

'Yes, mammy. I promise. I'll sort out this confusion and I'll be in touch, OK. I know what I want and what I have to do. There'll be no more trouble. We'll all be friends.'

'Gareth, I think you should listen to Nicky's side of things first,' said Mrs Smith, as she raised her frail body from the sofa, buttoned up her coat, put on her scarf and took directions for a taxi.

'Bye, mammy,' said Nicky, excitedly, walking her to the door by the arm. When he heard the outside hall door close behind her he turned to Gareth to pay his compliments.

'You fucking rat! I hate you, I hate you!' screamed Gareth. 'You've gone abroad, have you? Working overseas! You fucking coward!' He slapped Nicky repeatedly across the face then stood rooted to the spot sobbing, before falling down into a chair, removing his glasses and weeping into his hands. Nicky was ashamed of what he had done to him but he didn't dare touch Gareth either. He sat on the sofa, shakily lit a cigarette and stared at the pathetic wailing figure opposite him.

'I waited that day . . . that Sunday. I waited. The library was closed. I had nowhere to shelter . . . I waited. I waited through the rain. I worried about you . . . I waited and waited . . . I phoned your house. They said you weren't there . . . I thought you were on your way so I waited. In the pouring rain, I waited. I sat on those steps until six o'clock just to be sure . . . The police even stopped and asked me what I was doing. I got my death waiting and was sick with pleurisy for four fucking weeks and not once did you ring. And all summer you had a girl, you bastard! I phoned and was told you'd gone away . . . You ran away from me, from us, with your tail between your legs, you fucking moral coward! Have you ever met anyone like me before? Have you? Have you! You felt the magic – and you still ran away. You ran away. You ran away from me – you ran away from yourself! The excuses I made for you, Nicky,' cried Gareth between his gasps and racking coughs. 'Excuses. More excuses than history has ever known . . .' He went into a fit of sobbing and Nicky knelt on his knees before him. 'You ran away, you fucking ran away . . . And you came back, you came back, you came back . . . I felt your eyes, I knew you were there. Every day I knew . . .' and Nicky lifted up his smeared chin with its ginger down and one or two whiskers, kissed him on the lips and then they both hugged, and cried together and laughed together. Cried and laughed.

14

'TWENTY POUNDS, the taxi-driver charged me!' giggled Gareth, dabbing the trickles from his eyes. 'He'd waited on me while I was in your mother's. I came out and we had to wait. I said, "Follow that cab!" and he looked at me as if I wasn't right in the head, before joining in in the fun. We drove at a distance behind your mother's taxi. I was sure she would go to you rather than just phone so I was very pleased with myself when she came hurrying out. I could see from her stopping and looking at the front doors that she hadn't been here before. And do you know how much money I had in my pocket? Twenty pounds exactly! I met your father as well when I was in your place. It was very strange. I thought, "So, Nicky came from you." He's a nice man. He said, "I'll leave you to it," rather than make me feel awkward, and left the room. By the way, he doesn't know that Patsy Cline's expecting your baby. That was cruel, wasn't it? But no more cruel than you have been. What are you going to tell them tomorrow? What are we going to do, Nicky?' said Gareth, falling quiet.

'You and I are going to sort everything out,' promised Nicky, his mood infectious. Gareth smiled and sat up, full of hope.

'Yes! That's the spirit!' said the boy, before breaking into a cough.

'But first things first. Where do your people think you are now?'

'That's the other thing, Nicky. I've run away. When I saw you this afternoon I was frantic. I've been using a taxi instead of the bus if I haven't been feeling too well during the day. This afternoon we drove back, looking for you. I knew that it had been you. I've felt your presence for some time.

'Since September things at home have got worse. That marriage is over, if you ask me. And the fights! He beat my mother, you know. That bastard hit my poor mum while I was lying upstairs in bed. Anyway, because of everything – that and you and me – I'd lost all interest in schoolwork and have had to contend with nagging about my education from my father and lecturers. So, when I saw you today it was heavenly. It was as if there were a God! Then I got the idea of going straight to your house with that story to see if I could smoke you out. To see if you would take care of me. If I hadn't found you I don't know where I would have gone.'

'But I thought you said you'd run away. Do they know you've run away?'

'No, but they will when I don't come back.'

'Ah Gareth, we can't make things work like this. You said so yourself months ago. You'll have to go back.'

'No, Nicky! Please don't make me.'

Nicky shook his head. 'Gareth, that's asking for big trouble. You are going to have to go home –'

'I don't have a home! Aren't you listening!' He was visibly upset, as if he was being forced to undergo an impossible ordeal.

'Gareth, what I'm saying is this. You go home, OK? We see each other as often as we can, as friends, all above aboard. As friends, I said. Understand? Wipe that smile off your face – it panicked me before. As friends, is that agreed? Yes? Good. We'll be open and then when you're older we can decide our future. Listen, even this plan will shock everybody but at least we'll be within the law.'

'But what about tonight, Nicky? Let me stay,' he pleaded. 'We haven't been together in ages. I'd love to have a long yarn with you and I could sleep on the sofa. Promise.' He broke out coughing again.

'And what about your mother and father. They'll crack up.'

'No, they'll not. I'll telephone them and say I'm staying in a friend's. They said I could when I got better. They've been promising me that for ages. I left when they were in the middle of a row so they'll think I've been upset and want to stay with friends. They'll believe me, I swear.'

Nicky wasn't sure but Gareth begged him and he relented. 'OK. But we'll go out and phone now. It's almost half nine.'

'Brilliant! Oh Nicky, I love you! But I haven't forgiven you, you bastard, for this Madeline one,' he laughed.

'You must be hungry. I know you're a gourmet but would you settle for fish 'n' chips and peas tonight?'

'Fish and chips would be first class.'

'OK then, let's go.'

Gareth went to a telephone whilst Nicky queued for their carry-out. They walked back to the flat, the boy excitedly clutching the steaming, vinegar-leaking, greasy parcel like a hot-water bottle. Everything was OK, homewise, he assured Nicky as he shivered with the cold. But he was expected home before eleven the following day, which was Saturday.

Nicky had put plates to warm in the oven before they left and on these he now served the meal whilst Gareth buttered bread and insisted that the table have a cloth. He put out salt and vinegar and cutlery and they sat down to a table which at least was properly laid.

'Sorry I've no candle,' said Nicky.

'We've no television either,' replied Gareth. 'But we don't need one when we've got each other.'

Gareth deliberately munched the crinkly, crunchy battered ends of the fish like a giant locust masticating a leaf to make Nicky smile.

'Working-class!' he parodied.

Nicky mimicked him and Gareth shot his finger into Nicky's mouth. Nicky tried to bite it but the boy was too quick and laughed with every victory. When Nicky looked over, Gareth was dropping peas out of the pods of his nostrils where he had stuffed them for fun.

'You're gross!' laughed Nicky.

Gareth ate every scrap whilst sipping on a big mug of tea

and at the end soaked up with a heel of bread the last traces of food on his plate.

'That was gorgeous,' he said, wiping his mouth on a tissue-napkin. 'I would have loved a bis . . .'

' . . . cuit to finish off with,' said Nicky, dangling a foil-wrapped mint biscuit.

'Nicky! You know me so well!'

Gareth insisted on doing the dishes. When he returned from the kitchen he brought with him a bottle of vodka, a little under half-full, a bottle of coke and two glasses.

'Gareth!' said Nicky, reprovingly.

But the boy poured Nicky a vodka and coke and himself a coke. Handing him the vodka he said: 'Yes. You were saying?'

'Just as well you did that, young man, or you'd have been on the next plane out!'

Nicky turned up the heating.

Gareth sat on the sofa, with his feet tucked under him, and, between bouts of coughing, recommenced August's telling of the story of his life for which Nicky had an insatiable appetite. It lasted for hours, Nicky weaving in comparable episodes in his own life but not in the same detail.

'Are you tired?' said Nicky.

'No, I want this night to go on forever. Is that a chess set? Would you like a game, though I have to warn you, I'm very good.'

'I haven't played in a while. OK then. Set them up, I'm away to the toilet.'

The board was open on the table, the pieces ready for bat-tle, and Gareth was rubbing his hands with glee. 'Oh Smith, you are going to be well and truly thrashed for your forni-cating!'

As they played Nicky told Gareth about his schooldays, about his work at the post office and his best friend there, Ger-ard, and why he'd fought with him. 'I'm telling you everything, OK?'

'You know this hurts me, don't you? But I still want to hear it. And to think that you were with her when I was thinking of you day and night.'

'Sure, she'd a turn in her eye,' joked Nicky.

'She'll have a turn in her other eye if she ever looks at you again. But I think I understand how it happened. The important thing is now and forever, isn't that right?'

'Yes,' smiled Nicky. He lifted his knight, knocked the table three times with his knuckle, closed his eyes and picked a new black man out of the box into which Gareth had thrown captured enemy pieces.

'And what do you think you are doing?' said Gareth tetchily.

'I'm passing.'

'"Passing?" This isn't Scrabble or poker. Get your hand out of that box. Who taught you those rules? You can't just do that. You've touched that knight. You'll now have to move him.'

'No, I don't.'

'Yes you bloody well do! That's the rule.'

'Oh, OK.' Nicky moved his knight. Gareth checked with his bishop and smiled. Nicky was forced to move his king out of the back file, exposing it. Gareth brought up his queen: he was only four moves from mate. Nicky went straight into Gareth's back row, checking him with his queen.

'That was fairly stupid. I can take your queen. Didn't you see it?'

'Take it, you block yourself in, and I'll checkmate you in two moves. Don't take it and it's checkmate in three moves.'

Gareth studied the board. 'You're right! You're bloody right! That's brilliant!'

Nicky basked in the compliment.

'Who taught you to play like that? You've played before. You were better than you let on.'

'A friend of mine taught me years ago. It's the last thing I have to tell you. It's the most important because it's the real me. He died when he was your age.' Nicky's voice dropped an octave. 'We lived inside each other . . . Often, it was uncanny, because we knew what the other was thinking. I couldn't save him. At the time I thought I was going to die as well. I used to think about him every minute of every day for three, maybe four years afterwards. Loneliness became my twin. My life was awful, terrible, until you came back into it last June.' Nicky's ambiguity and his statement's joint application startled himself.

'I'm sorry. That just slipped out. But, it's just that . . . when I first met you the feeling between us was powerful, overwhelming, like the feeling between Robin and me. Robin was his name, did I say that already? No. You reminded me of him – although there's no resemblance, not even in personality. I can't explain it. In depth maybe. But there is a roundness about my life. All sorts of echoes and repeats as if the past can return as a key into the future, as if opportunities will come around again for reinspection and reinterpretation. You remember the day in the leisure centre we were sitting at the side of the pool and you said something about the sea and early life coming ashore. It was like Robin speaking. I experienced *déjà vu*. You thought I was catching a chill.'

'And do you think Robin's in this room right now, Nicky? Sitting beside you?'

Nicky was disappointed at his friend's facetiousness but when he looked up he saw that Gareth, this unfolding, complex soul, worth a thousand sacrifices, was being sincere.

'No. He's dead. But things do keep coming back and I can't explain it. Maybe I'm mad! When my mammy was here this evening I realised for the first time that subconsciously for years I've been harbouring the crazy suspicion that my father tried to drown me as a baby! That he resented me. Isn't that incredible! But it explains why I've always been a strong swimmer, a survivor, I suppose. I conquered water early . . .

'See the telescope over there, beside the window,' said Nicky, continuing, 'and those books on the cabinet? Robin's mother called over to our house a few months after he died, gave them to me and said that the family was moving. The house was too much, I suppose. The memories. I was shattered because just being able to look at his sister or brother in the street and see Robin's features – Billy had his teeth, Heather his deep blue eyes – helped me survive even though after his funeral I'd become completely disillusioned with God and life after death and all that. Oh yes, I also tried to commit suicide but that was a scream and I'll tell you about it another time . . . I couldn't get out the window!

'Anyway, Robin and I had a hut – or garden shed rather. A fairly big thing where we held our "meetings" or sheltered from the rain. The new people that moved in demolished the hut. I had heard that they were going to knock it down and asked my daddy to offer to buy it or get it lifted out because to me it was a bit of a shrine but he wasn't interested. Inside it we had a barrel – a sort of big cask with copper hoops which had been branded with some sherry manufacturer's name from Spain or Portugal, I think. It came from an old ship. But the new owners chopped it up as well. It sounds so stupid now, doesn't it?'

'No, Nicky. It's all you, part of what made you, part of your struggle. I've been raised with a silver spoon in my mouth. Listening to you, I realise that I've been very unlucky, actually. Your past is rich. The past has passed over my head, been uneventful. Nothing haunts me like that and I feel empty, as if I've missed a wealth of raw experiences. You've a great history. For you it's been a painful adventure. But can't you see: it's also been wonderful? You're my hero!'

'And now, Master Gareth, it's your bedtime. You can sleep in my bed, I'll lie on the sofa.'

'Will you come in and tell me a wee story, Daddy?' said Gareth in a cajoling voice.

'I will like hell!' laughed Nicky. 'I might even lock the door to stop you from sleep walking, you pervert! My God, I'm gonna have to stop cursing.'

Gareth removed his glasses, pressed a finger into the corner of one eye and removed the sparkling gem of a happy tear.

Nicky left him a nightshirt on the pillow. 'It's four o'clock in the morning!' he said. 'You wouldn't think it. Anyway, have a good sleep.'

'Night, night, Nicky. And thanks. I can switch out the light here, can't I?'

'Yes, just there.'

Nicky sipped the last of the vodka. He himself was remarkably sober and didn't feel like sleeping. Gareth had looked pale and he was concerned that their talk was a bigger drain on the boy then he realised. He had just placed his glass on the coffee table when he was startled by the front door being put in, heard the boots echo in the hall and turned to see his own door come crashing open with splinters of wood exploding at both locks.

15

' "NICHOLAS SMITH." What's this? No middle name? No? "D.o.b. 23/9/1969. Single. Occupation: Unemployed postal worker. No previous record." No previous record? Is that right, Nicholas? Video cameras miss you outside the public toilets?

'He doesn't say much, Ian, does he?

'Buggery with a boy under sixteen is a life sentence, Nicholas. Or is it Nicky? Ah! The eyes flickered. It's Nicky. Do you understand, Nicky? The boy's being examined by the doctor and the sheets and quilt have been taken away to forensics. If he's been indecently assaulted you could be facing ten years, or five for gross indecency. Why don't you help yourself and tell us about it?

'Place smelt like a distillery, Ian? That right?

'Nicky, I am one of the most honest, straight and liberal cops you'll ever meet and I think it would be good for my career and chances of promotion if you were to say something really incriminating! Still, if you want to remain silent, I hope you enjoy your retreat here.

'Those cuts been seen to, Ian? Good.

'Does it hurt, Nicky, to talk? Could you sip a cup of tea or coffee? We'll get you breakfast soon when the cafeteria opens.

'You don't think we have a cafeteria, do you! Or that we'll

feed you? Huh, you don't want to believe the media's presentation of us. Don't believe all you see on TV. That lip looks sore. Lucky my men arrived when they did or you might have been killed.

'The son of *the* Gareth Williams. We were certainly snobbing it there, weren't we. Weren't we, Nicky? Is there a legacy on the go or what?

'Hey! You can't go through life without talking! Everybody needs to talk. If this were civil war and you a hostage we wouldn't want you to speak to us. If you spoke we would hit you a crack across the mouth. We wouldn't want to hear. Know why? We kill strangers more easily. But when a man opens his mouth and tells us his story it stays our hand; it appeals to our common humanity. Even the truths behind the darkest thoughts can sometimes make uncomfortable sense and find resonance in the listener. Who is without sin? Who can cast the first stone? It's not so easy to pull the trigger then.

'The same thing could happen in your case, Nicky. I'd understand you. See your point of view. Sympathise with you. Help you.

'Think about it, OK? Think about it.

'By the way, I'm Detective Inspector Derek Wainwright and I'm in charge of this investigation.' The big handsome police officer rose from his cluttered desk and apologised to Nicky for the mess: the building was being redecorated in stages and this was his temporary office.

As Nicky was being taken to the waiting-room he was forced to step aside to allow a prisoner to pass. This man and two plain-clothes officers went in the direction which a sign on the wall in the shape of a finger pointing said, 'Interview Rooms'.

The door was locked behind Nicky. His back ached from the blows and kicks he received from the three henchmen and Gareth's father who broke into his flat. He couldn't erase from his mind the pathetic figure of terrified Gareth being trailed from the bed, screaming, 'I didn't mean it, I didn't mean it!' Then, seconds later, the uniformed policemen had came running in, pulled off the men who were beating Nicky and restrained the rabid Williams Senior. Nicky was asked by the police to accompany them to the station. He was unsure of his status because they were searching his flat when he left and they wouldn't let him put on a jacket, despite the temperature outside. People had gathered and were talking in low tones as he was led out. But there were no handcuffs and he couldn't remember any charges being mentioned. He was taken in the back of a squad car, where he sat between two officers, to a central police station. Here, they had asked him to remove his clothes which they labelled and bagged. He was given a boiler suit to wear and allowed to keep his own shoes and socks. The little money he had in his pocket, his change from the fish and chips, his watch and his laces, were removed, placed in a large envelope marked *Property* and sealed. He countersigned the inventory. The room in which he was presently placed was coloured a dismal pastel green and there was a smell of fresh paint from the corridors along the administration block.

Despite Wainwright's frank and relaxed manner Nicky had found him extremely menacing. He couldn't shake off a feeling of doom as if above the station door had been written the motto: *Abandon hope all ye who enter here.* He thought he could hear shouting and banging but it was so far away it could have been the creeping edge of his imagination preparing him for the worst. He ate the toast and sipped the awful tea they gave him. He was worried about Gareth, what they were saying and doing to him at this very moment.

I'm compromised but I haven't done anything wrong, thought Nicky. I've asked for my solicitor. There's not much more I can do.

'This Williams chap has some pull, Nicky, hasn't he? Friends everywhere.' They were back in Wainwright's office. 'Plenty of money, you see. I tell you, I wouldn't mind investigating him instead of you. Must be up to all sorts of no good, him and his politician friends. Between the two of us, Nicky – Ian, close your ears – did you give the boy one? Did you? I might see him before he goes home. What's he like? I suppose he's got long curly hair like a little girl? I've daughters myself, Nicky, and it's not very nice, you being bold like that. Where was I? Oh yes, Law and Order. I like a bit of meat to my crime, Nicky. Something challenging. Crime isn't like it used to be.

There's some real dotterels around today. I've three across the hall. Robbed a bank yesterday. They're for court on Monday. You should hear them allocating the proceeds – allocating the blame! It's a scream. One of them – Joe's his name – would scare the living daylights out of you. He's your archetypal villain. It strikes me that he was born premature or born before he was even conceived he's so malformed.

'Did you know that the average brain contains ten billion nerve cells and weighs 1,500 grams? Believe you me, Nicky, I've had boys in here with brains half that weight. Some of them hadn't even been taken out of their wrappers they were that new.'

A uniformed officer knocked on the door and Wainwright left.

'You've got a good man there, Nicky,' said Ian, leaning back, with his chair balanced on two legs. 'A professional. Does all sorts of charity work too. When he was younger, back in the sixties, he had long hair. Know what he did? Got people to sponsor a hair-cut. Raised money for charity. Still does parachute jumps for cancer research. I've a lot of respect for him. Do what he says and you'll not go far wrong. But tell him no lies. He hates lies. He can smell them even when they're being thought.'

Wainwright returned. 'Nicky, you could've picked a better day to be arrested. There's some great races from Cheltenham on television. Let's see . . . the 2.30. Here, pick me a winner. Run your eyes over the runners . . . Don't be so sullen. We're here to get the truth – and a few winners . . . Nicky, have you ever thought of joining the force? We need men like you.

'He'd make a good officer, Ian, wouldn't he?'

'Right size.'

'Yes. Right size. Let's see your feet. For God's sake, throw them up on the table to we check that they're not flat. Very unresponsive.

'Did Ian tell you that he and I were on the town last night? You should have seen that big eejit about three o'clock this morning, his head hanging out of his top pocket, he was that drunk.

'Isn't that so? Did you tell him about the wee Malaysian?

Another time, another time.

'Do you know, Nicky, that I haven't been home yet? But I don't hold it against you. No, I don't hold it against you. Duty calls and I'm your man. And my wife, she doesn't understand me. She's a real moan. Nag, nag, nag. The Super says to me, "Get your ass over here and apply your experience to this one." So the missus had to go to the wall. Nicky, never get married. It's a mug's game. Or, if you do, then marry somebody ugly and fat. Then you can play the field and she'll never leave you. And when she's sixty she'll come into her own. She'll be a beauty queen then, a friend and an ally while all the bimbos will be falling to pieces like old ruins. Breaking the law, you know, and committing adultery are very alike. Very alike. It becomes easier the more you do it. I'm a, a what's-it-called? A recividist or a recidivist. I can never get that word right and yet I deal with the chaps every day. A recidivist, that's it, that's it! How many times did you screw the boy, Nicky? No! Don't answer! I don't want to know!

'He said nothing, Ian. Play fair! He didn't open his mouth. Put nothing down.'

Wainwright reminded Nicky of someone, he couldn't remember whom. Someone from his past. Wainwright the detective. Detective? Detective! Suddenly, Nicky made a connection. Wainwright the detective, the hypocritical, bullying husband of Elizabeth, the woman on the beach all those years ago! Was this him? He shuddered as the wheel came around again, the past never leaving him alone. Yet for a few hours the previous night its weight had lifted from his shoulders and he felt liberated after his discussion with Gareth. He was sure this was Elizabeth's husband.

'Nicky, there's a certain *je ne sais quoi* about you. I suppose you've been told that before? I'm not insulting you, by the way. It's not fish odour syndrome you have! It's a certain magnetism. Do you know what I mean?' Wainwright punched the palm of his left hand.

'No, Ian. I have to say it. I like him! I do. I like him. He gives us no trouble.'

'But sure, you won't let him get a word in edgewise.'

'Ah now, Ian. Is that fair? Is that fair?

'Nicky, is that fair? I presumed you were saying nothing until you'd seen your solicitor. Where is the man? Where is that man, I ask you. Probably watching the races, where I should be.

'Ian, did you ring him?

'See, Nicky, Ian rang. He rang. Saturday's a bad day. I've told you that already. We're going around in circles here. I need a drink.

'Would you like a drink? Do you fancy heading over to Robinson's and we'll finish this off over there? It's Ian's round, Nicky.

'Do you remember the number, Nicky? Here. Look it up in the directory and phone him. Why do weight-lifters always rip these things in two? Is it because they can't find their number? We can get you a duty solicitor if you want but everybody thinks they're working for the cops. So do I.'

Nicky telephoned. The wife of his solicitor answered and said that she had paged him but that it would be a few hours before he could get there: he was out of the city.

'Ian, go and see how the case is progressing. Tell the boss Nicky's confessed to those four unsolved murders and can the three of us now head over to Robinson's. I'll finish the crossword.

'Smoke away, Nicky. They're your lungs.

'3 Across. "Engrossing". Absorbing. 8 Across. "Harvest." Reap. 9 Across. "Logical", Rational. 13 Across. "Postbag". Oom. Postbag, postbag, postbag. I'll come back to that one . . .

'1 Down. "Leg of chicken". Drumstick. 2 Down. "Fit to be lived in". Habitable. 16 Across. "Guilty person". Culprit. 24 Across. "Defamed". Slandered.

'One left. Just one left! Shit, shit, shit. 13 Across. "Postbag". Postbag, postbag? Take no notice of me. I always get my inspiration from the ceiling. Postbag, postbag . . .'

'How many letters are in it?' said Nicky, breaking his silence.

'Well, if it's a big bag, about two thousand. But a wee bag this size would only hold a couple of hundred!'

Nicky felt such a fool for he had heard that same joke on his very first day at work.

'Ian, Ian! You're back. Nicky spoke. I caught him a cracker.

The old one about the postbag.

'You're the third this week,' said Wainwright.

'Could I see you, boss?'

'Nicky, we'll not be long. This is called a "conference" in police parlance. Read the paper. If my wife calls, for God's sake don't tell her where I was last night. Tell her . . . tell her I was with you, all night. No. On second thoughts don't tell her that!'

'We've very little to go on,' said Ian. 'The boy's clear. No evidence of sexual abuse. There'll be no word on the sheets for a week, if you still want us to go ahead. The boy says they're just friends. But the father is in there with one of the bigwigs. He's insisting his son's been interfered with and is too traumatised to speak properly about what's happened to him. He says his son was lured to the house, that Smith was seen loitering about the college for days beforehand. You'd think he'd want to keep it quiet, given his connections. Williams and his wife don't hit it off. It was she who called 999, that's how our boys arrived there just behind the father, otherwise you might have been questioning him about a murder. The father's sent a car out to his house to get some photographs and the boy's diary which were found in his study. Says they're incrim-inating though Williams's solicitor said we can't read it all and the boss has agreed with them.'

'We'll see,' said Wainwright, who through the laminated glass door watched Nicky rotating his forefingers about one another.

Nicky was certain that he'd be released. His earlier fears had almost left him. The detectives were entering the room when the phone on the desk rang. Nicky lifted it, half in jest, half-seriously: 'Mrs Wainwright, Derek's been with me all night, I swear he has . . .'

Wainwright snatched the phone and waved a threatening finger at him.

'Honey, I'm sorry about that . . .'

' "Honey?" Who was that on the phone?'

'Excuse me a second, sir,' said Wainwright, beckoning his colleague to remove Nicky from the office.

A few minutes later Nicky was returned.

'Find that funny, did you?'

'You thought it was Elizabeth, didn't you?' said Nicky smiling.

'Elizabeth? Who's Elizabeth? Elizabeth who?'

'You . . . your wife,' said Nicky, flushing. 'You said you had daughters and I thought . . .' He realised he had been ridiculous.

'Elizabeth? My wife isn't called Elizabeth! Now sit down on that chair and don't get familiar again.'

'Now. Your name. Your proper name.'

'Nicholas Smith.'

'Father's name?'

'Harry.'

'Mother's?'

'Margaret.'

'Brothers. Any brothers?'

'No.'

'What about sisters?'

'None.'

'Oh? No sister to watch through the keyhole! Poor Nicky. That must have been a deprivation. How often do you think about sex, Nicky? Tell us. Go on, tell us! No? Well, did you know that men think about sex every six minutes? Did you know that one in seventeen men admit to having had sex with another man at some point? Come in, No 17, your time is up! One per cent of men – this is the group to which I belong – have sixteen per cent of the sex, in terms of partners in the past five years, and one per cent of women – the group which senior officers like myself have to trace as a matter of grave urgency – have twelve per cent of the sex. You have to admit, Nicky, I've done my homework. Do you know how I know all that? Do you know how I know all those statistics, Nicky? Do you? Do you?'

'No,' murmured Nicky.

'I'm reading them from this report sitting in front of me,' said Wainwright, chuckling. 'It's a study conducted by University College, London. Oh, and the other thing: women are more loyal than men. Ha! Try telling that to the prisoners, eh Ian!

'You think you're going home, Nicky, don't you. That's why you're so smug. But you're going to jail, my boy. Do you know what the prisoners will do when they find out what you're in for? Do you? They'll cut the dick off you. You'll be able to have a good look at all the wee goose-pimples and follicles on the end of it because it'll be held before your very eyes like a big lollipop.

'Ian, what do you call those lollies with the ice-cream up the middle?'

'I don't know. Quenchers?'

'No, not Quenchers. I don't think they make these ones anymore. It doesn't matter. Probably before your time.

'You'll be in with the bullroots – the fruits, the rapists the child-molesters, the perverts. What a menagerie! We had a mortuary attendant in here a few years ago. Remember him, Ian? What's this his name was?'

'Bert. Oul Bert.'

'Oul Bert, that's right,' laughed Wainwright. 'Sixty-three years of age. Used to throw buckets of hot water over the corpses of the young girls before he violated them. I asked him why he did it. Know what he said? "To heat them up." To heat them up! Did you ever hear anything like it? I was expecting something Freudian!'

I've strayed into a dark, ugly, violent and sick world, thought Nicky. How did I get here? How do I get out?

'You'll recognise him, Nicky, when you get up on the threes, that's the top landing in A-wing. He whistles all the time. What's this now he whistles?'

'"Danny Boy"'.

'"Danny Boy", yes "Danny Boy". You think I'm joking, don't you? Well, you're right. I have been. We'll just send you back to your room, get you some dinner. We'll finish our paperwork, you sign a few things and we'll get you transport home.'

'Thank you,' said Nicky with a sigh of relief. 'Thank you.'

'Not at all.'

Wainwright closed the file and Nicky was brought to the waiting room. He sat for ten minutes, twenty minutes, an hour. He wondered what was keeping them. He rapped on the door and was told it wouldn't be much longer. But another hour passed. He was given a greasy fry on a paper plate with a plastic knife and fork and tea in a styrofoam cup. He asked to go to the toilet and passed a cleaning lady on her way home who glared at him dressed in his boiler suit as if he was a suspected murderer. He was put back in the room.

The door at last opened and a constable nodded to him. But instead of being brought to the reception he was led in the opposite direction and was walked down a long corridor at the end of which was a room with dirty, smoke-stained walls, containing a table and three chairs.

In the ceiling a burning fluorescent light thrummed. It was four o'clock and the frosted glass window showed that it was a dark winter's afternoon outside.

He turned around and saw Wainwright and Ian walking down the corridor towards him with yet more files under their arms. 'In you go, Smith,' said Wainwright. Ian opened a folder and they began questioning him again about his personal details.

'We know from our enquiries,' said Wainwright, 'that you have an unhealthy interest in young children. Why do you give them money? Is it in return for favours?'

'What are you talking about?' said Nicky.

'Just answer the questions. It doesn't matter one way or another to me. In fact, if you keep quiet, the quicker I have a case and the quicker we get out of here. You don't have to answer any questions, understand? But if you do then I must warn you that they may be taken down and used in evidence against you. That's your caution. Understood?'

'I understand.'

'You got that, Ian?'

'Yes.'

'Are you prepared to go in front of an identity parade?'

'What do you mean? What have you done with Gareth? What have you got him to say?'

'What have I done to Gareth? That's a bit rich. For pity's sake, Nicky, the boy's only thirteen.'

'Fifteen. He's fifteen.'

'Write that down, Ian. "I knew he was only fifteen." Nicky are you sure you wouldn't like to be a detective? Jesus, I'd love to work along with you. We could join the firearms branch.

I'd be as safe as houses in all sorts of critical situations knowing that you were watching my back. And watching my back.
And watching my back. Have you any plans for Christmas? I
suppose you'll be spending it with mom and dad? It's a real
family occasion, isn't it. Know what I love? Christmas Eve,
around the hearth. Every year they show that Frank Capra
film, *It's a Wonderful Life* starring James Stewart. Have you
seen it? No? You don't know what you're missing . . . Have
you got a minute?

'It's about a really good guy called George Bailey who longs
to see the world and the wonders of this earth but who never
gets to leave town. He ends up carrying on the family's small-
town savings and loans business when his father dies. He gives
home loans to ordinary folk and even lends money to a prosti-
tute to help her make a brand new start. George is resented by
the town's misanthropic big financier – that means he doesn't
like people, OK? – whose name escapes me . . . Potter maybe.
Anyway, on Christmas Eve the whole town's preparing for the
homecoming of George's famous brother Harry, who's a war
hero. George wanted to be a hero but he had to stay at home
and look after things. You see, he's the real backbone of America, its moral fibre, representing all that's decent and fair. He's
a bit disappointed with his unremarkable life but he's humble
and he gets on with things and loves his steadfast wife Mary and
their kids.

'Anyway, George's uncle, whose name also escapes me – but
he played the part of Scarlett O'Hara's father in *Gone with the
Wind*. He spent the film saying, "Tara! Tara!" whilst crumbling black soil in his hands and staring at golden skies. Tara
was the name of the family mansion. Did you see that one,
Nicky? Nicky, have you seen any-blooming-thing! It's brilliant.
Brilliant! Scarlett marries everybody but the cameraman. And
everybody she marries dies – except Rhett. Great theme tune.
Scarlet's father goes mad at the end of the civil war. He climbs
on a horse and tries to jump a fence. The horse stalls but he
doesn't and he's killed on the other side. Tatie bread. Same
thing happens to Scarlett and Rhett's daughter, Bonny. Have
to say, as soon as she climbed on her pony I saw it coming.
That child was no actress.

'But, to get back to *It's a Wonderful Life*. George's uncle is to deposit the takings in a bank but crossing the snow-covered street he meets Potter being pushed in his wheelchair and slaps it up old Potter with a newspaper whose headline refers to Harry's homecoming. The money is accidentally wrapped up in the newspaper and comes into slimy Potter's possession.

'I could never work out why those particular week's takings were crucial. A bit of poetic licence there, but sure. With the takings missing, George's credit is suddenly called into question and his business plunges. Everybody wants to withdraw their savings. He is facing bankruptcy, disgrace and imprisonment. Don't worry, Nicky, there's no bankruptcy proceedings in your case.

'At home George is uncharacteristically short-tempered and Mary knows that something catastrophic has happened. He leaves the house and goes and gets drunk and, again uncharacteristically, gets involved in a brawl. Then he makes his way to the bridge over the swirling river – I love swirling rivers in films – and contemplates suicide. But someone else gets there before him and George dives in and saves him.

'This man whom he saves is called Clarence, and is a bit doolally. He tells George he's his guardian angel and has come down from up above to help George if George will help him in turn to get his wings. George is fed up with life and wishes he were never born and Clarence says, oom, maybe that's not such a bad idea, and grants him his wish.

'Well Nicky, the next part is fantastic! We see what happens when a good man was never around to influence events.

'George stumbles into the cemetery and what does he see but his brother Harry's name on a tombstone. Harry had drowned when the ice on the pond he was playing on as a kid broke underneath him. George says, "But I was there! I pulled him out!" Wee portly Clarence says, "You weren't there to pull him out, George. You were never born, remember?" George runs back home but it turns out to be an old ruin. He wasn't around to buy and renovate it. He goes to see his mother and she hasn't a clue who he is. Imagine that? Your own mother not recognising you?!

'He then runs crazily through the town. It's now called

Pottersville and is full of drinking dens, gambling parlours and whore-houses. George is going mad and thinks it's the fault of bad drink. He wants Mary. Mary'll sort everything out. Clarence says he mightn't like what he sees but if he hurries he'll catch her locking up the library where she works. Nicky, she's an old maid. She never met anyone, never fell in love, never knew the happiness of a husband, a home, kids. George calls her his wife and she's terrified when he wants to know where their kids are! She goes into hysterics. Ward Bond of *Wagon Train* arrives, except he's a cop. There's a fight and shots are fired at George, who runs back to the bridge and cries and begs God to stop it. He's truly sorry. He takes everything back. He wishes he had been born.

'Suddenly, he's really alive. His troubles are back but so are his riches – his family, his friends, their love for him – because, you see, Nicky, at the end of the day it really is a wonderful life. He runs through the town wishing everyone a Happy Christmas. He's deliriously happy.

'Everybody rallies to save his business and Potter is thwarted. In the last scene, it seems as if the whole town is gathered in George's house around the Christmas tree. Harry arrives to a tumultuous welcome and everybody is singing 'Auld Lang Syne'. The bell at the top of the tree tinkles and George's wee girl, whom he is holding in his arms, says, "Teacher says that every time a bell rings it means another angel gets his wings." George then knows that Clarence, his friend and guardian angel, has got his wings.

'Well, Nicky, I be in pieces at the end of that film. What did you do with the films that went missing? The blue movies? There's no video in your flat. If the cassettes are in Williams's house we'll find them, you know.

'Write down, Ian, "No reply."

'You definitely have the makings of a cop, Nicky. Ian, get up.'

'What?'

'Do as I say and get up. Nicky, come around to this side. Ian, you sit where Nicky is. Come on, jump to it.'

Ian stood beside Nicky, waiting, obliging him to change chairs.

'OK, Nicky. Ask Ian why he corrupted the boy.'

Nicky was tired from lack of sleep and his nerves were frayed. As time had passed he had become more terrified and as time passed events became ever more surreal.

'Are you going to ask him or do I have to do everything around here? . . . OK then, but don't think you're gonna just sit there and get your cheque at the end of the month!

'Ian, when did you first meet, eh, Gareth Williams. Young Gareth Williams?'

'Let me think. Am I allowed to look?'

'No.'

'Eh, late last June. The thirteenth, to be exact.'

'And how did it come about?'

'He was being attacked by some hooligans and I broke up the fight.'

'*Inspector* Smith!' said Wainwright. 'You haven't written down a word in the interview notes of what the suspect's saying! Look, here's a pen. You do know how to read and write? You simply write the questions and the replies – no embellishments. Like this. See?'

'Please. I feel sick. Can I go to the bathroom,' said Nicky. 'I'm going to be sick.'

'Ah Nicky! Not now! Ian was on the verge of confessing! OK then, if you must. Geneva Convention and all that.' Wainwright rose, opened the door and called to a constable who was sitting on a chair in the corridor. 'Take Smith to the toilet, please. Get him a few headache tablets as well.'

Nicky vomited into the bowl. It felt as if he threw up a week's food. His face sweated and he was shivering.

In his absence, Ian said to Wainwright: 'You know, it should be the boy we're charging. Some of the stuff in this diary is real heavy.'

'Smith's the one who's over eighteen and was giving in to his animal instincts but for the arrival of the cavalry. The diary indicated the way both were thinking.'

'Yes, but Derek, the scribblings in here could also be read as mere juvenilia.'

'Not in our hands it isn't . . .'

'Inspector Smith, you're back! I do hope you're better. Now, ask Ian a question.'

'I'm not well. Can I go home or can I see my solicitor?'

'Nicky! We've got Ian by the balls and you keep letting him off the hook!'

'I only asked a simple answer,' said Nicky, all muddled.

Wainwright pushed photocopies of Gareth's diary in front of him. 'Ask Ian about these, Nicky.'

Nicky read the diary entries for mid-June. His face flushed with embarrassment and humiliation. He had met Gareth twice that month but there were almost daily references to him after their first encounter. The entries were of an explicitly sexual nature about the boy's desires and fantasies. The ones for August, after his return from New York, were detailed and lurid. There were accounts of their few days together, their adventures, their first embrace on the mountain road which Gareth had exaggerated into a kiss. But there were also beautiful and moving expressions of love and affection, resting, however, on the perilously narrow ground of mere recent acquaintance but fully echoing feelings of Nicky's which stretched back in time.

'According to this one he nearly gobbled you in the car,' said Wainwright.

'No! It never went that far,' said Nicky.

'Write that down, Ian: "It never was meant to go that far."'

Ian raised his eyebrows but Wainwright winked.

'Stop it! Stop it!' shouted Nicky. 'I've done nothing wrong!' He pushed away his chair, fell to the floor and rolled under the table in the foetal position but with his hands over his ears. Wainwright got down on the floor and rolled up beside him.

'"Nothing wrong," Nicky! You stuffed him with brandy in the boat, you stuffed him with vodka last night and Lord knows what else . . . Nicky, I spoke to your father and mother on the phone. They're good people. They raised you to be honest, sober, industrious and clean-living. But you're a disgrace, aren't you! Aren't you!'

'No!' cried Nicky. 'I'm not, I'm not!'

'Oh Nicky, it's in you, it's in you. The truth is in you! I can smell the pure fresh air of the truth! I can smell the truth coming! It's coming, coming, coming, coming now!'

'Did you screw the boy, did you screw him?'

'No! No!'

'But Nicky, you love him, don't you? You told him you loved him – or was that another lie? Don't you love him! Don't you!'

'Yes, yes, yes! I love him!' cried Nicky. 'I love him, I love him and I would die for him!' Tears were spilling down Nicky's cheeks on to the floor.

I've said it. I've said it. I've told the truth. It's out. And it's over. It's over. I thought it would have been harder to say. But the truth of my love is such that I have been able to declare it. How surprising!

'I've nothing against love, Nicky,' said Wainwright, relentlessly.

'Nothing. I love my own nephews, Williams's age. Get up! Get up!'

Wainwright dusted himself down and Ian arose from the prisoner's seat. 'Now, get around there and sit in that chair.

'I've nothing against love, Nicky.

'There's Ian and I. We like each other. Because of our comradeship you could probably say that we love each other.

'No, no, Ian, don't turn your nose up. I do. I love you. And I would die for you.

'I would even pish in front of him, Nicky.

'In fact, we were pishing in front of each other last night, weren't we, love?

'But you know where we draw the line? Do you?

'Tell him, Ian. Tell him where we draw the line.'

'There's no way would I photograph Detective Inspector Derek Wainwright having a pooley.'

'Correct! You'd need a pretty big wide angle lens for a start. No, but seriously. Look at these pictures, Nicky. He's only a boy, a frail, ailing boy. Here's a full frontal. Here he's tweeking your nipple. In this one your tongue is in his ear – or maybe you're just whispering. He's somebody's son. He's innocent. This isn't what life's about. It's supposed to be wonderful. It's disgusting, isn't it? It's depraved. You make me sick with your talk of love. You're no George Bailey, Nicky. Clarence would never get his wings wasting his time watching out for you. It would have been better for everyone, for

Gareth, for your poor mom and dad, for you, if you had never been born. You and oul Bert and all the other bullroots.'

Nicky felt incredibly small. Smaller than the gnat of a summer's day which splashes against the car windscreen. Smaller than the tiniest mote of dust caught in a capillary of sunlight. Smaller than the core of an atom. And what made him so small, what made him collapse in on himself, was the oppressive gravity of intense humiliation. Wainwright had succeeded in making him feel infinitesimally small but universally, infinitely, dirty.

'Are you going to let the boy go to court and testify? Are you going to allow the contents of his diary to be published in the muck-raking tabloids and feasted on by every paedophile in the country?

'Stop feeling sorry for yourself. I hate self-pity – unless, of course, it's me's the subject. Nicky, we in the police have feelings too. It needn't all come out.'

'Please, what can I do?'

'Make a statement. I'm sure we can persuade the DPP to pick a lesser charge. Say, a drunken prank of unlawful imprisonment that went wrong. You'll appear in court on Monday. We can phone your people and they can be there to post bail. Later, plead guilty. We'll recommend leniency. You'll probably get a suspended sentence.

'I'll tell you what. Wait until your solicitor arrives. I know what you're thinking. "I can see the worm, but where's the hook?" Isn't that right? It's simple. What do I get out of it? I pack up and go home tonight and don't have to spend tomorrow questioning you. My boss is left happy. I'm happy.'

'I'll make the statement,' said Nicky. 'I want it over with.'

'Are you sure?' said Wainwright. 'You can have as long as you want to think about it.'

'I'm sure.'

'Here.' Wainwright nudged the interview notes and the photocopies of Gareth's diary towards Nicky. 'Go ahead. Destroy them.'

Nicky uncertainly took the papers, tore them up and threw them into the bin that the Inspector pushed towards his feet.

The two policemen left the room.

Ian said: 'You know that we received no diary entry for their get-together on the last Sunday in August and if it had been damning then the father would have given us it.'

'So?' said Wainwright.

'The boy said that Smith didn't turn up and was trying to end it and that it was he who went to Smith's flat last night.'

'Yes, and last night the boy's caught in Smith's bed with no trousers on. Listen, I'm tired, I've had no sleep in two days. Come on, Ian! Everybody's happy. The Super's off my back and everybody goes home.'

'You know he's not going home. The DPP's looking for something just like this even if we only charge Smith with picking his nose. We're handing him Smith's head on a plate even with the lesser charge.'

'You worry too much. What do you want to do? Give Smith a grant to go away and make a new start? Let's just get a statement. "I brought him or lured him to my flat. I was drunk. Didn't want to let him go. Made him stay, etcetera. I'm sorry, Mr Wainwright, it won't happen again."'

'I'll do it but it goes against my better judgement.'

Nicky made a contrite statement.

Wainwright then formally charged him.

Wainwright rose from his seat and offered Nicky his hand. They shook on the deal.

'Feel better?'

'No,' said Nicky. 'How can I raise my head again?'

'Feel cheated?'

'Yes.'

'Who by, me?'

'In part. But also by life in general.'

'Just out of curiosity, who's Elizabeth?'

'A woman who's life was ruined, just like mine, and by a man like you but in a different way.'

Wainwright was used to prisoners talking gibberish after they'd signed away their freedom so he listened patiently to Nicky and then said: 'I see.'

16

NICKY WAS TAKEN DOWN STEPS into the solid foundations of the building and placed in a police cell containing a bed welded at the joints and chained to the wall. At first it looked comical, until he realised that it was to prevent the prisoner from upending the bed into a makeshift gibbet to hang himself. Society made sure you faced the music. On top of a dirty pillow – on which were blotted stains of slabbers, faded blood and discernible teeth marks – lay a paper pillow-case and paper sheets. The mattress of compressed stuffing was encased in a thick rubber ticking to protect it against bed-wetters.

He had been lying down only about fifteen minutes when he was called for a medical examination by a young doctor. He told him he had no complaints to make.

Again, he hadn't been long back in his cell when he was taken out and brought to a room where he had a private audience with Baker, the solicitor, who had previously handled his insurance claim. He outlined the facts, as secretly agreed with Wainwright, and described his friendship with Gareth, which struck Baker as eccentric if not suspicious. He said he had been treated well and had immediately realised the folly of his actions the previous night and so made a statement admitting that he had intimidated Gareth into staying but didn't use any violence.

Baker asked him if there were not more. Nicky said that that was it. 'Are you sure?' Baker persisted. 'Yes,' said Nicky.

'What did the police say would happen?'

'That I'd get bail on Monday and if I pleaded guilty at the provisional enquiry – or something like that – a suspended sentence.'

'Do you want to contest the statement, challenge it?'

'No! . . . No, I mean. I want things over quickly. Then I shall move away from this town and start my life from scratch. Here, take this down; it is my parents' telephone number. Ring them, please, and tell them not to worry. Tell them also not to come here to see me. There is no need. Tell them I'll explain everything on Monday after my release.'

'You should think things over, long and hard. It would have been better to wait until I arrived before you answered their questions.'

'I tried to wait but your wife said you would be delayed . . .'

'A second ago you said you made the statement voluntarily. Are you sure there was no duress?'

'None. None whatsoever.'

'Are you sure you're telling me everything?'

'Yes,' said Nicky, hesitatingly; and he thought: the only people I need to explain myself to are Mr and Mrs Smith.

'What if bail is opposed?'

'Can that happen?'

'Of course it can. It isn't automatic. It depends on what the prosecution chooses to say. Depends on how many have been granted bail before you. The mood of the magistrate. What his wife said to him before he left home that morning.'

'I don't want to go to jail, Mr Baker,' said Nicky, the stubble of desperation beginning to show on his tired face. 'I don't think I could go through with it.'

'We'll do our best. I have to go now,' he said, tidying up his papers, 'but I'll see you before court sits on Monday. We'll be using your mother's address as your residence.'

'No, use my flat.'

'No, I'm using your mother's. It sounds more respectable. Are there any clergy you know would be prepared to speak up for you . . . give you a reference?'

'Not that I know of.'

'Oom. Right. That'll do for now. I'll see you Monday.'

After the visit Nicky was allowed an hour's exercise in a small yard behind the administration block. A policeman let him have a coat to wear over the boiler suit. Visible, inside one of the brightly lit rooms, were two young women, presumably clerical workers, engaged in an animated, but to Nicky muted, conversation. Their silent-screen laugh was like an augury of his seclusion from society. He summoned courage and asked his taciturn guard for a cigarette but he humped and muttered that he didn't smoke.

Back in his cell the last tea before breakfast tasted good and he ate the cold toast down to its last crumb. The deputy sergeant asked him if he had any complaints. He said no, and the door was locked on a long night.

He lay on top of the bed, his hands under his head and his bare feet crossed and let his mind wander.

But try as he might, his current predicament kept asserting itself, cleaving his mind into two opposites: that what was happening to him was really nothing – just one of those hiccups in life that had to be taken on board: that what was happening to him was absolutely catastrophic and that nothing, not even simple, taken-for-granted things, would ever be the same again.

He became very angry with himself.

What Wainwright did to me was to make me momentarily betray my true self by feeling ashamed of my nature. The real disgrace is that I am here because of love. I am not a pervert, a rapist, a child molester, a criminal. I can't be appalled at what I am.

But he realised that he would have to be cunning if he were to survive.

He burnished his convictions and marshalled his morale behind shimmering armour and saw his life in its true trail-blazing light. I've known these things all along! he laughed. Since I was six, anyway! Come Monday and Nicky Smith steps out into the world! Into a world which has to recognise his terms! I can be happy, I can be happy! And I shall see Gareth again! And damn the lot of them!

He lay down to dream but was disturbed by worries about court on Monday. Two fictional fates – one of which would turn to fact – vied, with the power of the future, to disrupt the present and deprive him of a good sleep.

As morning approached his army of convictions melted away into the night, just as he suspected they would, leaving him defenceless, vulnerable and prey to a thousand well-grounded fears. Depression deepened and he sweated regularly. What if I've been double-crossed? What if I don't get bail and am sent to prison? They'll murder me!

The passage of Sunday was punctuated by breakfast, dinner and tea, all served in his cell and eaten on his lap, against the background of a lonely silence in the corridor or, occasionally, distant voices; in the afternoon an hour's exercise in the same yard as before; and several visits to the toilet which he prolonged because it meant being out of his cell.

For some reason he kept expecting Wainwright or Ian to call in and ask how he was keeping. He found that he had to perpetuate a sense of his own importance – or go under – even though he knew that all that they really had in common was his prosecution, that to them he was a mere cipher and was probably the furthermost thing from their minds as they played happy families. But still he looked up, expecting them each time the door opened. He needed them. He needed their pact and the reassurance that everything was going according to plan.

After tea the guard unlocked the door and handed Nicky a big brown paper parcel and wished him 'Merry Christmas', even though it was still November. On the side of it was written his name in his mother's small but neat handwriting. He felt a surge of love for her and felt as if she were sitting at home in her chair at this very second and knew that he was showering her handwriting with filial kisses for all the days and nights she had given him her unqualified love. Inside, were new clothes which she must have especially gone out and bought for him that day: new clothes for court, among them the style of grey duffle coat which he liked best. Cigarettes had also been sent in and placed with his official property but the new nightguard retrieved them and allowed Nicky the packet.

Shortly afterwards he was asked did he want to shower and shave. He jumped at the offer to get cleaned up.

At about eight o'clock the door opened and he was told to

get dressed and to throw out his pillow case and sheets. He was
on the move. This time he was handcuffed. At the reception his
police escort signed some documentation and checked his property. He was taken out a back door to the courtyard which
sparkled with the rough sandpaper of evening frost. He was told
to climb into a poorly-lit prison van which resembled in dimen-
sions the cargo lorry he used to drive long distance. The policemen dealing with him were completely indifferent, whereas for
him the entire experience was traumatic. If one had said, 'Mind
your step, son,' Nicky would have been obliged to him the rest
of his life for those few words of concern. He was locked into
a vandal-proof metal box fitted with an aluminium seat. About
six other prisoners must have been loaded on before him because
he was the last and the count was carried out and concluded at
seven. When the engine started up some of these men began
shouting and joking to one another. Nicky remained silent and
hugged his chin into his duffle coat. He had often overtaken one
of these vehicles on the motorway without ever considering
that there were people locked and handcuffed inside.

The van trundled out of the yard and when it turned into
the street a cold draught whirled around his ankles. He wondered where fate was taking him, where he lay in the scheme
of things, and he closed his eyes tight the way he often did in
bed as a child imagining a monster outside.

The custody station to which he was brought backed on to
the courthouse. The cells were dirty and smelt of urine and disinfectant. Nicky's contained just one mattress on a sloping concrete base, no blankets and no pillow. From out the grill at the
top of his metal door he could look across at the cell opposite
where he could see two heads bobbing up and down. There was
shouting and laughing along the cell block and many of the prisoners seemed to be on first-name terms with their jailors. After
the main lights were switched off a yellow glare permeated the
grill and the gap below the door like a pea-soup fog.

Only about twelve more hours of this, thought Nicky, com-
forting himself. He alternately paced the floor and did press-
ups for several hours to exhaust himself. He thought about
Gareth and his state of health and hoped that his mortifying
ordeal in the police station, of being intimately examined and

then interrogated about his personal diary, hadn't caused a relapse. Nicky worried that Gareth might misinterpret his guilty plea as some kind of repudiation but then felt that he would understand his pragmatic stance.

He was woken early by borborygmus as his insides fermented and his intestines ballooned with gas beyond their capacity. He was in agony with cramps but the guard said he couldn't let him out until the morning relief arrived. Nicky waited and waited until he could not wait one second longer. He begged the guard to let him out but even before he heard the refusal he felt his bowels exploding. He whipped down his trousers and underpants and a pail of diarrhoea went splashing across the cell floor and up the walls. The backs of his trousers and shoes were pebble-dashed with faeces and his coat was stained with a brown fantail up the front. The stench filled the cell and corridor.

'For fuck's sake, could you not have held on a minute!' said the guard, opening the door. 'Get that mess cleaned up!'

'Somebody shit them, down there!' a prisoner called out amidst general laughter.

Nicky was struck dumb with humiliation and did as he was told. He cleaned up the diarrhoea with newspapers, then threw disinfectant over the floor and mopped up the remains. In the toilets he washed himself as best he could. He was weak-kneed and trembling and couldn't face his breakfast. At about half nine he was called for a legal visit and was told to take his duffle coat with him. He was again handcuffed even though the journey to his solicitor was short.

'Are you OK?' asked Baker. 'You're a bad colour.'

'They wouldn't let me out to the toilet. They wouldn't let me out to the fucking toilet!'

'I'll see the custody sergeant and make a formal protest.'

'No, no. It doesn't matter now. Things are nearly over, aren't they?'

'Let's hope so. We've only a few minutes. Are you sure you've nothing else to add to what you've already told me. No? Good. It'll be a while before I see your statement. That'll all come later. I'm not sure who's on the bench this morning. Just look respectful and dignified and remember that when the clerk asks you how do you plead, say, "Not guilty".'

'No! I can't do that.'

'It's only a formality. This is not the trial, you know. Relax, it's only a formality, OK?'

'Are you sure? I told them I'd plead guilty. We agreed.'

'Nicky, you have me very worried. I'll be extremely angry if I get hit up the teeth with something I haven't been told about. Now listen. You've to answer your name, etcetera, and you've to say, "Not guilty." OK? It does not prevent your pleading guilty at a later stage once we've fully assessed the evidence.'

'OK,' said Nicky reluctantly, having no one else to trust at that moment. 'Did you phone my parents?'

'Yes, and arrangements have been made for bail. I have to go across to the High Court but I'll see you in about an hour.'

'An hour!'

'Yes, you're well down the list. Another solicitor's watching for me and if you are called any earlier he'll ring me. Don't be worrying.'

Nicky was brought to a holding cell containing about a dozen prisoners. They were all talking among themselves in a babble though keywords surfaced occasionally: 'armed robbery', 'bail', 'cops', 'my brief', 'bastard', 'Wainwright', 'two-to-four maybe', 'joy-riding', 'maintenance', 'bitch', 'breathalysed'. Nicky put himself in a corner and kept his head down and no one bothered him. Prisoners were called out: some returned glum; others gleeful – those who had made bail. New prisoners were added to the throng and at one stage when the door was unlocked Nicky caught a glimpse of another packed room across the hallway. No one could accuse the police of being soft on crime, he thought. When he asked to go to the toilet he had to wait for ten minutes. The room to which he was brought was functional but the toilet had no seat and there was no paper, though he had kept some tissue from earlier that morning. On his return he noticed yet more holding cells and could hear raucous voices within.

At last his name was called. He sheepishly followed the officer with the clipboard through the twisting corridor and sat on a gym-like bench along with four other men when instructed to do so. All were nervous and someone had farted a terrible smell of fear. There was a flight of well-worn concrete steps at the top of which stood another police officer with a clipboard containing the court list, and beside him a prisoner waiting to go through the door. A young girl stepped out from the courtroom, accompanied by two policewomen, and was taken in the opposite direction, Nicky couldn't see where exactly. As the names were called he moved up the bench and a half-smoked cigarette was passed down. He thanked the youth who gave it to him. Suddenly he felt the need to go to the toilet again. His bowels seemed as if they were going to erupt. But then the police officer at the top of the stairs called, 'Nicholas Smith,' and his mind took possession of him. Nicky passed on the butt and climbed the steps, then waited.

The door opened and he stepped aside.

'Bail!' smiled the young man. 'Got bail!'

Nicky couldn't muster congratulations, so preoccupied was he with his own fate.

'Nicholas Smith!'

He walked through the door and was surprised to find himself in a dock like an opera box, standing above the seated public and two pews filled with solicitors and clerks. He quickly scanned the room and saw that he was below the judge's bench to his left where beneath a crest high on the wall sat the magistrate in a blue suit. At the back and sides of the court stood police officers. The courtroom was incredibly bright, spick and ornate with an elaborate corniced ceiling and cloth-like wallpaper of miniature golden trefoils. Nicky's eyes caught his solicitor but Baker wouldn't look at him, as if this were the convention or that to do so would have indicated human weakness.

He searched the banks of faces and found a familiar one with a little moustache, mostly grey but still flecked with some black bristles. His father, who had been watching him from the first instant, gave him the thumbs up and a smile of solidarity that seemed to call Nicky to his protection.

My da, thought Nicky. My great da!

Nicky sent him a smile. He couldn't see his mother but behind a figure who was whispering to a uniformed police inspector in uniform on the front bench he saw Ian. Directly opposite the prisoner in a reserved area was the court reporter and above him a big clock which showed ten past eleven.

Nicky couldn't understand the exchanges. He answered two questions the clerk put to him about his name and age, and later was to think that he'd answered some others. The figure beside the inspector was a Mr Collins for the DPP. He read out the charges. Mr Baker said he was appearing for Mr Smith and argued for bail.

Collins asked for press restrictions to be imposed and Nicky felt that Wainwright was keeping to his part of the bargain. He glanced at Ian but he was staring straight ahead like a soldier on parade with eyes front.

The magistrate asked Collins the reasons for the restrictions. He replied that the case was a delicate one, involving a boy of just fifteen from a well-known family. Police investigations were continuing. There was a possibility that it might have been an amateurish but nonetheless dangerous and menacing attempt at a kidnapping and ransom with the boy unwittingly going along part of the way. He had statements made by the accused which he wished to reserve for the present. They were awaiting forensic reports and a psychiatric report on the victim which could put a more serious complexion on the case. They were also studying photographs and a diary. There was a probability of further charges. The magistrate then directed the court reporter not to reveal the name of the witness mentioned in the charges, Gareth Williams.

Collins asked for Nicky to be remanded in custody for a month while the DPP studied the papers.

Nicky was aghast and his knees wobbled. He imagined everyone was looking in his direction and whispering. He wished the ground would open up and swallow him. As the prosecutor had been speaking the magistrate scrutinised the accused ever more distastefully over the top of his pince-nez. He understood the coded language of his learned friend but the public were none the wiser and if they saw anything in the dock it was a pathetic bungler not a terrifying monster. Nicky dared look at his father and once again he got the thumbs-up treatment. He felt so undeserving and was indebted to the old man for this solidarity which was like oxygen to a gasping man.

Impassively, Baker rose from his seat, said it wasn't his intention to waste the court's time nor supplant the function of a jury should the case go to trial – something that he doubted – but that the facts of the case supported the contention that the police had over-reacted. In fact, the boy, as far as he could establish, and this was something that the prosecution was dilatory in stating, was making no complaint whatsoever about Smith, who had a clear record. The prosecution was long on innuendo and short on specifics. He was, therefore, asking for his client to be remanded on bail on a surety reflecting the gravity of the charges and with whatever other restrictions the court and police saw fit to impose.

Collins jumped to his feet. If ever there was a case where bail should be denied it was in this one. Bank robbers in front of the court earlier deserved bail before Smith. Police believed that there was every possibility that witnesses . . . and there were four who could attest to the boy being held in Smith's flat, they weren't relying solely on the boy's word . . . that witnesses would be interfered with – 'interfered' was said with particular gusto – and he repeated that it was a delicate case involving the child of a respected and well-known family, a family who needed reassurance and security, the security of the prisoner's remand in custody.

The magistrate agreed with him, refused bail and remanded Nicky in custody. Nicky looked over at Ian, who shook his head from side-to-side like a soldier disillusioned with the war, before rising and walking briskly from the court. Nicky's arm was firmly gripped and he was taken downstairs to yet another holding cell containing prisoners whose destination was the city's notorious jail. Nicky overheard talk about a bank and assumed that the three individuals in conversation opposite him were the gang busted by the treacherous Wainwright. They deserved bail before he did! What a world!

'Smith! Legal!'

He entered a small room. Baker looked at him, didn't even invite him to take a seat, though Nicky slumped into it.

'You threw me in the fucking shit, there, didn't you?' said Baker. 'Sit down and tell me everything that's going on. One more lie and you get yourself a new solicitor, understand? I'd drop you right now only I wouldn't want that bastard, Ray Collins, to know that you wiped my eye. Now begin.'

Hesitatingly, in bits and pieces, jumping back and forth between events, Nicky told everything. He even felt better for it.

'I suppose now that you know I'm a . . . a . . . '

'A queer?'

'I can't say it.'

'Nicky, the queer's the one up on the bench with the glasses and the little gavel. If I were to talk out of school about his peccadillos you would be disgusted! It makes you wonder who has the right to judge who. You've been very stupid in not telling me all this at the beginning. It's not everybody hates gays. Is everything you've told me the truth?'

'Yes, everything.'

'Well, things aren't great but the evidence is mostly circumstantial. You say the boy won't make any incriminating allegations against you. Let's hope so. The diary and the photographs, bar one or two, are not your responsibility. You are being prosecuted for your hospitality last Friday night and because you are gay: the law plays to prejudice despite all the shite to the contrary. You are being prosecuted because Williams-the-stud probably hates his son, because of the muscle which Williams exerts in these corridors and shouldn't, because of internal politics between the police and the DPP, because of this and that. There is a possibility that the police meant to honour the deal you entered with them, or that Inspector Wainwright, whom I've had the pleasure of meeting before, doesn't care one way or another. He did nothing wrong, allowed you to phone, gave you all the opportunities you needed to wait on me, etcetera. But that was also part of his clever game-plan and it worked.'

'What choices do I have?'

'Oh, it's clear. You fight the charges.'

'What if they throw in gross indecency?'

'Are you afraid for yourself in jail or for the boy's reputation and future?'

'For both. I don't want anything of that nature in court. Gareth's ill at the moment and it would kill him. I swear, it would kill him.'

'Ray Collins has already more or less entered it into the

record though there'll be no press reports about that aspect. There's no guarantee it won't come out as a result of you contesting these charges. Isn't that how the police got you to make your statement in the first place. Now the prosecution's threatening to move it up several more notches. "Plead guilty to these more serious charges or we'll read out the diaries and show the photographs". It's blackmail, pure and simple. I don't think they can do it. It couldn't be in Williams' interest to have his son's adolescent musings – with all due respects – published. He must be pretty perverted to want to hurt his wife – and boy – in this way. Besides, under the laws of discovery we would have access to the diary and there are bound to be things in it that will exonerate you and damn him. Mr Williams may have bitten off more than he can chew. If what you say is true about the parents murdering each other then there would probably be details of that nature which the father wouldn't want exposed, not to mention, what's this she's called . . . "the floozie florist"! Even though they're not relevant to the charges against you he wouldn't trust us not to lose photocopies of them in Royal Avenue.'

'No!' said Nicky. 'That doesn't help me either! It doesn't matter that we can balance their threat to read out selective excerpts about me by the risk they take that details about Williams' private life might surface in some newspaper office. If Williams has bitten off more than he can chew and the case has a momentum of its own and he can't prevent the diary going to court and being read out it still damages Gareth. It would humiliate and destroy him, I tell you! I can't risk that. I'll plead guilty to unlawful imprisonment as soon as possible. That way they don't need the diary and the photographs or any evidence for a conviction. I want you to go and tell the DPP that.'

'And what if they see you running and add gross indecency. Don't you realise that they hate you people? You frighten them. Really frighten them. Will you plead guilty to gross indecency? You've heard what life is like inside for the sex offenders, haven't you? You'll be lumped with the worst.'

'Will we get notice of any new charges?'

'Yes, we should.'

'I'll kill myself first,' said Nicky gravely. 'If I am dead there'll be no trial, no hearing, no airing of what poor Gareth felt for me last summer. It'll be the suicide of a man awaiting trial on kidnapping charges.'

Baker was shocked.

'You mean it, don't you?'

'Yes, I mean it.'

'Don't think that way, son. It's not that black.'

'It's always been black,' Nicky laughed hollowly. 'Black was Robin's favourite colour. No wonder.'

He left his solicitor and waited for the policeman to unlock the gate to the cells but he was shunted down another corridor and silently obeyed. It had cubicles, each closed off with sliding glass doors. The officer shouted, 'Whoa!' and Nicky stopped. He slid open a door and told Nicky to go in. Nicky sat down. If Wainwright or Ian were coming to apologise it was a bit late now. He heard steps approach, the officer opened the door and stood aside and in came his mother and his father who appeared to be about to tackle the policeman for his lack of manners. Mrs Smith immediately burst into tears and Nicky jumped to comfort her.

'Five minutes,' said the officer.

The three settled around the table, Nicky and his mother holding hands. All that Mrs Smith could see was the boy, the height of innocence, who climbed on the back of an invisible horse and kicked up silver spurs of splash as he galloped through the puddles and down the street to school along with his friend Robin. All else was over her head.

'I don't understand anything, Nicky,' she said. 'That boy, Gareth. I thought he was very nice. But he came to you. I'm proof of that. Did you know he has no sister? He's a proven liar . . . But then when the police raided they found him in your . . .'

'Mammy, daddy, I have something to explain. It is very hard for me to explain. But the truth is important to me. You may want to walk away from me and I will understand.'

'Nicky,' said his father. 'I know what you're going to say. I'm not so stupid, eh! You're our son. Our son. Through thick and thin. Understand? It's not easy to take or go along with but you are a good person. You are no rogue. We've a lot to learn from each other. We will support you, don't worry. I've to see your solicitor later in his office. I knew something strange was going on in court because it was the police inspector, the one in uniform, who dealt with most of the other cases. But just before you were brought in there was a lot of activity around the bench and that man Collins took control. Not see me shrugging my shoulders?'

'Yes, I did. I did. But I was looking for mammy.'

'Oh Nicky, I would have died if I'd seen you brought in with all those chains,' she said, still gripping his hand.

Nicky and his father laughed. She's so simple, so straight, thought Nicky. How will she understand me when things become clear? She'll be horrified. And if things get worse, if I have to kill myself, how will they cope? Daddy'll understand. Daddy'll understand.

The policeman called the visit. It was time for Nicky to go to jail.

'I'll be up to see you tomorrow,' said his father, shaking his hand with a firm grip. 'We'll get you whatever you need. Be careful. OK?'

'I love you both,' said Nicky. 'You're a father and brother, daddy. Mammy, you're a sister and mother. I'm sorry for everything, for all the hurt, for all the cruel things I've . . .'

'Stop it!' said his father. 'There's the saint there,' he said, pointing to Mrs Smith. 'You should see what I put her through for years. And you know what she said to me, Nicky? Do you? Once when I was as close to the edge as it is possible to go, she said, "You're the best thing that ever happened to me." You saved my life, didn't you, Mrs Smith! Well, you two are the best thing that ever happened to me and, I'm ashamed to say, it has taken me twenty years to say it.'

Mrs Smith smiled. This is my family. All back together. My family.

17

NICKY CRIED OUT IN PAIN as the podgy Vaselined finger penetrated deep inside his rectum and searched for contraband. The gouty medical officer had hippo nostrils and ran his gloved finger in circles inside the prisoner like a vet his arm up to the elbow in the birth canal correcting a calf in the breech position, except that he was hoping to pick up a thread lassoed to a package. He withdrew his finger and told Nicky to drape himself in the towel which lay on the tiled floor below him. His own clothes were being thoroughly searched and his duffle coat was deemed a prohibited article of clothing because it had a hood. His two remaining cigarettes were confiscated and removed to his 'property'.

'Hold out your right hand . . . deep scar, index knuckle to wrist, three inches.'

Another warder noted down his colleague's comments. In this way the surface of Nicky's body was mapped for every distinguishable mark. It was like an autopsy, but one revealing the progress of life, from the first survival scrapes of childhood down to the extant wisp of fading white left on his back by one of Madeline's nails. They even found the tiny white pockpit in the lobe of his left ear which he had allowed Robin unsuccessfully to pierce with a hot pin, and about which he had forgotten completely.

He was weighed and his height measured. He was given soap, toothpaste, a razor and a brush and told to have a bath and shave. His clothes were returned to him.

'Your number is one-seven-one-one. What is it?'

'One-seven-one-one.'

'Seventeen-eleven, for short. Don't forget it. Now stand up against the wall. Hold this.'

Across his chest he held up the small blackboard with his name and prison number chalked on it whilst they photographed him.

'Turn to the side and hold the board at shoulder height.'

He held the board awry and the irascible warder roughly corrected him before he was photographed in profile.

Through an underground passage. A half dozen gates were opened and locked, some both manually and electronically. Down more steps. The base. Everywhere the effluvia of men. Everywhere the smell of carbolic soap. A black polished floor, a yellow line.

'Stand at the yellow line when the SO addresses you.'

SO. What's that? thought Nicky.

'Number?'

'One-seven . . . I can't remember the rest of it.'

'Well, you better. It's one-seven-one-one. What is it?'

'One-seven-one-one.'

'One-seven-one-one, SO.'

'One-seven-one-one, SO.'

'You're here for the night. Don't want to hear a peep out of you. Tomorrow you'll see the governor and will be sent to the wings. Collect your pot, water-gallon, plate, knife, fork, spoon, mug. If you wanna do your pops, your load, your numbers – whatever you call your shite – do it now. Get your dinner over there, from the orderly. You're in cell 10.'

The orderly stood behind a table laid out like a field kitchen. He gave Nicky a generous helping of potatoes and cabbage with the sausage and gravy. The new prisoner went to take a slice of bread but the orderly gave him six rounds.

Nicky's cell door was locked behind him without any

further word being spoken, though he heard more remands being taken through the same induction. He felt hungry but his stomach was full-up with fear. *Three days ago I was walking down the street. It's incredible.* He sat on the lower bunk of the frowsty beds and tried to forget his circumstances so that he could eat. He sat his plate on the plastic chair and it slid to equilibrium, spilling some gravy on its minor descent. Recessed high in the wall, though actually at ground level outside, was the window. It consisted of inner bars – four verticals and two horizontals; and outer bars – eight verticals and two horizontals. *I'll not be cutting my way through them,* he joked. A round heating pipe ran at floor level along the back wall, below the window. It made a crinkling, expansive noise, perhaps as the heating was raised with the drop in temperature.

He looked at his plate: the food was gone, and his cup was empty, and there were tastes in his mouth. *Well, I'll be.* He wiped the sides of his mouth with the back of his hand. On the top bunk he made up his bed from the pack on the lower bunk and lay on top of it.

The electricity dribbled through the low-wattage bulb which hung at the end of a twisted flex from the white-emulsioned ceiling.

He stretched out his fingers and examined his right palm, its abstruse wrinkles and skittered lines. *Shit. I thought that was a hair growing there. No it's not. It's only an eyelash. Right in the middle of my lifeline. My ninety-year-old life line!* He relaxed his hand and it reverted to the prehensile mode. He outstretched it again until it was fully contoured and the skin blanched. He became objective and thought: *what an odd-looking, funny bit of limb . . . just like a monkey's.* He studied it through to the bones and back again until the relationship between his hand and his brain grew distant, faded and became lost. Instead of familiarity the hand became strange. *Uh-oh,* he thought. *This could be how* rigor mortis *sets in!* It became strange, then eerie, then totally alien and made his flesh creep. So he made his fingers and thumb into a wigwam above his palm and then opened them several times. *That's coming from my brain . . . that's better! Better not try* any tricks between my mind and my brain, in case my mind doesn't recognise my brain! Where would I be then!

He looked at his fanned fingers and aligned them. They're knock-kneed! My bloody fingers are knock-kneed! More light filtered through the gaps than was excluded but these were the fingers that he'd broken in his mid-teens. If they were webbed I'd be a duck . . . or a champion swimmer. He became amazed at his hands. Not bad looking. The servants of humanity. Hands that can plant seeds; hands that write poetry; hands that touch; hands that do dishes can feel soft as your face . . . For God's sake, be serious. He's got the whole world in his hands. Hands that can love. Hands that can kill. The hand that Gareth squeezed with all the life that was in him and said, Nicky, I would die for you.

There is no doubt about it: I am here. Right now. Nowhere else. Not in the past. I am here now. My hand is running down the cold wall of a cell. My prison cell.

'It's been seven hours and fifteen days . . . since you took your love away . . .' Fuck, I'm no singer.

His wall was banged and he knelt down to the pipe.

A voice said: 'That you, Joe?'

'No, it's Nicky.'

'Nicky who?'

'Nicky Smith.' Nicky felt excited, communicating with another prisoner.

'Where's Joe?'

'I don't know.'

'What are you in for, mate?'

'Kidnapping.'

'Kidnapping!' said his next-door-neighbour, followed by a whistle.

'What about you?'

'Armed robbery. Is Joe not in with you?'

'No, I'm on my own.'

'Try the next cell.'

'Joe?'

'Hello.'

'Joe?'

'Yes, who is it?'

'Nicky Smith.'

'Who?'

'Nicky Smith.' Fucking – the Scarlet Pimpernel, does it matter!

'What do you want?'

'A fella's looking for you in Cell 9, I think.'

'What's he want?'

'Hang on . . . Cell 9! Joe's in Cell 11, I think. He says, what do you want.'

'Fuck all. Was just asking.'

'Joe?'

'What?'

'He says the grub was OK, wasn't it?'

'Hasn't changed much . . . What are you in for, mate?'

'Kidnapping.'

Cell 11 replied: 'Kidnapping! Who'd you kidnap?'

'A businessman's son. Holding him for a ransom.'

'Phew, they'll hit you for that. Were you nollared?'

'Eh, yeh. Nollared right.'

'Bit like ourselves. Who done you?'

'Wainwright. Know him?'

'Wainwright, that bastard. He done us. Here, I'm away for a wank. I'll maybe see you tomorrow on the wing.'

'Right,' said Nicky, feeling a lot better now that he'd broken the code to the underworld and apparently impressed one or two of the most dangerous men in the country. How can you live without lies? he thought. They are important little links which connect us to possibilities the truth denies – survival being the principal one. They oil the machinery of existence, allowing us the parts to engage each other. And we even deceive ourselves to hear a lie as a truth because truth on the whole is cruel. Just call me Aris-whatever-to-fuck-his-name-is-Totle. Then he remembered where he was and the smile vanished from his face. Then the guard lifted the flap to check the prisoner and switched off the light.

The next morning he was told to empty his po in a sluice in the toilets and to leave it in the state he'd found it, which actually had been smelly and scaled. He washed, got his breakfast and was told to fold up the blankets and sheets and gather up any belongings. He followed the warder up to the top of long, wide stairs where they waited at an air-lock – a pen where one gate is locked before another is opened.

They entered the circle, which was actually partly hexagonal in shape but was at the hub of the radii of four wings. It contained administrative offices for governors, chaplains and welfare workers. Along one side, behind bullet-proof glass, was a large control room which monitored on short-circuit television screens the four wings, the base, the exercise yards, the hospital, the walls and the perimeter. The control room was also in radio contact with the observation posts and the IRF – an instant-reaction-force of special riot-trained officers.

Four spiral staircases from the circle allowed vertical access to the second and third landings of A–, B–, C– and D–wings, though movement of prisoners was, again, limited and controlled by turnkeys inside a series of air-locks.

He was told to wait outside a door marked 'Governor'. A few moments later he was called in.

'Prisoner! Stand to attention!'

Nicky's hands twitched by his side and longed to be at home inside their duffle coat where they belonged. He couldn't understand the rules or directives that he was expected to absorb in a two-minute address. He was a little relieved that at the finish he was handed three pages of printed rules, guidelines and advice. He was told he was going to A–wing and was to obey any order given by the class officer.

'Any questions?'

'Will I be able to get a visit today?'

' "Sir." '

'Sir.'

'Does your next-of-kin know you're here?'

'Yes, I spoke to them yesterday, sir.'

'The welfare officer will phone for you. You'll be seeing him next.'

He saw the welfare officer, declined to see the chaplain, and was examined by the doctor, a man of unkempt appearance with thick, black, greasy hair who spoke into a hand-held dictaphone like an executive.

His escort then walked him over to a heavy metal door and

pressed a bell. An observation hatch opened. They were scrutinised and the door's electronic locks reluctantly vacated their mortises.

'A–wing! One on!'

Nicky now entered the jail proper. It was incredibly vast, incredibly drab and incredibly noisy. Gates banged, sending down the wing shuddering waves that could be felt on the hairs of one's neck. There was the continual jangle of keys; the hissing sound of escaping steam; the clanging of metal mop-buckets; the ringing of bells on the consoles above the door of the class officer on each of the three landings as prisoners called to be allowed out; the shouting of male voices; the creaking of trolleys overloaded with blankets, sheets and towels; the thrumming of an industrial buffer polishing the floor. An entire world, a Bastille cut off permanently from the outside world with no possibility of ever being breached or liberated.

Nicky followed the officer in front. They went through another locked grille at the base of stairs connecting the ones to the twos – parlance for the ground floor and the landing above. On the twos he stood outside the class office, which was merely a converted cell. His escort handed in a folder containing his file and then departed. A cell card was filled out. In the space for religious denomination was written 'None'. Once again he felt utterly alone and helpless. This new world was completely unfamiliar despite the scenes of inside a prison one saw on television regularly. Imprisonment, the corollary of crime and punishment, was a constant, essential, feature of society but still one that generally remained an impenetrable mystery.

'You're in the Napoleon Suite, cell 20. Yard'll be called in about ten minutes if you want to go out. Or you can sit in and polish your shoes. Follow me.'

The door of cell 20 was opened and Nicky stepped in. Two pairs of eyes in gazes of apparent resentment immediately looked up at him.

'You've company,' announced the warder grinning.

'Any sign of the yard?' asked one of the prisoners who was in his early twenties, stocky with rich, jet black hair.

'Soon, Al. Soon.'

The door was banged.

The stocky fellow turned down his transistor radio. He had been lying on top of a single bed, separated from bunks by a narrow aisle, with just enough space for making the beds. On the lower bunk was a haggard-looking weedy man, in his late twenties. The man the warder had addressed spoke.

'My name's Alan Burgess. Or Al.'

'Nicky Smith.'

'Are you not saying hello, Seán?' said Al.

'Seán O'Neill's the name,' said the man on the lower bunk.

'You're on the top bunk,' said Al. 'Was there many in the base?'

'I'm not sure. There was a few.'

'Not much space on the landings. C–wing's being renovated and we're overcrowded. But I'll not be here too long. I'm up for my PE shortly, then I'm walking! Spare bed then!'

Better learn all these terms, thought Nicky. He jumped up on the top bunk, his long legs dangling over the edge. O'Neill was quiet and just lay on his bed picking bits of fluff from the mattress above.

'What are you in for?' said Al.

'Unlawful imprisonment.'

'Who'd you lock up?'

'The son of a big businessman. Ransom. But the cops hit the place.'

'Many of yous arrested?'

'Just myself at the flat. Don't wanna say how many were involved, you know.'

'Yeh, no problem,' he said. 'It's none of my business anyway but there's fuckers in here'll think it's theirs. Are you going down?'

'Not if we can put the frighteners on the boy.'

'Right. Right. Demanding money with menaces myself. The case'll definitely fall at the PE. The witness has seen the light. "Happy days are here again",' he sang as he rolled a cigarette for himself, thought for a moment and asked Nicky if he smoked. So he made him one but said rhetorically to O'Neill: 'Hey, skinny hole, when are you going to share some snout?'

Doors could be heard being unlocked and banged as the prisoners on the ones were sent to the exercise yard.

'Send on the twos!' bellowed the voice of a senior officer.

'Have you no coat?' said Al.

'They took it off me.'

'Here, stick this old one on or you'll be foundered.'

They went down to the ones, queued, were frisked and then were allowed into the bleak yard. It was about a third the size of a football pitch and indeed a bit of a game was picking up even though the tarmac was slippery with a heavy frost. On three sides were huge walls topped with razor wire, security lights and cameras. A grey powder of dry damp with the outline of a sprawling ivy plant clung to one wall three-quarters way up in an attitude of failed escape.

The fourth side was the mountain of A–wing block itself: a huge basalt frontage rising out of the ground with an inter-fenestration of two hundred barred slits, and below each slit the lime streaks of pigeon droppings like huge tears; a vast slated roof; and, where roof and stonework met, a mansard of lengthy spikes over which it would be impossible to climb should the windows be breached. The brickwork around the last two cells on the top landing, the ones closest to the gable, shared with part of the wall a stained, damp look. Al said the cause was a small explosion over twenty years before which had left tiny cracks.

In one corner of the yard were two smelly toilets with broken cisterns. A short distance away on metal posts was a small open shelter with a corrugated sheet roof under which the men could huddle and shiver if it were raining or snowing. All movement was monitored by a manned observation post inset into the most northerly wall and by cameras.

Nicky stuck like a limpet to Al. O'Neill had gone off on his own.

'Never trust anybody with thin lips,' said Al, as they strolled across to one of four benches bolted to a wall. 'They're usually informers.' He introduced Nicky and his crime to a few of his acquaintances and, in asides, pointed out other prisoners who needed watching, who was in for what, who were the tobacco and drug barons and who the cut-throats. New prisoners came on: among them the ones charged by Wainwright with armed bank robbery. One of them was real ugly. Joe, no doubt.

By nature diffident, it was essential for Nicky's survival that he blended in as anonymously as possible, even if he was only going to be here for a short stay. His cover-story needed to be convincing to these professionals. He was relieved – felt dangerously important even – when told by one of the hoods in their company that there had been a small item about his case in the previous evening's *Telegraph*. Only the really elite among them ever made the press so this lent him some credibility.

The morning was bitterly cold, the air thin and clear. To the left and right of the tarmac track, around which the group of four men, including Nicky, were now walking, glistened frozen phlegm and spittle. Steam came out of the men's mouths as they spoke and Nicky found the spectacle humorous. You could get used to this life, he thought. No wonder jail doesn't deter. Most of their conversation was about sex. Al was talking about their cell-mate, Seán O'Neill, and presumably embroidering a story he had heard.

'So O'Neill comes home early from the night shift and there's his mate in bed with his missus. He starts crying: "Ah, Sarah! Ah, Rab!" and almost fainting, falls on the side of the bed. "How could you do this to me. Ah, my life's ruined. Ruined!" His wife gets up and puts on a dressing gown and says, "Seán! What's up? What are you talking about? It's not like it seems. Nothing's happened, honey. People came back for a few drinks last night and we were all tired and just fell into bed and asleep."

' "Is that right, Rab?" says Seán. "Is that true?"

' "Sure you know it's true," says Rab, not believing his luck. "I was steamin'. Didn't even know who Sarah was when you woke me up."

' "Oh, thank God for that. Thank God, for that," says O'Neill. "Is that honest? Are yous being straight with me? Ah, thank God for that, thank God. I'll go and make some breakfast. What would you like, Rab?" '

The men all laughed at Al's perfect mimicry of Seán's voice, Nicky included.

Al made a pit-stop for the toilets and said he'd catch them

on the way round. The ball was kicked high, struck one of the walls and was deflected on to the roof of the shelter were it remained, caught up in the barbed wire.

'Hey, big lad! Jump up and get us the ball, would you?' said a bearded man in his late twenties to Nicky. Nicky felt in obliging mood and asked for a fireman's lift. He then pulled himself up onto the roof, gingerly stepped over the rolls of barbed wire, recovered the ball and kicked it down. When he came back to the edge of the roof the person who had helped him up had disappeared.

'That was a stupid thing to do,' shouted Al. 'Stand on my shoulders.' This way Nicky got down without having to jump. 'Them cunts would set you up very handy. Not see that sign?'

Nicky read the board screwed to the wall:

> Any activity recreational or otherwise which causes an inmate to be raised supported or suspended above head height will be deemed a breach of establishment rules

'Let's hope you're not reported by the screw in the box,' said Al. They hadn't walked three laps of the yard when Nicky's name was called over the tannoy.

'Seventeen-Eleven. N Smith. Visit.'

Al explained that you didn't rush off the yard but did another two or three laps just to show the other men that you weren't 'a heavy whacker'. So, even though he wanted to run to his visitors, Nicky shammed nonchalance.

'Who's the dick?' said Patterson, the bearded man who'd got Nicky to climb up and get the ball, to Al after Nicky had left the yard.

'He's all right. This is his first time in jail.'

'What to fuck age is he?'

'I dunno, about twenty-four or -five.'

'He mustn't have had much of a life,' he said scornfully and his cronies laughed.

'He's OK,' said Al. 'You stay off his back . . . He's OK.'

'We'll see if he's OK,' said Patterson, who despite his diminutive size, was one of the chief bullies on the wing where rivalry resulted in a delicately balanced set of scales.

Nicky was escorted through the wing, went downstairs to the search bay, emerged at the other side, and came up concrete steps, through more locked doors, to the visits. The warder said: 'Box Four.' He counted the numbers painted along the walls between partitioned spaces containing fixed rectangular-topped grey tables and fixed wooden-bench seating. He spotted his father's face. The old man rose and they shook hands and embraced. Then they sat down opposite each other.

'Well, is it OK? Has anybody harmed you?' asked Mr Smith.

'It's fine, daddy. I was moved on to A–wing this morning and was called off the exercise yard just there now . . . Where's mammy?'

'Ah, she couldn't make it. She's dying with the flu. Maybe it's as well she couldn't make it, Nicky. She did nothing but cry after yesterday's visit. I don't think it's a good idea if she sees you in here, do you?'

'No, you're right. I'll drop her a line tonight. We're allowed to write a few letters a week.'

'I saw Mr Baker yesterday. He's a good solicitor. You're for the High Court on Friday morning. He could have put you up tomorrow but there's a judge sitting he didn't want you to appear in front of. His daughter was . . . was raped. I'm sorry. I know it's got nothing to do with you but Mr Baker said there'd be no chance of getting bail from him under the circumstances. So, he's holding back until Friday when you should get some other judge more neutral.'

'Did he say what he thought the chances were?'

'He said we'd a good chance. You have no previous record and despite what was hinted at there's no evidence of anything wrong having been done. He still doesn't know if they've got a statement from the young lad which goes against you. Nicky, why did you admit to holding him against his will when you didn't? None of this need have happened.'

'Da, you've no idea what it's like in a police station. I was never in one before. I was all confused. They were threatening me with worse things and I fell for it. The man responsible is that Detective Wainwright. You never seen him; he wasn't in court yesterday. But he spoke to you and mammy on the phone last Saturday . . .'

'We never spoke to any detective last Saturday, Nicky.'

'Are you serious? He came in and told me he'd spoken to you. What a fool I've been! . . . Daddy, I'm really terrified that I could just disappear and get lost inside the system . . . I don't think I'm going to get bail, which means I could be here for three or four months to the preliminary enquiry when it'll be sorted out when I plead guilty to unlawful imprisonment. It's the only way I can get out . . . How's my mammy really?'

'She'll not be in court. But I'll be there. Know who drove me here this morning? Dan Leckey. He's a really good neighbour and sends his regards. As does everybody. Your Aunty Kate and Uncle Tom. Uncle Brian. Everybody. I've left in money for you. £25. I hope that's enough for you to buy whatever you need?'

'Daddy, that's great.'

'I've also left in a parcel. There's fruit, biscuits, cigarettes, more clothes, two newspapers, including last night's *Tele*. There's a new pair of runners as well – size 10. But if they don't fit we'll get you new ones.'

'Daddy, I'm overwhelmed. I'm not worth it, am I? When I think of all the trouble I've given you and mammy.'

'It's not just as black and white as that . . . Look, to be honest, I can't talk about the other thing. I thought I was OK, yesterday, but I find it hard, difficult. Bloody embarrassing, if you must know. I don't even know if I can ever come to terms. But your mammy, never. She still doesn't know exactly what's going on, though she's not stupid. I blame that young fella, Robin Coulter, for a lot of this, you know. He was a bad influence on you, Nicky. I always felt it odd the grip he had on you. He almost drove you to your death.'

Nicky smiled. 'Da, I should be angry with you for saying that. All I will say is, don't be silly. And don't be hitting me a crack again. You pack some punch!'

'I really can't understand it, Nicky. I can't. I saw that wee girl what's-her-name . . . Madeline Taylor. A great girl. I'm sure everybody's after her – '

'Where did you see her?'

'Your mammy and me met her yesterday. There were queues for the number 8 so we got the number 9 instead even though it meant a bit of a walk from Montside. She said you wouldn't harm a fly; it was all a set-up. We were talking to her outside the post office.'

What a life I've led, thought Nicky, and he loved all the friends and neighbours he'd known. And, once again, reminded of friendship, he thought of Gareth. He'd love to visit a real jail like this but not one with me in it! And not one with me in it as a result of him!

Suddenly, his father's countenance cracked and his eyes filled and he put his hands over his face.

'Ah, Nicky! Nicky! Nicky! What have you done to us!' he gasped, between his tears. 'Nobody was asking for you, son, nobody! I had to get a taxi here. Some of the neighbours have avoided your mother and me, apart from that woman, Mrs Russell. She was the only one who called but you know what she's like. If this gets any worse it'll kill your mother. I don't even think I can face people in work . . .' His voice was shaking and Nicky's deep, heavy, sad and bewildered breathing oscillated in step with his father's.

'I thought I could have come to terms with what you are but it's hard, so hard . . . It's im . . . possible. Impossible . . . I'm sorry, I'm really sorry.'

Nicky touched his father's arm and squeezed it. Once again he felt like the loneliest person in the world.

'Da, don't be worrying. It's not fair on you and mammy. But you know what the joke is? I haven't even done anything homosexual! Do you know that?'

'Shoosh, Nicky, be careful these bastards don't hear you. I should be stronger, I know. I've fooled myself for years with believing that I was fairly liberal because of my experience when I needed people's grace. That time last July your mom told me you had stayed overnight with friends I laughed at her naïvety and said it had probably been a girl. I should be acting better, Nicky. For years I wasn't a good father and suddenly because of this situation it seemed that we were all drawn closer. But still I find it hard.'

'Da, you're doing great and I thank you.'

The warder set down the pass and said that the time was up.

'Already?' said Nicky.

His father looked at his watch. 'Actually, they gave us extra. Look, I'm sorry for what I just said.' He was trying to compose himself. 'I'll be in court on Friday morning with the deeds of the house. Let's keep our fingers crossed.'

'Thanks Da. Give mammy my love.'

As his father reached the exit Nicky shouted to him like a litigant: ' "I'll see you in court, Mr Smith!" '

Nicky was returned to the wing. Nobody cares about me – apart from my parents, that is. Nobody cares. Exercise was over so he was to be sent up to the twos and back to his cell.

'Smith!'

He turned around and saw the SO.

'Come here!'

Nicky obeyed.

'Did you climb up on the roof of the shelter during exercise?'

'Aye, just to get a ball.'

'Weren't you told only this morning that we didn't want any trouble from you?'

'But I didn't know you weren't allowed until I saw the sign.'

'You're being put on report. Don't step out of line again.'

He went back to his cell feeling despondent.

'Where's Seán?' he asked Al.

'Down with welfare. Sure he's never away from it. He has them phoning home about three times a day to say hello to his wife. He can't read or write, you know. Here, wait till you see her.' He went to the door and looked through a gap in the jamb to check that Seán wasn't on his way back, then removed an envelope from Seán's bedside locker and took out a photo.

'What do you think of her?'

'She's a nice girl,' said Nicky.

'She'll not be long lonely, I can tell you.'

'What's he in for?'

'Fired a shotgun through a neighbour's window who he thought was making eyes at her. You should see the wee skirt she wears on the visits. But she's dead thin lips.'

At 11.45 there was a count carried out, followed by the call of 'Unlock!' Doors were opened, eight at a time. As Nicky,

Seán and Al came out of their cells with their mugs, knives, forks and spoons, and waited for the stair grilles to the ones to be opened, Al spotted some prisoners from the threes move along the catwalk above to a segregated canteen.

'Bullroots!' he screamed. Patterson, behind him, took up the taunt: 'Go on, you fuckin' bullroot bastards!'

Soon, the men moving along the ones joined in with the chants of hatred.

'Nonce bastards!'

'Bullllroooot!'

The prisoners in the protective unit felt the abuse, kept their chins tucked into their chests and scurried in silence to their canteen.

'Who're they?' asked Nicky.

'Them's the queers and the child molesters,' said Al. 'I'd love to cut their balls off and shove them down their throats, the fucking perverts . . . There's another one! Quick!' Al jumped over the rail, onto the reticulated safety wire for a better view, and shouted: 'Root! Root! Root! You fuckin' root!'

Nicky thought it wise to join in but just as he was about to shout, his heart wouldn't let the words out of his mouth and he felt shame and despair for even contemplating swimming through the dregs by drowning others.

The remands from the ones and twos, after queueing and receiving their dinners through a hatch in a screened counter, ate together in the groundfloor canteen. The canteen was actually a large wooden structure, an adjunct to the old A–wing proper. An observation post built high up into the wall overlooked the room. The warder on duty here had a master control over the television. The canteen doubled as a recreational hall in the evenings between 5.30 and 7.30 and also contained snooker and table-tennis tables.

Once again Nicky attempted to keep his distance. He would have preferred his own society but also needed warning if anyone should suspect him. As he ate his stew his tooth almost broke on something sharp. He was about to examine the foreign body when from out the corner of his eye he noticed at the next table Patterson watching him. So, assuming composure – because the toe-nail in his mouth had a nauseating effect on the contents of his stomach – he inserted it between his upper gum and cheek and finished his meal. He rose from the table with his plate licked clean and rubbed his stomach with evident satisfaction. He beckoned Al for his plate and went to the sinks to do their washing-up.

Back in their cell before 12.30 the three men went to bed, like the rest of the prisoners, for their lunch-time siesta. Nicky took the toenail out of his pocket. It was shaped like the head of an axe and was discoloured down one side.

How did he get nicotine stains on his big toe! He must fucking smoke with his feet! But this is a bad sign, him having it in for me.

At two o'clock the flap on the door was lifted and another count was made. Then bells started to ring as men once again vied to go to the toilet.

'When do we get our parcels?' said Nicky to Al.

'It'll be down in the parcels office on the ones by now. Hit the bell and ask to get out. I want to get a cup of tea anyway.'

About a half-hour later Nicky was let out to get his parcel and Al went to the boiler on the landing for three cups of hot water. On his return journey Nicky met Patterson, who occupied the cell next to him.

'Smickers,' said Patterson, addressing Nicky. 'Did you get any fags in?'

'Eh, yes.'

'Lend's twenty until the tuck shop comes in. I'll fix you up tomorrow.' Patterson had thick, sensuous lips, a bit like Madeline's. He pursed them regularly as if anticipating trouble and his lower lip which hung over his beard appeared chapped like the facets on the rind of a pomegranate.

Nicky gave him one of his two packets but received not a word of thanks. The three men in the Napoleon Suite, Cell 20, A–2, ate Nicky's biscuits along with the tea Al had made. They talked some more about the jail, although it was hard getting anything out of Seán. His trial was just a week or two away. He was hoping to plea-bargain for a two-year sentence. When Al was out of the cell he asked Nicky would he write a letter for him to his wife and Nicky obliged. Seán suddenly came to life and stood watching Nicky turn his speech into sentences.

That evening at association Nicky indicated to the warder in control of the air-lock that he wanted to go to the toilets. The latrines and wash-house were adjacent to each other on the ones and a few men at a time were allowed out to shower and shave if they had a visit early the following morning. Nicky was sitting on the toilet, privacy rationed to just the trunk of the body by a swing door about three feet square. Along the tiled floor crawled a variety of cockroaches examining the lip-end of discarded butts and the cores of apples or bits of bread which littered the corners.

Suddenly the door was kicked in, scaring the heart out of him, followed by two buckets of freezing cold water which came at him like huge punches. Patterson and one of his mates stood laughing at Nicky as he automatically jumped from the seatless, bare ceramic bowl. His jeans and underpants were around his ankles, a piece of crumpled, brown-stained toilet paper was in his right hand and water dripped down his face and jumper. He was a sight.

'What was that for?'

'A wee welcome from the boys.'

When he returned to the canteen a cheer went up. He had just experienced an initiation but he would be careful from now on.

He sat on top of his bunk and composed a very simple letter to his mother about all the kind, new friends he had made. He said that if all went well in court on Friday she'd perhaps see him even before the letter was delivered, 'given that the post office has fallen apart since I left!' But he also added that if he were refused bail she shouldn't worry about not visiting him, and, in fact, he would be suggesting to his daddy that he take just one visit a month.

At about half-past ten Al declared: 'Yes, it's that time again, folks.'

'Not again,' bemoaned Seán. 'It's the same every night.'

'Nature's nature, my friend. It's like sex to women. They gotta have it every night.'

Al put two brown paper bags into his metal bin and squatted over it. The place stank from the warm steam of his faeces. He then lifted out the bags, twisted the top, stood up on his bed and threw the bag out the window where it landed and splattered in the exercise yard below.

'There's another mystery parcel for the cunts tomorrow,' said Al with satisfaction.

'What do you mean?' asked Nicky.

'The work crews for our yard are all bullroots from D-wing, sentenced men. It's their job to lift the mysteries every morning,' he said with a satisfied smile.

18

'THE SCREW'S JUST AFTER telling me that Seán got whacked with three,' said Nicky, standing on the threshold of the cell with a mug of hot water in either hand and with one ear on the landing to hear who was being called for a visit. He had a huge black eye, like a panda.

'He'll be sick,' said Al. 'Must send his wife a sympathy card! I've kept her address,' he smiled. 'Ach, he wasn't the worst. Left us his teabags. Three years is still a short sentence. He'll get it knocked down to two on appeal. He'll be over in D-wing. We'll probably get him as an orderly after a while.'

Two weeks earlier Nicky had been to the High Court. Beneath the ornate ceiling and huge chandeliers, in front of a bewigged judge sitting austerely below a shield bearing the legend *Dieu et mon droit,* the lawyer representing the DPP, Ray Collins, rehearsed the deposition and innuendo he had made in the lower court. Mr Baker was cogent in the points he made concerning the application for bail. To refute him, Smith called upon Detective Inspector Wainwright who stunned Nicky with the aggressive glance he shot him. Inquiries were continuing . . . great danger of witnesses being interfered with.

There was no doubt about it, thought Nicky, but that Gareth's father had a powerful and evil influence over the lawkeepers. The judge had no time for the defendant and dismissed the application. Nicky turned and saw his father in the public gallery with his head between his hands. Then they both waved.

Afterwards Baker had come down to the cells and said he was very sorry but that Nicky could see that they were up against it. They could make another application later when there was a change of circumstances: for example, if the DPP delayed supplying the results of the forensic tests or the depositions.

Nicky had also been allowed a fifteen-minute visit with his father. His dad had returned to work. It wasn't so bad. He wasn't telling Nicky any lies this time – people had asked for him. Nobody could believe he'd been charged, never mind imprisoned. Nicky hoped that his cheerful response to his father's dissimulation looked convincing. But he returned to jail as if he'd been sentenced to death. There, Al told him a letter had arrived. It was actually a card and he removed it nervously from its envelope. It was from Sonny:

> Dear Nicky,
> You do get about! This is just a few lines to let you know you are in our thoughts and –
> [Here, the censor's stamp obscured some words]
> – you in a few books and magazines. If there's anything you need don't hesitate to ask. I would also like to visit you if you want to send a pass out to the shop.
> Take care.
> Sonny

He had cherished the card. Then he thought, fuck, if they saw Sonny in the visits they would think I was a fruit. He blushed to the roots of his hair at his own unworthiness. I didn't mean it, Sonny. I didn't mean it. But you know what I mean. He had to be careful. One man was removed on a stretcher during the week, having been kicked unconscious on suspicion that he had squealed about drug deals on the wing.

The company of Al was good insurance. He was held in a certain awe because of his long criminal history. He was intelligent and ruthless. The last time he had been in jail he bit off a man's nose during a fight. During a gang war outside he also once took a saw to a rival's leg and even though the police arrived at the wood yard and saved the man, the victim made no formal complaint. But Al was disgusted with the Mickey Mouse charge on which he found himself currently incarcerated. He knew that Nicky was so amateurish he was a joke, but nevertheless he liked him. Nicky grew to like him also and wondered was his environment starting to harden him. He realised one night that he'd told Al all there was to know about the movement of cash in the post office. A half-hour later Al laughed and, impressively, added greater and more accurate detail.

So Nicky became a jailbird, acclimatised to the pattern of lights on at 7, beds made by 7.30, requests taken at 7.45, breakfast at 8, and the rest of the monotonous daily routine. He no longer heard the pressure valves sneeze when the airlocks were opened or the heating pipes crepitate in the middle of the night.

Patterson was pushy with him at every opportunity and three days previously had put one of the prisoners, Robert Cranmere, up to a fight. Cranmere had been one of the robbers in the base with Nicky.

'Fuck, but you certainly knocked his bollocks in,' laughed Al triumphantly, when Nicky returned from three days in the punishment block, his eye now black. He had been adjudicated by Deputy-Governor Harris, who sentenced him to fourteen days loss of remission of sentence should he be convicted, fourteen days loss of all privileges, including parcels and evening association, and fourteen days cellular confinement and loss of radio. Since there were no empty cells they just let him stay with Al when he returned to the wing.

'Near broke my knuckles,' smiled Nicky, as he set down the mugs of hot water. Nicky had fought like a savage when Cranmere poked him in the chest just once too often on the landing. The warders had to use their batons to get Nicky off.

Nicky and Cranmere had ended up in adjacent cells 'on the boards' – as the prisoners called the punishment block – but they didn't communicate through the pipes or out the windows. They were exercised separately for an hour each day in a tiny dank yard, where it took thirteen seconds to walk from one wall to the other. A single chair was screwed to the ground should a prisoner feel tired but it was more likely to make him feel that he was to be bound and shot. Nicky walked up and down in such a fashion that the two guards had to keep shifting back towards a slow-dripping overflow pipe which they didn't notice. Eventually, the water caught one of them on the back of the trouser leg and Nicky chuckled.

Presently, he said to Al: 'Quick, put your ear to the wall.'

'I can hear nothing. What are we listening for?'

'Shoosh, any second now . . .'

The noise of Patterson retching and the faint sound of something splashing on his bare cell floor could be made out. Nicky tittered. Oh yes, Patterson had finished his tea OK and found the clippings of Nicky's ten toe-nails tied in a little ribbon of denim thread at the bottom of his mug.

He told Al what he had done and his cellmate roared with laughter. Macho Patterson, hearing the laughter, couldn't acknowledge even with a curse that one had been put over him. When Al recovered he told Nicky to be careful, that he wouldn't always be around and that Patterson had a long reach. He said that Patterson had once gouged out a fella's eye.

Each evening Nicky had some privacy when Al went down to the canteen for two hours' association. He was also alone when his cellmate was on visits with his glamorous girlfriend. Nicky went around for a half-hour with one eye closed, seeing if he could read or put his finger exactly on marks on the wall or put his spoon into his mug. He tried to lift his cup and found his coordination wasn't too bad - just a bit off to the left. If I lose the other eye it'll be just off a bit to the right. During these periods when he was alone he would lie on top of his bunk smoking roll-up after roll-up, staring at the ceiling, amazed at his simple life which without warning had branched into something incredibly complex and dangerous. He worried about Gareth constantly. He thought about the diary entries and how passionate and obsessed the young boy had quickly become, short though the occasions were that they had been together. He felt the same way. He loved and missed him. He begged the future to reveal itself, to hint at a happiness comprising their fates coinciding. He had drifted through a wasteland of several years before a vital new chapter in his life had opened only for the next pages to have been ripped out.

He drew joy from the memories of their times together. He had no regrets. If life with its abundance of tragedy, cruelty, suffering and violence held any meaning and purpose it did so in terms of the magnificence of love and its experience. He had felt the pulse of its greatness that day on the mountain with Gareth. The entire universe had appeared in the glint of Gareth's eye, the power of all creation in the leap of the heartbeat he had felt at a certain moment in their happiness. He knew he should be satisfied with having glimpsed something so pure and perfect, which many never ever experienced. But he craved more. This life was the only thing we were certain of. What we hold is all that we have. He wished he was an innocent child again, believing in worlds within worlds, mysteries, miracles.

He thought of Madeline and laughed. He could understand her. She was after pleasure in the here and now also – it was her security. Her mother had died young and she was taking no chances in missing out on experiences. She skated on the surface of thin ice with all the gaiety and nervous excitement of a kid. It was a great attitude, he supposed. She was going so fast that her speed would take her over any crack in the ice that would drown most others. She had earmarked Nicky from years earlier – or so she had claimed; took him when the time was right, saw his limitations, tired of him quickly – what superb judgement! – and moved on. Wasn't that her prerogative? He was puzzled by her material kindness. Perhaps, generosity and ruthlessness, he thought, *can* cohabit. Look at Al. No, he didn't regret having been with her. And the widow? The widow! What a gag. Coulter would have a scream if he was here now and I was to sit and tell him what I'd been up to since he left me. Wonder would he be jealous because of Madeline or because of Gareth? What a world we live in. What a world we create.

'I leave the day after tomorrow,' said Al.

'It's come so fast,' said Nicky with real regret. 'Are you sure you'll get out?'

'Yes, I'm walking, no problem. I'll leave you my radio, I'll see the class officer and get ownership transferred on to your file. You can have anything else that you want. I'll be giving the rest away tomorrow. I've ordered extra snout from the tuck shop, which should keep you going until you're off punishment.'

'I'm going to miss you,' said Nicky.

'Sure when I shoot all your witnesses you'll walk it too!' he laughed. 'Seriously, though. You watch yourself. Patterson's crew will certainly have a go at you now. Kill the first one you can.'

Nicky smiled. 'I couldn't kill anybody.'

'That's what I thought when I was a kid. But you know what I mean. Get the boot in first, the way you did with Cranmere. Generates respect. See those men, they're all tramps. I've filled you in on the lot of them. Not an ounce of loyalty or honour.'

Al had certainly been Nicky's mentor, had filled him in on every prisoner of any significance, all the scandals, who he thought – but couldn't prove – were informers, which screws were bastards, what deputy-governors were jockeying for positions, who had their hands in the till, every small detail about the workings of the jail, every detail about the lay-out and geography of the prison.

That Thursday night Al returned fifteen minutes early from association, covered in that day's food slops and laughing hysterically. 'Give's my towel and wash-gear,' he shouted to Nicky through the flap. The warder unlocked the door and Nicky handed him his toiletries.

'Normally, I don't go in for this crap! The lads . . . they ambushed me. A going-away present,' he laughed.

He went and showered and returned soon after. Then, when they were all locked up for the night he said to Nicky: 'Fancy a bit of blow? I tried to get a bottle of vodka as well but the screw let me down. Here you are.'

Nicky took the reefer, lit up, drew on it hard, sending the smoke deep into his lungs, held it for as long as he comfortably could and then exhaled.

'That's good,' he said, smiling.

The guard switched out the lights at eleven but Nicky and Al talked on into the night. The security lamps around the yard illuminated the back wall of their cell so that they could still make out each others' faces in the gloaming.

Al spoke about his life of crime since he was a youth. He made it sound respectable. Nicky didn't know what to make of it; he was sick of judgements. But he did ask him about his attitudes. 'Al? Why do you hate the bullroots?'

'They're the scum of the earth. When I was a kid one of them had a go at me. So let's change the subject . . .'

When Al left the following morning Nicky felt very lonely. After slopping out, and brushing and mopping his cell he was locked up. Outside it was a bitterly cold but sunny December day. Chilled sunbeams chinked through the bars of his window, spreading shadows across the wall like fingers raised in farewell.

A warder unlocked the door at a quarter to twelve with the good news that Al had been released and the bad news that since Nicky was still on punishment he had to surrender the radio.

He joined the rest of the men in the dining-hall for dinner. During his meal he kept getting hit on the back of the head with chips but could never turn quickly enough to catch the culprit. Eventually he lost his temper, kicked back his chair, jumped to his feet and shouted: 'The fucker that's doing that has the balls of a nit! Stand up and fight! Stand up and fight!'

Immediately, everyone cheered, 'Yee-ha!' – prison argot for expressing triumphalism or satisfaction. They started banging their tables, knowing they had provoked him, and the cutlery and plates danced towards and in some cases over the edges of the tables.

'Yee-ha!' screamed Patterson, grinning, and again the banging increased.

Nicky smiled to show that he could take it and sat down. Only one more chip was thrown at him that lunchtime and he didn't flinch.

After lock-up that night he was doing press-ups on the floor when he heard one of Patterson's cronies at his lark out the door. Sometimes the banter generally would be funny; often it was cruel.

He heard references to 'your favourite Sunday dinner', and 'me and your daddy miss you', and 'Irene Coulter rang and asked after you', and he realised that what was being read out was a letter from his mother that he had never received. He bit his tongue rather than show weakness. He wondered how he could compromise, what price he would have to pay to get in with Patterson and have the dogs called off. But he knew that Patterson would never accept him and, more importantly, that he could never swallow the gangster and his bullying ways.

Some days he was given peace but most days one of the factions thought he was good value for a slagging or some practical joke although they were still uncertain of his measure. By mid-December Nicky found that he was walking the yard on his own whilst the others went around in groups of three or four.

He made another court appearance, was further remanded, and had another visit with Mr Baker,who said he was confident that they'd be going to trial in late January on unlawful imprisonment charges solely. At least that was some relief, said Nicky. Baker asked him how he was finding jail: he said he was surviving.

The next day he went down to the dining-hall for breakfast as usual, having collected his milk carton from the ledge above his cell door. He got a plate of cornflakes from the warder at the hatch and sat down at a table. He poured the milk over his cereal but it came out like tapioca and stank. He checked the date: it seemed correct. He looked at it again. Someone had scratched out the old date and carefully printed a fresh date. The milk was six days old. They are so fucking petty. He decided that he would never take milk again. He drank a pint of black tea. Patterson rose from his table, rubbed his stomach with satisfaction, the way Nicky had once done, walked over and sat down beside him.

'Smickers, we're belatedly raising funds for Children in Need in the run-up to Christmas. Everybody's decided to chip in a score of quid. I'm the local organiser.'

The whole dining-hall was watching.

'We'll be looking for your twenty pounds before Friday.' Patterson put his repulsive arm around Nicky's shoulder.

'Take your arm off me,' whispered Nicky.

'Twenty-five quid.'

'Take your arm off my shoulder.'

'Thirty quid.'

Nicky pushed him off but Patterson revealed a razor blade between his fingers and ran it across Nicky's lower lip like a dragonfly skimming a stream. It smoothly sliced his skin and the blood came out and looked at the horror of the world. Nicky punched Patterson but two others jumped on and one swung a dixie with full force into Nicky's face, breaking one of his front teeth and sending him to the ground. He felt like saying: listen lads, I'm just a postman, why are you doing this to me? They knew to stop before the warder in the observation post pulled the alarm bell. Fights were common but a prolonged fight was usually a sign of murder.

Injured, he limped out of the canteen holding his mouth, blood dripping between his fingers, as a large minority of prisoners yelled, 'Yee-ha!' and stamped the floor.

The principal officer met him when he returned from the hospital after getting his wound stitched. He asked him what had happened and who had attacked him. Nicky said he didn't know.

That day, instead of going to the yard for exercise, he opted to stay in his cell. Later, he went down to the dining-hall but instead of joining the others at the tables he took his dinner, and his tea, back up to the twos where in the quiet of his cell he had some peace. After the 8.30 lock-up he put a piece of tin foil on the end of his fork, removed the bulb and stuck the fork into the holder until the foil connected with the points. The lights fused in six cells, including Patterson's. Doors were kicked and banged and shouts went up for the night guard. Nicky giggled and he thought his laugh sounded funny through his one front tooth. He replaced his bulb. It took the night guard about twenty minutes to establish the cause of the uproar, then go back down to the ones and change the fuse. His boots could be counted coming back up the seventeen wooden steps of the metal stairway. He lifted the flap on Nicky's cell but the prisoner was lying on his bed reading a book. When he had gone Nicky jumped up and fused the lights again. There'll be no fucking love letters written tonight.

Eventually the guard gave up and the six cells were left in darkness.

Another day Nicky was charged with refusing to obey an order when his class officer told him to mop up a spillage on the landing which he hadn't caused. He was served with a charge sheet and summoned to yet another adjudication.

'Prisoner! Attention!'

Nicky stood between two guards with his hands in his pockets. They were forcibly taken out and so he put them behind his back.

Deputy-Governor Harris looked up.

'You with us again, Smith. You're quite a subversive in this jail, a bad influence. Probably think you're a hard man. Let me tell you, you'll not be a hard man with me. Smile all you like, sonny boy, you're only making things worse for yourself.'

Harris's eyes bulged as he spoke. He was about forty years of age with a small moustache. He talked a lot but in between his silences he thrust his tongue into the wall of his left cheek as if he was a schoolboy sucking a gobstopper. When Nicky had previously appeared before him – for having a haircut without first seeking permission and for not being properly attired at the subsequent adjudication – he had detected a *frisson* of excitement run through Harris as he passed sentence. He struck Nicky as a sadist yet someone probably so sanctimonious that he didn't allow his kids to whistle on Sunday.

'Do you wish to have any legal representation?'

'Yes.'

'Overruled. I believe you're capable of understanding and answering the charge yourself.'

Evidence was heard that Nicky was ordered to mop the spillage outside his cell and had refused, claiming it was urine from another prisoner's pot. Nicky was asked if this were true. He agreed. He was sentenced to loss of tuckshop and evening association for seven days to run consecutively with his previous loss of privileges. The worst part of the punishment was that he was deprived of tobacco.

Before he left the governor's office Nicky stated that he wished to see the Board of Visitors about being continually victimised and unduly punished. Harris advised him against the request – if his complaints were not upheld he could be charged with maligning prison officers. Then he stuck his tongue in his cheek and his eyes bulged. Nicky ignored the less-than-subtle threat.

With the decorations up on the landings and a Christmas tree on the ones, with the Salvation Army brass band and choir carrying out their annual performance in the circle, Nicky decided that the atmosphere was perhaps right for him to strike a truce and begin taking his breakfast and dinner again in the company of the other men. So he returned to the dining-hall. He was ignored except by new prisoners who hadn't realised he was *persona non grata.*

On the second day he sat alone, eating a piece of white bread and margarine, drinking black tea, staring into space. It was just after 8 a.m. and someone shouted to the warder in the observation post to change the channel on the television. Men rose from the tables with their plates and carried them to the sinks. Others played pool even at this early hour. There was a hubbub of conversation. At the sliding grill at the far end of the dining-hall a few men stood talking and laughing: they were too far away for Nicky to catch the joke.

Suddenly, behind him, a hooded prisoner leaped up on a table and slapped a wet newspaper across the bullet-proof glass of the observation post in the wall. Nicky turned to see what was happening and felt a noose clamp around his neck. He shot his hands to his throat as it was being tightened and his fingers got caught inside the deadly collar.

Someone shouted: 'Smith raped a child! The bastard fucked a child! That's why he's in here!' Chairs and tables were overturned in the rush to get at him. An angry sea of voices cursed and vilified him and provided a tidal wave of support for his killers. He was kicked and punched and his shirt was ripped from his back. The strips of sheet, knotted together into one long rope, were thrown over one of the wooden eaves in the ceiling and the hooded executioners winched with all their might until Nicky's feet were kicking and frantically running through empty space. As they hurriedly tied the end of the sheet to the bars through one of the broken windows, someone threw a bowl of porridge into his face which splashed across his chest, someone else a cup of hot tea. The warder in the post was screaming through the Tannoy for the prisoners to immediately vacate the dining-hall. He hit the alarm and the bells began ringing.

Prisoners rushed the grille when it opened and the warder there abandoned his post and pushed his way through to where Nicky was dangling. The breakfast guard ran up the room also and whilst one of them wrapped himself around Nicky's legs and took his weight the other used a cigarette lighter to burn through the sheet. The prisoners caught between the air-lock were chanting, 'Yee-ha! Yee-ha! Bullroot can fly! Bullroot can fly!' Then they booed as Nicky was cut down and began coughing and vomiting on the floor. Getting his fingers under the noose had almost certainly added a crucial minute to his life.

All the prisoners in the canteen at the time of 'the incident' – Deputy-Governor Harris had refused to call it attempted murder because the sheet hadn't been greased; he claimed it was just 'a scare' – were put on general lock-up. Patterson took a judicial review of the arbitrary nature of the punishment and the court ordered the administration to reverse its decision.

Nicky was kept overnight in the prison hospital for observation. Upon his return to the wing, Harris interviewed him in depth about the rumours that his charges were really related to sexual offences. Nicky denied them. Harris said that if they proved true he would be moved into the special unit on the threes as quick as he could 'unzip his flies!' He would be making enquiries with the outside authorities and meanwhile Nicky-the-troublemaker was to be placed in a cell on the threes, a former storeroom at the end of the wing which was being prepared but which was just outside the special unit. 'A sort of half-way house,' smiled Harris.

19

Dear Mammy and Daddy,
Just a few lines to say that everything is fine. Time is flying by, isn't it? Some of the lads were saying the other night
that time goes in even quicker when there's no visits. The
visits over the holidays are packed with noisy kids so I
think it best if I don't see you until the New Year and we'll
set a date in my next letter. OK? Am reading some good
books. My cellmate got released and I'm now on my
own.
Love,
Nicky

NICKY FELT A LITTLE BIT more secure in his new cell and
didn't mind that it was cold and damp and so close to the boiler
house that one could hear the roar of air and oil burning in
the furnace each time the thermostat went on. The less he left
his cell the happier he was although he probably would have
been better off in the special unit regardless of what society of
men it held. But he was terrified of being transferred there –
as if the transition would suddenly turn what he felt for Gareth
into something incredibly sordid and shameful. On his first

days in A–wing he had heard the whistling of the tune 'Danny Boy' and looked up to the threes to see a harmless old man with a mop and bucket. But that harmless old man turned his stomach and frightened him so much that his hands visibly shook and Al had even asked him what was the matter.

Since the attempted hanging he had been seized with nightmares. He left his cell only to slop-out and fill his water-gallon. He turned down the offer of the statutory hour's daily exercise because it meant being exposed to danger travelling to and from the special yard. His meals were brought to his cell but he was afraid to eat all but bread in case someone poisoned him. Fortunately, his former cell mate Seán O'Neill was now on orderly duties on the threes and often gave out the dinners. When he was in charge the food was safe. He also supplied Nicky with the lifeblood of tobacco.

I shouldn't have saved myself. I always said I would kill myself before I would allow my mother and father to be disgraced or Gareth to appear in court. And yet we are half-way there, the public accusation must come shortly. But still I hang on to hope and am scared stiff that these ones here'll kill me.

He climbed up to the recess high in the wall and released the cleat on his window. The window on horizontal hinges fell away from the casement and the bars towards him. Fat flakes of snow silently fell across the city. He put out his hand and caught a few of the stars carrying the light of heaven to earth and he smiled a small smile, this paradox of human nature, humour in the midst of woe, as he remembered Robin and him lying in thick snow and making angels. Then he returned to jail with a thud.

'Root! Root! Smith's a fuckin' root!' They started up again, the prisoners below him on the ones and twos.

'Bulllllroooot!'

'Root! Root! Root!'

'Hang, hang, hang the bastard!'

'Roo-ute; Roo-ute!'

They wouldn't let him be. He stepped down from the window and stuffed some sheets of toilet paper in his ears. But they didn't diminish the noise, only made him look ridiculous, scarecrow-like. He looked through the tiny gap in the jamb in the act of coming closer to his invisible accusers.

'Root! Root! Root!' They peeled back his skin.

'Root!'

'Nicky Poofter, a willie woofter!'

'Yehhhhh!'

'You bastards, you bastards! Who's a poofter? Who's a bull-root! You're the bullroots!' he screamed back. The tirade of abuse from below became more truculent and unrelenting.

'Bulllllrooooot! Bulllllrooooot!' Sing-song.

'Ouch! Ouch! Yehhhhh!'

Fuck off, would yous.

A warder came along the twos for a count, lifting up the flaps, checking each cell. At some doors he paused for idle banter, took possession of a newspaper or a pornographic magazine through the jamb and delivered it through the side of another door further along. Nicky saw down to the twos that he was at Patterson's flap, talking and laughing.

When he came up to the threes for the count he did the special unit first before lifting the flap on Nicky's door. Nicky had taken a few steps back. The warder saw the tissues protruding from his ears, shook his head and, without warning, switched off his light.

'Turn the light on! I'm supposed to be innocent until proven guilty! Turn the fucking lights on or I'll . . . I'll . . .'

'Or he'll . . . Stuff! Stuff! Stuff your kids!' There were cheers of laughter at the punch line followed by the doors being banged. Nicky's light was quietly switched back on and he whispered, 'Thank you sir, thank you.'

'Bumboy! Bumboy!'

Nicky began to boil with fury again. His thoughts stampeded, tripped over each other and became dammed in his head. His reasoning was choked by the continuing chants and he would have gone screeching up the wall by the quick of his bitten nails if it offered some relief and distraction. He head-butted his door, scuffing and reddening his brow, and his whole frame shook convulsively. He struggled to control his respiration.

'Buuuu-ullll! . . . Buuuu-ulllll!'

'Rooooo-ute! . . . Rooooo-ute!'

Nicky conjured up the scene of an armed robbery. He knew this scene would be immediately recognisable to the men who had been in the same police station as him and later in the base on that first night. The other prisoners would also soon get the picture. They knew that the driver of the getaway car had been forced by a traffic warden to move away up the street from the front of the small bank after the others had rushed into the building. There had also been unflattering rumours of the gang's conduct in police custody.

Nicky stood close to the gap in his door through which his voice could travel the depths of the wing.

Nicky was now in the bank.

' "Freeze! Don't move and nobody'll get hurt . . . Just try it mate! Just make my day! That's better. Joe! . . . aw shit! We agreed not to use our names! Joe, watch these ones!" '

Nicky changed his voice.

' "What did I tell you about names, you fuckin' dick! Check those drawers." '

' "Joe! Joe! The car, the fuckin' car's gone!" '

'Bullroot's good with his voice,' said one prisoner on the twos to his cellmate. 'Shoosh! Listen! You couldn't pay for this!'

' "Ding-a-ling-a-ling-a-ling-a-ling-a-ling . . ." '

' "The alarm! Quick, let's get outahere!" '

' "Whiaow-Whiaow-oh-Whiaow-oh-Whiaow-oh-Whiaow!" '

' "It's the fuzz! Quickly, out the side door!" '

Nicky's voice now became drollish but supremely confident. He was none other than Detective-Inspector Derek Wainwright.

Though the gang had successfully fled the immediate scene and dumped their weapons, three of them had been arrested shortly afterwards.

' "Okay Richard, I've read you your rights. We got your driver and he's admitted everything. He's looking a deal." '

' "My brother-in-law, Peter, would never have squealed . . . [gasp]." '

Nicky pushed his licence with the burlesque right over the top.

' "Thanks, Dickhead Cranmere. We didn't know Pete was driving on this job!" '

'Fuck up, bullroot, you bastard!' screamed Cranmere, but he was drowned out by cheers and laughter.

Wainwright crushed the empty styrofoam cup from which he had drunk his coffee and threw it into a nearby bin. '"We know you were on the bank job, Joe. We found hairs on the balaclava which genetically match yours . . ."

'"But that day I wore a wig . . . aw shit!"'

'Root! You're a dead man!' shouted ugly Joe.

Nicky now visualised a different scene: the bully – remand prisoner John Thorpe, self-made widower – tumbling home to his pregnant wife, Liz.

The bricky's boots were covered in wet, clinging mud. Nothing like caking them in the squelch of mother earth, like getting jam over your face when you were three or four. He had one hundred and eighty quid coming off the site at lunchtime before his horses fell and he had ten quid left as he shambled out of the pub. Nicky kicked his cell door a tremendous bang and Thorpe-the-bricky had slammed his front door shut. Nicky pictured his wife, a consumptive Olive Oyl lookalike. She used to have beautiful teeth but now she was trying to get used to dentures. She looked at the hall. She had already scrubbed it three times because of what the kids had walked in. She looked at it: filthy again! He couldn't even have bothered to clean his boots on the mat. She had been warned by her mom but she thought she could have reformed him . . . if her cracked ribs could stand the course.

Nicky's mouth was twisted and he gruffly slurred and slavered.

'"Liz! Where's my dinner! Where's my fuckin' dinner, you skinny fat bastard!"'

'Bullroot's great crack! Thorpey hasn't caught on yet!'

She had been through this so many times before. It was the preamble to a smack across the face. Nicky's heart palpitated like a captured sparrow's but he drew upon the last vestiges of her courage: '"It's . . . it's in the oven. Where . . . where do you think it is?"' she piped out.

'"Don't you answer me back with your cheek! Get it out here!"'

'"Get it out," is right!' cackled someone on the twos but he was told by others to shut up and listen.

'"Mary, get your father's dinner out of the oven, child."

'"I told *you* to get it, Flagpole. *You*! Now get it!"'

As Nicky ferociously kicked the cell door a number of times, he had her shout: '"Please don't hit me! I can't take much more! Watch the baby, John! Please don't hit me! I'll get it! Ouch! I'll get it, aghhhhh!"' he screamed pathetically.

'"Daddy, daddy, daddy! Please leave mummy alone, please don't hit her! Please, please, I'll get your dinner!"'

Nicky stopped. There was a second or two of uncertain silence and he wondered had he shamed them.

'Bullroot!' shouted Thorpe. 'I'm going to hang you right!'

Then it seemed as if the entire jail was in chorus again as they chanted: 'Root! Root! Root! You're a fucking root!'

It just went on and on and on and Nicky turned in circles but couldn't escape the noise. He pulled the hair on the crown of his head till lumps came out. He began to howl. He cried bitter tears. He cried until his crying turned to uncontrollable sobs.

'Bulllllroo-oot's crying! Bulllllroo-oot's crying!'

'Crybaby! Crybaby! Crybaby!'

He fell to the floor in a heap, in despair as if at death's door.

Oh God, please, please help me. If you exist, have pity. I never meant to do anything wrong. Never. It was the way I was made. I never meant to do any harm. I am so, so afraid. Please forgive me . . . please help me . . .

The chanting was trailing off, either finally or for an intermission, and as the silence fell Nicky heard a tiny crackle as something hit the ground just inches from his face and knees. It was a cockroach and it ran to find refuge. He wondered where it came from. They usually came up through the floor close to the outside wall, making their way through catacombs in the old mortar. He looked upwards. In the corner of the coved ceiling there was a tiny dark spot. He watched, fascinated. The spot seemed to become larger and, like a caterpillar devouring a leaf, out of this munched hole the head and spindly antennae of a big curious cockroach appeared. It slid, tumbled out and fell to the floor like the first one. Then took off like a skateboard. Nicky jumped on top of his bedside locker and with his plastic knife gouged out some pebbles of old plaster and then loose cement from between the bricks in the ceiling. It was tough but it held promise. He was feverish with excitement. He knew that there was a connecting space above the ceilings of the cells on the threes – Al had told him. If he could get into that space he could crawl through to the circle and over to C–wing which was closed down for renovation, its far gable covered in a lattice work of scaffolding. Over there he would have to take his chances that he could knock through the slates in that deserted part of the jail and get on to the roof. There would be no time for a dry run because in addition to the night guard carrying out a check his cell was also searched daily. Once he dug through he would have to go. This could be a way out! Freedom! And he thought no further than that. Escaping this jail, its Pattersons, its Harrisons, their attempts to destroy and murder him.

'Yee-ha!' shouted Nicky out the door. 'Yee-fucking-ha!'

As they climbed into their beds or went back to writing their love letters they thought: he's fuckin' flipped at last. Bullroot's flew over!

Nicky was hungry. He prepared tinder from sheets of toilet paper carefully twisted into small logs in such a fashion that they would burn slowly without smouldering excessively. Then he pulled back his fusty blankets and faded sheets and leaned his mattress lengthwise over the head of the bed and on to the wall. He upturned his metal wastepaper bin – his 'barbecue tray' – and on this platform placed some of the logs in a pyramid. Its pinnacle would reach to just a few inches below the exposed reticulated wire spring of his bed – his 'grill' – when he slid the barbecue tray under. He tried his lighter. The flint sparked but the wick was too dry and he almost despaired. He removed the barrel and blew into the cotton wadding thus forcing the residue of petrol and fumes towards the wick. He struck the flint wheel several more times until a flame-bud appeared which he nursed until he lit a taper and from it the toilet-paper coals of the barbecue. On the flat spring he set a milk carton filled with water and then slid the bin below it, occasionally feeding and stoking the fire. The barbecue's flames were modest but within minutes the base and sides of the carton, now brittle, had blackened without melting and, within, chains of bubbles, swaying like a sea-anemone in a warm current, burst onto the surface with a boil.

'Yee-ha!' Nicky cheered again. It would soon be supper time. He delicately removed the carton and poured the hot water over the tea bag in his cup and placed it on the thick heating pipe along the bottom of the back wall. On the grill he now put his bread to toast. The cell had become quite smoky and he laughed.

He withdrew the bin and dropped a paper bag snuffer over the dying embers, threw back half his mattress for a seat and then unwrapped a dollop of margarine and spread it over his burnt toast which he then merrily began munching. His tea now brewed, he wrung the bag and flicked it from the end of a pink plastic spoon out the window.

'Aghhhhhhhhhh . . .' he shouted, trailing off, imagining the fading scream of a suicide as he hit the ground three floors below. He swirled the steaming black tea in his pint mug, lapping up all the pimples of condensation on the inside. He was engrossed by a snake of flickering light wriggling on the surface. As it settled he saw the dull reflection of the underside of his large nose and small nostrils, his split lip and the gap of his missing tooth.

He looked up at the tiny hole in the ceiling and winked.

20

THE SCRATCHED AND DENTED brown metal door yawned open.

'Visit,' declared the warder.

'Visit? I don't have a visit.'

'You have now.'

'Is it a legal?'

'No, it's an ordinary. I'll call back in five minutes when you're ready.'

Visitors were like postmen. They could bring good or bad news, yet they were a vital service to the prisoner – a great tribute to the prisoner. Someone is giving up their time, making arrangements, perhaps having to reschedule another appointment, preparing themselves, thinking about the prisoner, gathering news, rehearsing anecdotes, travelling a journey, laying out money, becoming a confederate and suspect, waiting to be searched, and then called to a room for those precious, anxious, fumbling, thirty minutes.

Nicky became flustered and dressed quickly. Fortunately he hadn't got too much time to think or worry. His door opened and the warder said: 'Right.'

He gingerly peeked into the landing. There were plenty of warders about. His escort was waiting at the class office at the other end of the grilles of the special unit through which he had to travel a short distance to the stairs. He was wearing his black shoes for combat purposes, rather than his runners. The twos and threes were fairly empty. Of course, he thought, they're out in the yard. He came down the stairs without any bother or abuse – just a few glares from prisoners who were, like him, surprised by an unexpected call for a visit and had come in from the yard to dress hastily.

At the end of the ones, Harris came out of the PO's office. 'Smith! A word with you.'

Nicky stepped into the PO's office.

'We should have new accommodation for you today,' he smiled.

'What do you mean?' said Nicky, anxiously. I've a fucking escape on and am going over the wall tonight! You'd almost think he knew!

'Well, Smith, the governor, Mr King, has spoken to the office of the DPP and, surprise, surprise, there's more to your little charges than meets the eye. Isn't that so? Any day now you could be brought out to court. You shouldn't be in with the ordinary prisoners, should you. You belong in the special unit along with your own kind. I'm sure the board of visitors will even agree with me on that – for your own protection, understand,' he smiled. 'The BOV will be in this morning to hear your complaints against the staff. I look forward to that. We've a file on you that thick. Have a good visit.'

Nicky felt as if he had been punched stupid. It looked as if he was going to be charged after all and he was going to be moved into the secure unit where the prisoners were monitored regularly in case of suicide attempts and where the least unusual noise – like the ceiling being removed! – would be snitched on. He felt drained as he entered the visits.

As he approached the box he had been allocated his visitor rose from the seat. It was Gerard and he looked pleased to see him.

'Gerard! Gerard! What a surprise!'

As they shook hands, Gerard pulled Nicky towards him and embraced him. It was a significant gesture of friendship and Nicky, despite his misfortune, appreciated the wealth of human kindness.

'Oh Nicky, what have the bastards done to you? Look at your face – and your neck!'

'I've had a bit of a rough time,' laughed Nicky, almost crying he was that glad to see a friendly face.

'Why didn't you call me back, Nicky. I left you a number of messages? Anyway, it's water under the bridge now. First things first. I've forty quid in my mouth for you. Just a sec. I can't talk properly. There, that's better. Money's always handy in jail.' He looked to see where was the warder patrolling the aisle, bent back, stuck his hand down the front of his trousers, removed a package and furtively passed it to Nicky. 'You may put that between the cheeks of your arse. I was once here myself! I heard you were on punishment and I didn't know whether you were getting smokes. That'll keep you going for a bit.'

'Gerard, you're great!'

'OK. Now listen. Gareth phoned from New York . . .'

'Gareth!' Nicky's heart leaped.

'Yes. He's there with his mother. He's been seriously ill for some time. He sends his regards. He phoned from a hospital clinic. He told me to tell you that he thinks about you day and night. Mrs Williams has left her husband. Gareth says he's made no statement against you, he'll not be testifying in court and not to worry. His father's a bastard and has been behind everything. Forced him into psychiatry after your arrest. But Mrs Williams and Gareth fled. They went to her sister's over in America. Nicky, that man's a raving lunatic, by the sound of things.'

Nicky was full of excitement and could hardly speak. He made Gerard repeat everything.

'How did Gareth contact you? How did he know to?'

'It seems you told him about me.'

'That's right! Of course!'

'I got another call from him yesterday. I don't want to worry you unnecessarily but he seems to be very ill. He coughed the entire conversation, became very tired and a nurse ended the conversation.'

Nicky became grave for a few seconds.

'Gerard. Thanks for bringing this news. And listen. I am sorry for fighting with you. From the bottom of my heart thank you for not judging me.'

'Nicky, Nicky! You owe me no apology. You did me no wrong, except you damaged the stick you bought me! But listen, I shouldn't have said what I said that day. I apologise. The world's crazy, as I'm sure you've discovered. But what makes it go around? Eh? Love. Or so they say. Years ago I fell in love, you know,' he laughed. 'It was before my accident. I fell in love and it was brilliant. Sheer heaven. But it was a while before I could do anything about it. She was about nineteen, very sweet, full of life and passion. Every conversation with her, every little joke, only thickened the plot and I began to just wonder if it was possible that despite the obstacles one day she'd agree to go out with me. I harboured this fantasy, was patient with it for many years. I hesitated in asking her in case she said no and in case I lost the dream – because, you see, the dream itself was something I lived off. Well, eventually I asked her, even though by this time I'd had my accident and my leg was banjaxed. When I'd been in hospital she had sent me flowers and a lovely letter. Then, one day after my wife had left the ward, she arrived! When I asked her if she would go out with me – her eyes lit up. She really liked me, you see! She asked me about my relations with my wife and I told her that I was very, very unhappy which was, in fact, true. I'm separated now, Nicky, by the way.

'So, she agreed to see me and it was perfect, absolutely perfect, and it lasted over two years. But often during those two years she broke it off. But then we'd get back together again and for a few months my life would be wonderful. You know what I'm going to say next, don't you?'

'I haven't a clue.' Nicky just wanted to go back to hearing Gerard's account of his conversations with Gareth all over again, in case he remembered something new, a sentence or a word even.

'Then you came on the scene.'

'Me?'

'Yes. You and Madeline. Did you really not know? She said she'd mentioned a married man to you. I spoke to her after our row. She'd been on holidays. Anyway, that's why I was so angry with you. It was jealousy. That's why I said those things, to put you off. Fuck, she wasn't pleased with me when I told her what I'd said!'

Nicky was amazed.

'She loves life, Nicky, and she fascinates me. But she's still very young, a tearaway. She'll shower you with gifts one second and the next she's off with someone else on another one of her adventures! I used to be deadly jealous sitting at home with the missus in front of the TV on a Saturday night visualising Madeline out dancing with her friends . . . My wife and I were never really happy, Nicky, but what's incredible is that that's not how she sees it. She thinks we were. Anyway, enough of me.'

'Does Madeline know why I'm in jail and what it's all about?'

'Maybe. I don't know. But here, tell me again what I should tell Gareth. He knows I'm up today and he'll be phoning me back.'

'Tell him, tell him . . . Tell him everything's going to be OK and not to worry. Tell him I think about him all the time too. Tell him that before long it'll all be sorted out . . . Tell him I miss him.' Nicky's head was bowed in bashfulness as he made the last point. 'That's if you don't mind.'

Gerard grabbed him by the neck and shook him, then said, 'Sorry! Hope I didn't hurt you. Your message is as good as delivered,' he smiled. 'Is there anything else I can do?'

'Pray?' suggested Nicky, half-joking.

'One of mine's worth a million times the faithful's,' he laughed. 'Done.'

'Oh yes, and tell my ma and da I send my regards.'

'Will do.'

As Gerard was leaving Nicky felt like shouting to him, *I forgot to tell you about the great escape I had: do you think I could have pulled it off?*

Having heard from Gareth put him in excellent form. He couldn't see how the DPP could press ahead with their threats. But the law could be a monster with a life of its own, Al had said. Then a thought struck him like a blow to the head and he felt faint and had to lean against the wall.

Gareth was dying!

His escort asked him was he OK; he had turned very pale.

'It's Robin all over again, Mister,' he replied, enigmatically. 'It's the story of my life.'

'Wait a while, son. Take your time. Get your breath back.'
He fell into a chair. Yes, it was true. Gareth was going to
die on him. The end of all stories is death. He drank the water
they gave him, said he was now OK and got up to return to
his new cell in the unit alongside those who had raped,
molested, committed incest.

'Smith!' said the PO on the ones. 'The BOV is ready to hear
your complaints about harassment and persecution.'

'I no longer want to make them. I withdraw them. I apologise to the deputy-governor.'

'Good man,' said the PO.

As he reached the top of the stairs the principal officer's
voice bellowed petulantly: 'A–3! Send down Smith to the ones!'

'Back down again,' said his escort. 'The BOV must want to
see you.'

The tape-recorder was switched on and the hearing began.

The Deputy-Governor read out a long report on Nicky's
behaviour. There were insults to prison officers, insubordina-
tion, interfering with prison property, several assaults on other
prisoners. By the tone of their questioning two out of three
members, including the chair of the panel, clearly sympathised
with the difficulties of the deputy-governor. The third member had been responsible for not accepting Nicky's withdrawal
of complaints. Harris spoke of the natural resentment ordinary
prisoners had for sex offenders, there being a pecking order
of the criminal and the depraved and Smith, clearly at the
lower end, had left himself and the prison authorities vulnerable by not declaring to the interviewing governor upon arrival
that he was still being investigated in regard to other, even
more deplorable, offences.

'Nicholas Smith, Number 1711. Mind if I call you Nicky?'

'No.'

'How do you feel about being moved into the secure unit?'

'I don't want to go.' He stared earnestly into the brown eyes
of the lady posing the questions.

'The deputy-governor says it's for your own safety. And look
at that terrible weal on your neck where the others tried to

hang you. And they knocked out your teeth as well. Don't you want to move?'

'I like the cell I'm in. I feel safe in it. It has a good view. I can see over the city. On a clear day I can even see the sea.'

Harris, the PO and the other two members of the BOV, clearly had no time for Nicky's eccentricity. They had no time for Nicky. But the third member was persistent and questioned him further about all that had happened to him in the jail. All the squalid pettiness of the prison authorities was laid bare, their double-standards exposed.

Nicky said: 'I haven't killed anybody, robbed anybody, raped anybody, thrown thousands on the dole, started a war. My conscience is clear. I shouldn't be in jail. I'm innocent.'

'Yes, well, you *would* say that,' said the chairman of the board, an elderly, smartly-dressed patrician.

At the end of the inquiry it was clear that Nicky's allegations were to be thrown out – despite his ally – and that he was to be moved out of the end cell where he had been so tantalisingly close to a break-out. He was to be categorised as a sex offender. He was sent out of the room and waited outside for the result of the adjudication, a mere formality. Next, Harris and the PO came out chatting animatedly. The deputy told him to take his hands out of his pockets. He stood for a half hour, couldn't fathom the delay and felt a bit panicky as the Tannoy announced the yard lock-up. Soon, the men from the ones and twos would begin streaming in. After what seemed like an eternity Harris and the PO were called back in, then Nicky. The room was hot and there were several red faces. The woman smiled at Nicky. He could almost trace the feeling that poured from her. Nicky smiled back at Jane's beautiful mother, now quite slim. He noticed her elegant hands, her slender ringless wedding finger. She had made it! She had come through!

'Well,' said the chairman. 'We, er, have decided that you have been treated quite harshly. We have expressed our opposition to moving you into the special unit. Clearly, you would consider it a further form of punishment. I am sure Mr Harris here will accept our recommendations. Mr Harris?'

'Eh, yes. Yes. He can stay where he is for the time being. But should there be a change in the nature of the offences he is facing we shall move him. PO, take Smith out.'

'Mr Smith? Nicky?' said the woman whom he hadn't seen in over nine years. 'Merry Christmas. I hope your case goes well for you. Maybe next summer you'll be holidaying by the sea.'

'Thank you,' said Nicky. 'Thank you!'

Back in his cell he fell on his knees, joined his hands in prayer and with his eyes raised to heaven he declared: 'Oh God! You are the Almighty! You are wonderful!'

It would be about fifteen minutes before dinner arrived. He toyed with the idea of asking Seán O'Neill for a metal serving spoon. Could he be trusted? Could he be bought? Wasn't he already smuggling Nicky tobacco despite his ostracisation? Yes! He would take the chance.

And Madeline! Just imagine! Gerard had been the married man! And, and, and most important of all – Gareth had phoned! And was phoning again! Oh, everything was falling into place! Thank you, God, thank you!

When his door opened Seán was there with his dinner. Nicky had only seconds to spare.

'Seán,' he whispered. 'Can you get me a metal spoon?'

'A what?'

'A spoon.'

'Hurry up, there. We haven't got all day,' said the warder, closing the door.

Fuck you.

Nicky wolfed down his food. He waited until the warders went out to lunch and only a skeleton staff remained behind before climbing up on his locker. He scraped at the hole with the metal hook of a coat hanger. He worked furiously. After about an hour's work he straightened out what was left of the hook and pushed it into the hole. It seemed to meet no resistance at the other end. He laughed. He stripped his bed and covered up his window with the sheets and blankets and stuffed toilet paper around the door frame. He blocked the bottom with a towel, then removed the light-bulb and the cell was immediately plunged into almost total darkness. Where to fuck am I. He moved along his bed, found his locker, stepped on it and looked upwards. Nothing! He moved back and forth. Last night I heard my momma singing a song. Whooooowee.

Chirpy chirpy cheep cheep. Suddenly he saw a little pin of light. It was hollow at the other end! He could get through! But he would need that spoon. He cleaned up his cell, covered in the hole with wet bread rolled in the dust of the white emulsion and made up his bed.

At about half two he put his metal tray out on to the landing.

'I need to go to the toilet,' he begged the officer, a different one from earlier.

'Serious business, is it?'

'Yes.'

'OK. Wait here, son. I'll be back in a second.' He left the door open. Seán came up to collect the tray.

'Seán. I need a metal spoon desperately. Can you do it for me? I'll give you money. Anything!'

'You're not going to kill somebody, are you? Or kill yourself?

'No! No! I swear.'

Seán smiled. 'I'll leave a spoon behind the cistern in the toilets after the half-four lock-up. But I'll have to report it missing at half six.'

'Can't you wait until tomorrow?'

'No, Nicky. I'd be in big trouble. But nothing'll happen. Landing spoons end up in the kitchens with the dixies by accident all the time. That's what they'll presume. Don't worry.'

'Seán, you're a gentleman. Thanks a million. Here. Take this,' said Nicky, holding out a twenty-pound note.

'Forget it, mate. You'll need it.'

Nicky got out to the toilet again and smuggled the spoon back to his cell. It was about fourteen inches long. For three hours he quietly rubbed the point of the handle along the concrete floor until it was quite sharp.

All through the evening he smoked. He was on a continuous high. At about nine o'clock, after the guard checked him through the flap, he moved his bed towards the window. He then dabbed a sock in water and marked out a rough circle in the ceiling. He made himself a wide-brimmed, paper hat to catch the dust and began digging into the soaked mortar between the bricks, exploiting the hum of the boiler-house on the other side of the wing. It was so easy it was unbelievable. The dust and pebbles fell away and were covering the bed and floor. He cleaned his cell up for the eleven o'clock check and lights out. Then he went back to work. But when he listened at his door for the signature tune of the midnight news he could hear no radios, just a low murmur of music. Fuck, it must be after twelve and I haven't even removed a brick yet.

It became tougher as he proceeded but eventually he loosened a brick completely. Instead of falling through it jammed between the others. Still, he felt an upward draught pour through the joints. His window was wide open and he worked by the light of the security lamps. After the earlier little flurry of snow the sky had cleared. A wind came up and the air vents on the roof rattled occasionally. His fingers were cut, his hands paralysed with pain, his arms and back cemented in an arc. But he worked on. Then three bricks fell out together and he felt like squealing with joy. At one stage the bricks were falling out so easily that he had trouble catching them before they crashed over the floor. I'm bustin' for a pish. He went to his pot in the corner and was urinating when his flap suddenly lifted and the arc of a torch hit him up the face. He dropped the pot and its contents splashed over the floor and ran out the door. The night guard laughed at his paper hat.

'You scared the living daylights out of me!' shouted Nicky, forgetting that he was in the middle of an escape. The guard snapped the flap closed, laughed again, and continued on down the landing. Nicky began to shake, realising how close he had been to discovery. But, at least, he was over the last check until seven in the morning. He now had a clear run. He stacked the bricks in the corner. The hole was opened wide enough to accept his body. He climbed into the roof space and looked around. A large metal grille the length of the wing separated him from the air vents, but he was able to touch the rafters and the cold slates. He went back into his cell, put on warm clothes and a zip-up jacket and threw over his shoulder his escape kit: a rope he had made from strips of sheets tied together, and a specially designed blanket. They'll be making a film about me!

He said cheerio to his cell and went back up into the freezing roof space. He had to crawl along at a snail's pace as he crossed the top of the cells of the special unit. Half-way down the length of the wing he heard a pigeon cooing in stress. He was afraid it would panic and create a stir. Shoosh. He put his finger to his lips. Shoosh. Then it saw who he was.

Good luck with the escape, Nicky!

Thanks!

It shut its lids and went back to sleep.

As he approached the circle his heart sank as he saw that access was denied by a gate built into the grille. I was mad to start this. Imagine. Me, a nobody, thinking I could escape! What a fool I am! But he crawled on anyway until he came to the gate. It's as rusty as fuck. The first thing I'm gonna do if I get out of here is stop cursing. He took out his spoon, put it between the metal lattice work and prised down on it. The laths snapped so easily that he wanted to laugh. Whoever built this jail should be sacked! He made a hole, slipped under and continued around the corner. He looked down into the circle. It seemed like hundreds of feet below. He could see no sign of activity and went on, past the entrance to the roof space of B–wing, until he came to the entrance to C–wing. Here, he discovered that the grille was lying open, probably to allow the trade-crews to carry out repairs. Must have been expecting me! He crawled in. C–wing seemed much brighter. All the lights burned. But when he looked up at the air vents what he saw was the first blue of a dawn sky appear around the rims and he knew that he was hours behind schedule. He was so tired he could have curled up where he had halted.

He moved quickly to the far end of the wing, towards the gable; then had to rest for about ten minutes. He stood up and examined the slates for a weak spot. Once again he used the handle of the spoon and with considerable force cracked open a slate which shed a triangle of itself and revealed a clear blue sky, a sensual sight for starved eyes. But the noise he made had been so great that it frightened him and he sat motionless for several minutes to see if he had alerted anyone. He broke off another piece, then found that he could prise off other slates and lift them through.

He stuck his head out, like a periscope emerging from the heavy depths of darkness, and enjoyed the view so much that he forgot he was on a mission. He took a fit of giggles. Nicky

Smith. Postman! The great escaper! A fucking postman! First class delivery! He lifted himself through the narrow space of the rafters. It's as well I don't have Sonny with me! Fuck! I'm only remembering now! I said something like that before when I was blocked. There was frost on the slates and Nicky experienced a wave of vertigo, then queasiness in his stomach. He looked over the side of the gable. Scaffolding, as promised! It always looks rickety – ever notice that? He climbed up to an air vent, belayed his sheet-rope to it, tested it for purchase, threw the rest over the side and began his descent. He came to the end of the sheet but didn't have far to drop to the platform though he had to be careful not to lose his toehold. He landed on the bouncy planking and let his body billow so that his weight was spread out. He wondered if the cameras monitoring the length of the inner wall were wide-angled and could see him. He was now only a jump from the perimeter wall and, had he wanted, could have leaped from the scaffolding over it but he would have broken a leg if not his neck on the other side. Instead, he went down a level, inserted the long spoon through holes at the end of the blanket making a fluke, and put his hands into loops at the other end. He jumped up at the wall at an oblique angle, flicking the blanket at the crown of barbed wire. The blanket enmeshed itself in the sharp metal burrs and the spoon took hold and gave extra purchase. Nicky swung like a pendulum along the wall. He swung his right leg up until it caught the coping stone and he pulled himself slowly up. But he couldn't get under the wire as planned because the spaces between each rivet, where the circular wire was fastened to the coping stone at tangents, were too narrow. He was completely enervated. His legs were trembling, hands cut and bleeding but he raised his trunk through one loose loop, then he stood up and took slow strides through the wire. He momentarily flinched at the sticky wetness around his bleeding calves and thighs. He was seconds away from freedom. A dog ran up to the bottom of the wall and wagged its tail, encouraging him. You're for a tin of Pedigree Chum, my friend!

Suddenly, the alarm bells began ringing, drowning his ears in noise, ringing with such force that he imagined the sound swelling like a bubble over the entire jail and encapsulating him. Next, the siren wailed its nerve-plucking scream and

Nicky couldn't stand the pace any longer. He was finished. He saw the warders running out into the yards. Some of them seemed to jump like Keystone Cops when they saw that a prisoner was on the perimeter wall and so close to freedom. I wish they wouldn't do that. It's so funny!

Nicky looked towards the horizon where the gold leaf of the sun was beginning to show over the sea of eternity. I did my best, everybody! I did my best. Then he tottered and fell back into the jail, his body cracking as it thudded on the concrete path of the catwalk.

Through the vent-hole in the wigwam of prison officials that stood over his corpse Nicky's gaze was settling at infinity, the last registration on his retina already having mixed and died with that faint chaos of the ending.

'He looks so peaceful.'

'Peaceful and happy after the rough time they gave him.'

'He was a bullroot, what do you expect.'

The doctor knelt down and examined him carefully, checked his pulse and heart. He pronounced him dead. 'He must have broken his back when he fell. Did anybody see what happened?'

'I saw it. He just couldn't go any further. It's amazing he travelled this far. Then he just dropped like a stone.'

A blanket and a stretcher were sent for. The doctor closed Nicky's eyes and drew a heavy blanket over his body.

And then the swallow appeared. Fixed and hovering, high above Nikolai. Waiting. Watching. Always.

Nicky lay dead but couldn't help chuckling. I've got *rigor mortis*, my eyes are shut, there's a blanket over my face, I've got a quack and four screws standing over me, and still I can see my old friend up there in the blue sky!

The swallow tipped its wings and began an accelerating swoop.

You're a bit late! shouted Nicky in his old, joking, philosophical way. I've already fallen to my death!

No.

In the next scene it is Christmas Eve and the pure snow is fluttering down. Nicky, in his duffle coat with his hood up, hands in pockets, turns into the narrow confines of Bank Street towards the red glow in the windows of his favourite tavern, an old white-washed establishment which predates the rolling heads of the French Revolution and where Madeline first ate all his peanuts as they looked at the snapshots of her life.

He enters the busy premises where the people are in great festive cheer and looks through the arches and over the smoky sea of faces, towards the fireside and the spitting roaring logs where a lonely, dispirited, unpopular man drinks on his own and combs his fingers through his dishevelled pomaded hair. Nicky pulls down his hood, smiles, and reveals that he now sports a quick-growing beard. He unbuttons his toggles, shakes the melting snow off his moired duffle and walks forward. He looks up at the bodhrán on the wall and the old sea-pictures and smiles again. The spiders in the far corners of the ceiling goose-step out to hear the crack. Nicky takes down a chair from a lop-sided stack and shouts to the barman, 'A gin and tonic for me and one for the road for this gentleman.'

He puts his arm around Wainwright's shoulder.

'Look at you. Look at the state you're in. You've been on the drink for days; you haven't shaved; you haven't been home. You know you can be a good man if you try, Derek.'

Wainwright looks up: his bloodshot watery eyes are sunk in a beaver's nest of wrinkles.

'Thank you, thank you, for those kind words,' says Wainwright.

The drinks are set down on top of an old wooden barrel serving as a table and Nicky pays for the round.

'Don't I know you from somewhere?' says Wainwright.

'Possibly,' replies Nicky with superlative aplomb.

'Oh well. I suppose you've read all the papers and have heard what's happened? It's that that has me this way. I had a case, you see, a few months back. I arrested a dangerous villain. A threat to society. So I put him away. I fixed him properly. The DPP and I had to twist things a bit. Didn't let on to my mate, Ian, though he sussed me out in the end. But we got the pervert on the essential, irrefutable points . . .'

Nicky removes his gloves and Wainwright looks at the scar on his hand.

'Are you sure I don't know you from somewhere? In the newspapers? On television?'

Nicky smiles.

Mrs Russell comes up the bar and approaches the two men by the fireside. She takes out a little box and says to Wainwright: 'Hello, sourpuss. Here, take a pinch of snuff, the best in Ireland. It'll lift your spirits.'

'Go away, woman, or I'll have you arrested!' says Wainwright.

She slaps her thigh and laughs. 'What a scream you are. Think this town is yours? What about under the mistletoe?'

'Go away, you ugly woman.'

'Ah, Derek,' says Nicky, 'you've still a lot to learn about human relations.'

'As I was saying. I screwed the bastard well and good. He was a bullroot, you see. A fucking queer.'

'Derek. The best thing you could do now is to go home to your wife and kids. They need you. They love you.'

'Anyway. Will you let me finish? We had him well and good. But the next thing you know he escapes! I can't believe it. Nobody knows how it was done. After all my hard work . . . And now I'm in trouble. Are you sure I don't know you? Wait a minute! Hold it! Did you always have a beard?! I k-n-o-w y-o-u. You're him! You're Nicky Smith!'

Wainwright shouts to three men sitting at the long wooden counter: 'Quick! Come to my aid! Help me make a citizen's arrest!'

On hearing this alert two of them immediately jump up from their seats and rush to the fireside duo. But instead of grabbing Nicky, Gerard and Ian overpower Wainwright and pinion him to the chair.

'Ian! What are you doing?' screams Wainwright in disbelief.

Nicky roars with laughter. He looks towards the bar where his father holds up a glass of soda water and lime, toasts his son, then holds up in his other hand and shows him a single red rose, the best Christmas present he could give to the greatest queen in the world. Sonny shuffles over and planks himself on the detective's knee until Wainwright turns blue in the face.

'Well, Derek!' says Nicky. 'Justice is being seen to be done at long last. Everything is falling into place. Faith, you must understand, is the mistress of the universe! Faith! Not power! It was nice of you to show up at my getting-out do!'

He turns and waves goodbye to everyone and they all wish him well in his new life. Even strangers are privileged to have set eyes on a true man.

Nicky leaves the bar and goes out into the busy streets, athrong with people with their mixed histories, with their plans and bright hopes. Through the snow he runs, waving and shouting, 'Merry Christmas!' to everyone he passes. Earlier he had gotten through to Gareth. He was weak but he was going to recover. Gareth was going to recover! The happiness between them was simply indescribable. Nothing could suppress or crush them. They were going to find a life: people would have to change to suit them and their ways. Mrs Williams had arrived in the ward during the conversation and ended the call. But Gareth was confident that given assurances she could be won around. Possibilities are to be found over every horizon.

On and on Nicky hurries, down Donegall Place, crunching the snow in the pavement, laughing like Santa Claus, winking at the children, past City Hall and its gigantic Christmas tree standing like the shape of a palm raised in peace but decorated with a blazing galaxy of lights and its bells ting-alinging as angels get their wings. He shouts his congratulations to the choir on its excellent carolling, and runs down May Street where the cars beep their horns in celebration of his freedom. Through the Markets and on towards the bridge he dashes, his and Robin's bridge where they stood as children and wished for the mysteries to be answered, the bridge where the swirling river carries its perpetual waters into the sea, and where the swollen sea brings the gift back upstream,

Over and over again: over and over;

On and on: on and on;

On and on until there is no end but the promise

of And . . .

There is no end but the promise

Of And . . .

And